THE CHRONICLE OF
THE WELL

AWAKENINGS

DEBORAH BARWICK

Published in paperback in 2016 by Sixth Element Publishing
on behalf of Deborah Barwick

Sixth Element Publishing
Arthur Robinson House
13-14 The Green
Billingham TS23 1EU
Tel: 01642 360253
www.6epublishing.net

ISBN 978-1-908299-95-6

British Library Cataloguing in Publication Data. A catalogue record for this book is
available from the British Library.

This is a work of fiction. Names, characters, businesses, places, events and incidents
are either the products of the author's imagination or used in a fictitious manner.
Any resemblance to actual persons, living or dead, or actual events and places is
purely coincidental.

Deborah Barwick asserts the moral right to be identified as the author of this work.

Printed in Great Britain.

To 'The Horsemen' without whose suggestions,
encouragement and faith this book
would never have been finished.

PROLOGUE

WELHAM: 1616

Extreme fear had heightened her senses to almost unbearable clarity. Colours were nightmare bright; sounds, strident and jagged. The rare breeze which lifted soft tendrils of ebony-dark hair at her temples also wafted the cloying sweetness of overblown summer blossoms through air made heavy with anticipation.

The rope securing her wrists, the noose around her neck, chafed and rubbed, and she could feel the splintering coarseness of planking beneath her bare feet.

In front of her, a mob ebbed and flowed. Her friends, people of the hamlet, all now standing in judgment of crimes she had not committed and could not begin to comprehend. Surely James would come soon. Her eyes jumped from face to face, searching, hoping. The man she loved, respected both within their small parish, and in the wider community. He could diffuse the situation with a word; make the crowd understand their terrible mistake. At his command, the angry horde would heed his message and disperse. Perhaps there would be mutterings and sly glances, but James would deal with these deftly and diplomatically.

He would take her home to Damara then, soothe her raw skin, and talk about their future once more.

Soon. Soon he would come.

They would be married, as he had promised, and he would shield and protect her from all ills in their new life together. She would eventually find it in her heart to forgive her neighbours for their treatment of her today; and they, in turn, would understand how wrong they were to doubt her intent, or the signs they believed they had received. Her eyes searched the throng once more, desperate for sight of her champion.

'Please!' The whisper escaped through parched lips. 'Have mercy. My babe… I carry a child. An innocent child. Have pity.'

An audible gasp rose from those closest at her plea, and murmurs began to pass between the ranks. Two words took shape and formed into a chant-like rhythm, creeping towards her in hissing accusation.

'Witch. Whore… witch... whore,' and she took a ragged step backwards as if to escape the terrifying taunts. Her fear now reached new and dizzying heights, and she wondered wildly whether she could bear the shame. Belatedly, she realised the impact of her heartfelt admission as the mob's mood darkened still further, becoming ever more threatening. The faces below her appeared distorted, ugly in their misguided fervour; faces she had known all her life now turned against her in judgement.

She saw him then, to the back of the crowd, standing nonchalantly, arms crossed over his broad chest. Relief washed through her at the sight of her lover. Now, he would reason with the villagers, explain their mistake. Now, he would stride to where she was held, bound and powerless, and take her home to Damara. His status in the small community would ensure that his words were heeded, and this nightmare would become a thing of the past.

His voice rose then, with authority above all others and cut through the air like a knife, the intonation slow and clear so as not to be misunderstood.

'The Lord's words tell us that a witch shall not be suffered to live. The Bible shows us that whoring cannot, *will* not, be tolerated. This woman is twice fallen, and can have no other justice but death.'

The crowd had quieted as he began to speak, and now an eerie silence spread across the gathering. Not a bird could be heard calling in the thicket, and even the wind stilled. Her breath had caught in her throat at his words, the very heart of her rent in two.

Betrayal.

Her beloved, father of her unborn child, condemning, denouncing her before her peers. An icy calm washed over her, replacing in an instant the previous fear. She spoke in a low voice, now chilling in its hatred.

'James Brunton, you are cursed this day, you *and* your kin, for what you do. Damara was yours for the taking. You have forsaken your claim both to her, and to me. My innocence and intent are beyond your understanding. I take my babe and leave this life with a pure heart.'

Her eyes locked for an instant with those of her erstwhile lover, catching a momentary flash of fear, gone before it could be noted by others. Anger now curling his handsome features, he nodded crisply to an unseen acolyte behind her.

Had she been given time to react, she was bound and imprisoned, no means of escape or hope of rescue. A heavy thud of booted heel against planking. A sharp push against her shoulders, triggering again the overwhelming fear. An unexpected feeling of release as she was momentarily suspended, feet free of earthly bounds. A cruel snap of rope against tender flesh, and her world dropped into darkness.

WELHAM: 1987

His name was called, as expected.

'Could you come to the front, please,' and she beckoned him forward, her grandmotherly face a study of sympathetic concern.

He arranged his own features into what he knew to be a parody of sadness. He had practised in front of the mirror many times over the last few days to perfect this moment. Bowing his head – a nice touch, he thought – he tried again to manufacture some tears but, frustratingly, this seemed beyond his ability.

He reached the front, taking his time, milking the moment, savouring the attention. Mrs Lockhart placed both her hands on his shoulders and turned him gently to face the class. He allowed himself to be handled – just this once.

Her voice above his right ear burbled on, in language suitable for her audience, explaining to the other pupils about grief – his own, in this case, he supposed – about being kind to one another during 'this difficult time', and ultimately about death – but only a far away, fluffy sort of dying. Not at all like real death.

He had seen real death. It was his own mother being spoken of now, and he had been there when she died. It had not been pretty.

He understood that he should be feeling sad; but in truth he had never liked her very much. Her main purpose in life, it seemed to him, was to thwart any fun or adventure. He could still hear her voice, within his head, sniping and snapping at yet another supposed misdeed. And she had never understood any of his hobbies or interests. She wouldn't be missed, not by him.

Nor by his father, he suspected; and he almost allowed his lips to curl unconsciously upwards. That would never do; to be caught smiling while Mrs Lockhart talked about his dead mother. He regimented his thoughts to the present, and rearranged his features to that of despair once more.

Raising his eyes, for he had kept them suitably downcast until now, he scanned his classmates. Few, apparently, wanted to meet his gaze. Some looked to their teacher, others to their own clasped hands. A couple of the girls were actually crying, and he almost pitied them their tears, their weakness.

Almost.

Only one stared back. Openly challenging. The dark-haired girl who sat across the table from him. He knew her name but refused to say it, even inside his own head, for acknowledging it gave her power. He knew that she knew this. He felt that she might also know the truth about his mother. And the thought excited him.

Finally, Mrs Lockhart patted his shoulders kindly, and sent him back to his seat, her discourse exhausted. He allowed shoulders to sag and feet to drag just a little, in what he hoped was a grief-stricken way, as he made his way solemnly through the class to his seat at the rear-most table.

The girl's eyes never left his and he tried again, as he had in the past, to bend her to his will. She resisted; without effort, it seemed, and this irked him. How dare she defy him?

At the same time though, he welcomed her challenge. There was a thrilling expectation of honing his talents at her expense, of her obvious humiliation at his hands; and then, when she begged for mercy, of crushing her like an insect.

He held her eyes across the table, and his own darkened in anticipation.

WELHAM: 2016

ARRIVAL

She had dreamed again of him last night, his body splashed in red by the insane paintbrush of a vengeful god. Death injuries hideously obvious, he reached for her, pleading yet angry. She had awoken with his ravaged face still fresh in her mind. The intensity of these nightmares always faded on waking, to leave her with mind-numbing grief and a grinding weariness which shadowed her as she dragged her way through each new day.

Now the snub nose of the reliable old Volvo edged around the undefined verges and blind corners of narrow country lanes. Anna, at the wheel, heaved another inward sigh, and wondered for the umpteenth time at the wisdom of this decision. She glanced at the passenger seat. She couldn't see his face as he looked blindly at the passing foliage.

'How'd the last exam go, Jake? We haven't even had chance to discuss it yet.' She was talking for the sake of it, but most of the journey had been silent and she felt a need to reconnect with him before they arrived. Not long to go now, if she remembered correctly.

'Yeah, it was fine. It went okay. Nothing I wasn't expecting. Is it much further?'

Jake, her son, and anchor in recent months, met her gaze and gave a half-smile. She could always rely on Jake to stay calm in the face of most crises. He had unknowingly been her rock on more than one occasion, but this nineteen-year-old had had more than enough to bear these last few months; and supporting a grieving mother was well beyond what any youngster should have to cope with. Anna had tried to spare him, as much as she could. They each had their own demons to fight.

Her world had fallen apart on that night in January, when a knock on the door had brought the news of her husband's death. For the following few weeks, Anna had drifted in a fog of disbelief; she functioned, she existed, but actually living seemed to be something she couldn't quite grasp hold of. Eventually, an instinctive urge to run for home, to lick her wounds, wormed into her consciousness. She began to make plans to move back north to Yorkshire.

Anna had set herself the task, when it became clear that a move was the best possible solution, of finding the perfect property; a fresh start for her small family. She had spent many hours, while Jake made a pretence of revising, trawling through internet property sites, making telephone calls and, finally, making the journey north to view shortlisted properties. Perhaps, she admitted now to herself, finding some solace in keeping busy. Anything rather than to think and to feel.

Jake had shown little or no interest in her endeavours, accepting blankly the need for change, a new beginning, but avoiding any input or involvement in the project. She could recall it now, facing each other across the kitchen in Winchester, his eyes devoid of expression.

'Whatever you decide, Mum. Honestly. It's fine by me.'

Anna had wondered then whether it may be delayed shock. Or perhaps he was indeed indifferent to his surroundings. Thankfully, he seemed to rally somewhat when his A Levels had been completed, but by then the final decision had already been made.

Several appealing propositions had already been viewed when

she first saw Damara Cottage. Set a little distance outside of Welham Village in the northern-most corner of North Yorkshire, she had felt an immediate attraction, a feeling of belonging. A homecoming. And all this before she'd even opened the front door.

The inside of the property could, and should, have been a disappointment but Anna was looking beyond the cosmetic. The décor had obviously been neglected for quite some time, and had fallen into shabby disrepair. There were even signs of possible vandalism – raised floorboards, and the freestanding kitchen units were slightly askew and out of place – but the estate agent assured her that all would be attended to should Anna 'decide to proceed with the purchase'.

The trick, she thought, was to be able to see past the need for redecoration and new carpets, and instead imagine cosy rooms made warm by the open fires. She could picture herself and Jake feeling secure and safe within the solid masonry, could see the gardens flourishing with summer blooms and scented herbs.

The proportions of the cottage were perfect for their requirements. A roomy porch at the end of a winding cobbled path gave way to a large kitchen-cum-dining area, and she looked forward to scrubbing down the old Aga to bring out its true potential.

Beyond this, a sturdy oak door led to the sitting room, which extended for the whole width of the rear of the property, with large French windows allowing views over the wooded countryside beyond. Three good-sized bedrooms, and a snug but well-appointed bathroom, were upstairs, all accessed via the narrow and steep wooden staircase. There was also the cellar – she had only peeped down the darkened steps thus far – which was clearly huge, and would, as the estate agent had so earnestly pointed out, 'cater for all storage needs'. No garage, unfortunately, but with a large garden and no near neighbours, Anna was sure that any improvements they wanted to make would be no problem.

Damara Cottage would be a complete culture shock when compared to their Hampshire property but she was sure that, in this case, different was good. Anything that distanced them from the past few months could only be an improvement.

And so, the wheels had been set in motion, solicitors and surveyors employed, contracts signed and exchanged, and Damara Cottage had become the property of Mrs Anna Freer two days previously.

They'd spent the last evening rattling around the almost empty shell of their four-bedroomed, smartly modern, detached house in the suburbs of Winchester. Jake worried her. He had a heavy-eyed inertia about him, so unlike his usual enthusiasm for life that she wondered whether they should think about a trip to their new GP. Perhaps bereavement counselling, which she had previously refused for both of them, would have to be considered. He still functioned, was the caring and supportive son he had always been, but a light had gone out inside him. She understood that feeling very well. Jake's health must be a priority if he didn't show signs of improvement very soon.

Most of their furniture had been packed and sent ahead in the removal trucks during the day, with only camp beds, a tiny portable television, the kettle and the microwave remaining.

And here we are, thought Anna. *Almost there.*

A signpost ahead signalled 'Welham 2 miles', and she began to recognise the route that she had followed with the estate agent on her previous visit. Excitement sparked, touched with apprehension. Would her choice of home meet with Jake's approval? She directed the Volvo around the next left turn, which would take them through the centre of the village, before the final half mile to the cottage.

'Nearly there now,' she told him. 'Our cottage is about half a mile further on.'

He nodded, showing a welcome spark of interest now that they were approaching the end of the journey.

Welham was charming, and exactly as she had remembered it; the main street dotted with the obligatory butcher, bakery and grocer. Centrally located was the village public house, The

Wishing Well, the frontage of which gave off a well-kempt and welcoming aspect. Anna guessed at around sixty or seventy private residences arranged in a haphazard grouping around the central area, of varying shapes and sizes, but all built using the traditional local sandstone, and all with a look of care, and of pride in ownership.

'Where's the gym? Or even a supermarket or cinema?' complained Jake, in true teenager-style, and only half-joking.

'Bright lights there may not be, but there's a pub,' replied Anna, 'and that's a good place to start looking for a part-time job.'

A Levels under his belt and results pending, Jake had told her he was as yet undecided about what his next move should be. Always more inclined towards artistic rather than academic pursuits, his dream was to open and run a gallery selling his own photographic landscapes. Confidence in his ability, and lack of finance were, of course, the drawbacks to this grand plan. He was taking these summer months to make some tough decisions about his future; whether to enrol into a suitable course at the local college, and then study photography – or a related subject – at university. Or to take a gap year, and a deep steadying breath, before having to even think about his options.

Anna spotted the almost-hidden right turning to the far side of the bakery, a wooden signpost on the corner confirming in faded, white-painted letters:

Welham Farm
Damara Cottage

And below it, stencilled in black onto the fence,

Mad Alice Lane

Jake turned to her. 'Seriously, Mum? Mad Alice Lane? Where are we, the Village of the Damned?' Jake craned his neck over his shoulder to get a closer look before turning back to the track ahead. 'What's around the next bend, the Gingerbread House?'

11

She steered the car into a tiny, one-track country lane, smiling at his mock horror.

'These little villages, they have a lot of history, Jake. There'll have been a really interesting reason for the name originally, but we'll probably never get to find out.'

A grunt was the reply, but he was looking about him with more animation than she had seen for quite some time.

They passed the rear of the bakery and a couple of residences, crunching over a cinder-like surface, and then progressed into open farmland where the tiny road dwindled to a rutted farm track. Cattle grazed on one side, sheep to the other. A copse of trees directly ahead hid from view any buildings beyond, but the mood in the vehicle had lightened noticeably at the thought of the long and tedious journey finally ending; and of investigating their new home.

The Volvo continued cautiously along the track, Anna aware of and avoiding the many potholes, until the tiny lane took one final sharp bend and split into two even smaller access tracks. The other fork, she knew, continued for a further quarter mile or so, to their nearest neighbours at Welham Farm. She slowed the car to a stop as they took their first view, together, of their new home.

'That's it, Jake. Damara Cottage.' Anna looked at him. 'What do you think?' Her last words caught in her throat as she felt a sudden and unwelcome lump of emotion. She forced it down by sheer effort of will. It shouldn't be like this. They should all be living happy and uneventful lives back in Winchester. Or at the very least, Peter should be here with them, enjoying the adventure of a new start. Despite her best efforts, Anna's eyes began to sting at the unfairness of life.

The battle was all but lost, the enormity of the moment overwhelming her. In another minute, she might very well be sobbing openly in front of her son. Not something she had ever wanted or intended.

Peter. Father, role model and mentor to Jake; husband, lover and best friend to Anna, had been killed in a road accident just six months previously. It was just 'one of those things' said the police. 'Nobody's fault; just one of those things'; but the loss had turned the Freers' world upside down.

He had been driving home from work, only ten minutes from their house. Ten minutes from safety. The lorry, travelling in the opposite direction, had a tyre blow at the wrong moment on a blind corner, and veered into the oncoming carriageway. Neither driver had time to react in any meaningful way, and although not a head-on impact, Peter's Audi took the brunt of the encounter on the driver's-side wing and door. Unfortunately, the lorry came out better in the one-sided battle, and Peter's life was the prize it took.

Anna felt no malice towards the other driver. She could even feel some pity at the thought that he would carry the burden of the accident for the rest of his life, poor man. What she did feel, though, was anger. Anger at whatever malicious fate had decreed that she would be widowed at the age of 39; the same fate that would leave her son without a father. The unfairness, and particularly the randomness, were what she was finding it impossible to come to terms with.

Since the accident, she had tried to present a strong and positive face to the world and, more importantly, to Jake. In doing so, she sometimes managed to fool herself into coping with the awful situation they found themselves in. But right now, facing this new challenge without Peter by her side, Anna was struggling to find strength to keep her feelings in check.

As if understanding his mother's mixed emotions, as he so often did, she felt Jake's large, warm hand slip over hers, giving it a gentle press. He was wise beyond his years, this son of hers, and she blessed whatever gods had smiled down when they had given him to her. Somehow, his mere presence gave her the necessary resilience to cope for just a little while longer, and she gave herself a mental shake.

'It's the gingerbread house.' He smiled to take the sting from the words. 'No, it looks perfect, Mum,' he said softly, his eyes fixed on the cottage. 'You've done good.'

She squeezed his hand in thanks. Swallowing the lump and

blinking back unshed tears, Anna unconsciously squared her shoulders. She raised her eyes to Damara Cottage.

'Ready, then?' Jake's low voice beside her. 'Time to investigate this clapped-out old shack you've found for us. Where do we start?'

DAMARA

The inside of the cottage was blessedly cool after the stifling confines of the car, and Anna noticed immediately the quietness. An expectant silence; as if Damara Cottage was waiting to see who these new inhabitants could be; and what fortunes, good or bad, they would bring with them.

Could they be happy here, this little family of two? Would this change be good for them? Or were they just running away from old problems, never really dealing with, or solving, anything? Only time would tell.

She wandered slowly between the downstairs rooms, pointing out to Jake aspects which she hoped might sell the place to him.

'The stairs are off the lounge, and you need to watch your head on the lintel. When it was built, people were much shorter than you.' Anna grinned at her son and he snorted back.

'I've got used to ducking. It comes with the territory. We need one of those signs. What was it?'

Anna knew the one he meant. They'd seen it in a pub when Peter was alive, and it brought his memory crashing back.

'Duck or Grouse,' she replied, forcing a smile and hoping Jake didn't catch her thoughts.

She hoped that in time he'd feel the same way about the cottage as she already did. In truth, he seemed more animated since their arrival than she'd seen him for… well, a long time.

Thankfully, she noted that the estate agent had followed

15

through on promises. All loose boards and skewed kitchen units had been repaired or re-seated. Most, if not all, of their furniture seemed to have been left in the correct place by the removal company too, and she made a mental note to send a letter of thanks to the director. A good start.

Being quite specific about locations, and using a colour-code tagging system for the delivery men, she had anticipated that their belongings would arrive well ahead of them. Knowing, too, that she and Jake would be far from up to the task of rearranging the heavier items after their long, hot and tedious journey, Anna had spent many solitary hours micro-managing their move. Tomorrow would be the time to start taking stock, and making Damara their own. For now, it was enough that they were here.

Jake, too, was experiencing things far from ordinary. He was aware, as was his mother to a lesser extent, of the vibrations within the building, but was far from overwhelmed by it. Rather, he embraced the sensations, the new ideas, which seemed to spring unbidden into his mind.

The vibrations flowing now within the cottage seemed strong. Clearly events both positive and negative had taken place on this spot over past years, but specifics remained misty and beyond his grasp. Now, though, the strongest feeling seemed to be that of waiting. But for what?

His eyes were drawn to a small door to the left of the Aga. The cellar, he presumed. The urge to see for himself what lay beyond the closed door was almost overwhelming.

Almost.

He turned away decisively, aware suddenly and acutely that his previous attitude had changed drastically since entering the cottage, and much for the better. A switch had suddenly flipped within him, reversing all that was negative to the positive. Gone, or at least significantly reduced, was the seemingly bottomless pit of grief which had opened abruptly and completely beneath him on that night the police had knocked on their door with the grim news of his father's death. Gone too was any anxiety or confusion as to what the future might hold for him.

He had blundered his way through his A Levels, previous hard work and natural talent scraping him the grades he had been predicted, but the joy had gone out of life for him. He had acknowledged to himself, on various occasions and quite dispassionately, that this was the auto-pilot he had heard mentioned in the past. He recognised this dissociation now – from the inside out.

Jake's clarity of thought, however, had come very sharply into focus upon entering the front door of his new home. Problems – previously impossible mountains to climb – now became challenges to be embraced and overcome. He felt completely and willingly engaged in his own life again.

Following his mother through the kitchen and into the living room, he listened to her plans for redecoration, ideas for brightening and warming the flagged flooring, whilst being conscious all the while of the cottage 'watching' them. It was not an unpleasant sensation. Merely one that Jake had never before encountered.

A narrow door to the right of the lounge led straight on to the steep, dog-leg staircase.

'Have you decided which bedroom's yours, Mum?' He raised his eyes, looking forward to seeing more of this fascinating place. A small smiled curled his lips.

Upstairs, their personal belongings had been left, packed into crates and boxes. The removal team had more than exceeded their remit, and Anna noted with satisfaction that Jake's blue-coded boxes, along with her own yellows, were all in the bedrooms she had previously designated for the two of them.

For herself, she hoped for the larger of the two front-facing chambers. It was bright, airy and had a lovely view of the garden and the approach to the cottage. She crossed her fingers that she'd got it right, and that Jake would pick the rear bedroom, opposite the bathroom. He would appreciate the privacy it afforded, both from herself, and from the world in general and was by far the larger of the two remaining rooms.

Facing towards the woods, and beyond them the hills and vales of Welham Moor, she was also hoping that he might find some inspiration to continue his photography. This view, she had thought on first seeing it, could not but help to calm the most troubled of souls and Jake had recently had more than his share of cares. Enthusiasm for his art had been instantly squashed on the night of his father's death, as if nothing beautiful could survive in this new world of grief and loss.

His voice carried across the landing. 'This one, Mum. Can this one be mine?'

She smiled. He hadn't even seen the other two yet. 'Good job I know you so well,' she called. 'That's the one I thought you'd like. Otherwise we'd have spent the evening hefting our furniture between bedrooms.'

Anna hoped that, in time, the third, smaller bedroom might provide a studio for Jake's photography. For now, it would serve as a store to enable them to organise their lives from the many boxed belongings with no permanent home as yet. The small but well-furnished bathroom completed the first floor and, now appreciating the floorplan of Damara Cottage, they returned downstairs to make a hot drink and rustle up a hasty supper. They had eaten a hot lunch at the motorway services on the journey so as not to have to worry about cooking on their arrival. The Aga, although a welcome challenge for the future, seemed a step-too-far to cope with on their first evening.

By mutual and unspoken agreement, they decided to eat at the kitchen table. The view from the front window was spectacular as the late evening sun turned the landscape into a blaze of glorious colour; a balm to the emotional and physical exhaustion just now beginning to catch up with them. It had been a long and tiring day, and she was anticipating a restful sleep in their new home.

The door to the basement, as yet unexplored, remained latched shut in its shady corner. As he sipped his coffee, the feeling of being watched was, for Jake, now stronger than ever, had seemed to magnify as soon as they returned to the kitchen. Sitting at the table, sandwich and mug before him, his back towards that shabby little door, the tiny hairs at the nape of his neck began to prickle. He wondered whether his mother was aware of the energies swirling around them, although he had to admit that mostly what he had felt thus far had seemed positive. Even the strange sensation of continually being observed was merely disquieting, rather than frightening. Again, 'waiting' popped unbidden into his head.

The companionable silence was broken by his mother.

'Well? What do you think? Does it pass muster?'

'Mum, it's perfect.' Jake meant it. 'The right thing for us.' He paused, smiling, unsure how to continue. 'It's got a nice feeling too. Welcoming.' Again, the hesitation. 'Like it wants us to be here. That sounds a bit mad, doesn't it?'

He glanced from beneath dark lashes, trying to gauge his mum's reaction. Would she think him crazy? He'd never spoken to anyone in this way before, and it was more than a little unsettling to finally share these thoughts, even with his mother.

'No, not mad. Not at all,' she replied.

Jake's breath left in a tiny whoosh, and he realised he'd been holding his breath, waiting for her answer.

'It feels like home to me already,' Anna continued, giving a self-conscious chuckle. 'Now *that* sounds silly! I knew as soon as I walked through the door though – when I first came to see the place – that it had a good vibe.'

She paused for breath, gabbling as he knew she always did when nervous, but seeming relieved to finally have the chance to talk.

Relaxing back into his chair, Jake waited for her to continue.

'I just hoped that you'd feel it too?' she questioned. 'It's such a big step to take. For both of us, but especially for you. I didn't want this to be a bad decision.'

They'd had little time for chatting over the past weeks. The demands and chaos of moving house seemed to have taken over their lives. It was nice to sit still at last. To reconnect.

'It feels good, Mum. Honestly. But can I ask you something?' He wavered again, worried still about how much he could share without toppling over the edge of his mother's perception. 'And this is going to sound really spooky. Do you have a feeling of being watched?' He paused. '…or of maybe the *cottage* watching us?' His relaxed appearance belied the uncertainty.

There it was. Out in the open. Now his mother would tell him not to be so silly. That he was being over-imaginative and that, nice as Damara was, it was just a pleasant place to live. Nothing more, nothing less.

He prepared himself for the words, for the disappointment of being alone in his awareness, but they didn't come. Instead she leaned towards him.

'I *do* know what you mean. The atmosphere in here? It feels welcoming. Warm. Like we've lived here forever. We've only been here a few hours!' Again she laughed, a musical sound that had been absent from their world for many months now. Jake found himself smiling with her. Perhaps Damara Cottage was already beginning to work a kind of magic on them both.

Changing the subject abruptly – he was still doubtful as to how far he wanted to pursue this line of conversation – he asked, 'Did you go down into the cellar when you first looked around? What's down there? Any electricity? And is it big enough to make into a dark room, do you think?' He knew of his mother's hopes. That he would regain his interest, his passion. He knew, too, that his words would bring happiness.

The urge to explore the underground chamber for altogether different reasons was strong though, and the desire to turn towards the door oddly compelling. He resisted the temptation. For now. Tomorrow, in the sensible light of day, would be time enough to investigate below ground.

'Only a quick peek,' Anna replied, apparently unaware of his internal conflicts, 'and there's a single bulb, but it looks like there'd be a lot of work needed to make it into anything but a storeroom. A bit damp and musty. Still, it could be a project.' She laughed again. 'But if you want to have a look down there tonight then you're on your own. I'm on my last legs and can feel my bed calling.'

He shook his head. 'No chance. Maybe tomorrow though.'

Of one mind suddenly, and with tired smiles, they gathered their used crockery. By mutual unspoken agreement, they left them on the counter to be dealt with tomorrow.

'Bed?' It was more suggestion than question, and with a nod, Jake granted that he was more than ready for sleep.

With a last longing look at the innocuous little door in the corner, he followed his mother upstairs.

WITCHES AND WARLOCKS

His dreams that night were remarkable in their clarity and intensity.

The woman was beautiful beyond words. Black, lustrous hair that ebbed and flowed around an elfin face. Eyes deep with wisdom and kindness. Her clothing was white, a loose garment which did nothing to disguise the perfection of her body beneath, and she was surrounded by an aura of pale lilac light. He knew he was still sleeping, but the knowledge merely heightened his senses.

Seemingly without movement, she was beside him then, and placed a pale hand upon his shoulder. Although he felt no physical contact, he was imbued immediately with a sense of her. Aware completely of all that she knew. Of all that she once was. Her name, however, remained elusively beyond his grasp.

Jake's head swam with sounds, smells and scenes of a life lived to the full. Snapshots of happiness, of helping and healing, of time spent with friends and neighbours. And of the tall man. Her love for him had been deep and intense. Most of all, though, was Damara, her connection to the place spiritual, her mission beyond his ability to understand.

But you will understand, she promised, although no words passed between them.

Visions then, of dazzling brightness, blinding in their precision. A murmuring crowd. The same man, his clothing dark, a snarl distorting handsome features. And feelings. Of fear, of betrayal, of anger – and of sadness. Intensely now, there was sadness.

Jake awoke with a jolt, to sunshine slanting through the gap in the curtains, the dream, in all its intensity, still clear in his mind. The aching sorrow lifted quickly though, a heavy blanket raised with ease, leaving him surprisingly energised and excited.

Lying still for a few moments, he allowed his thoughts to settle, making certain they would not disappear like morning mist upon waking. He knew without doubt that this was a dream unlike any of past experience, that Damara Cottage and the beautiful dark-haired woman were inexorably linked.

He was also now convinced that their coming here, he and his mother, at this time, was something that was meant to be. Pre-ordained? Fate? Destiny? Jake wasn't sure of the words to describe the conviction, but he was certain that his future was somehow entwined with Damara Cottage.

With her.

Mid-morning found the Freers in the centre of the quaint little village of Welham. Provisions were needed, and both were keen to explore their new surroundings. They had already had a friendly reception in both the butcher's shop and the small but well-stocked convenience store, and were now heading towards The Wishing Well for a well-earned cool drink before carrying their purchases the half-mile back to the cottage.

Jake had made the decision immediately on waking that, for the time being, he would keep his experiences and thoughts to himself with regard to Damara and his dream-lady. His reasons were two-fold.

Initially, he wanted to be certain what the vision wished to tell him, what she wanted of him. Also, and far more mundane, he was unsure of the reception he would receive. Talking over dreaming of a beautiful woman with his mother didn't sit comfortably with him, however innocent it may be.

Their purchase and possession of Damara had been crucial. He recognised this to be true, but was as yet unsure what could be of such importance. Or, indeed, what part they each had to play.

He wanted to be confident of his own beliefs before voicing them. Even to his mother.

The coolness of The Wishing Well was welcome after the heat of the summer sun, and the décor was charming in a sturdy and comfortable way. The boarded wood, which floored the entry and surrounded the bar area, gave way to a richly-patterned red carpet stretching the length of the room. An inglenook fireplace dominated the far end which would, no doubt, make for cosy evenings during the dreary winter months. Deep leather sofas and armchairs, with accompanying low oak tables, completed the homely feel. The brass fascias, and the foot rest on the bar itself, gleamed with a sheen of frequent polishing. If the landlord wanted to create a welcoming ambience then he had certainly achieved his aim.

This same landlord stood now behind his bar, the epitome, Jake thought, of a village publican. Balding head, rosy cheeks, broad smile, and attired in cravat and braces atop a shirt with rolled up sleeves, he completed the perfect scene. His welcome was no less warm, and his voice boomed in bonhomie.

'Hello. Please come in. What can I get you?' A sweeping gesture with burly forearm displayed the beverages on offer. 'Something cooling on such a pleasant day?'

Seated on high stools beside the bar, cool and very welcome lemonades before them, the thought crossed Anna's mind that Mr Brunton, their genial host, had an obvious talent for story-telling.

He began with, 'You've probably been wondering about Mad Alice Lane then,' and at their eager nods, he continued with his narrative. 'You'll have seen the road name as you turned towards home, I'll warrant.' His bushy eyebrows raised in query and, at their affirmative returns, he continued. 'It's so-called after a certain witch of these parts who was hanged for her craft back in the early seventeenth century. And a bad and wicked woman she was, if accounts are true. She lived in your cottage, Damara. Did you know that Damara was the name of a pagan goddess? Of the hearth and home, if memory serves me.'

Anna caught Jake's look of surprise and pleasure at this snippet of interesting and personal information and, at the landlord's questioning look, she nodded encouragement for him to resume, even though a fat worm of suspicion twitched. She suspected that much of this local legend had been either invented or, at the very least, embellished over many years in the telling; most likely to entertain holiday-makers over a pint or two, or those new to the area such as herself. That aside, and taking everything with a very large pinch of salt, it was certainly interesting to hear about Damara and the surrounding area from one who had obviously lived in the village all his life.

'Well,' said Mr Brunton, 'she plagued the village with her black arts and curses until the good folk of Welham eventually rose against her and called in the Witch Finder.'

Jake hitched forward, elbows on the bar, and Anna could almost read his mind. *This is getting interesting.* She smiled, glad to see him involved and attentive once more.

'It was a time when charms and witchcraft were still a part of everyday life. People believed in the powers of good and evil, and in the abilities of those using magic. Mad Alice was one such.'

Mr Brunton had thus far been pottering around the back-bar, drying and replacing glasses as he spoke. Now he leaned opposite Jake and stilled as he became more engrossed in his tale.

'Her deeds were well-documented if you've the time or inclination to look. You can find records, written after her death, which'd turn your hair grey if you gave them credence. Awful things happened in the village during her lifetime, the blame for which were laid fairly and squarely at her door. And rightly so, to my mind.'

His certainty was absolute and Anna wondered about a

community where such fables were still believed. He had seemed such a rational man on first meeting.

'The Witch Finder made a proper job of cataloguing her many misdeeds,' he went on, 'and they make for miserable reading.' He raised his hand and, using his fingers as counters, ticked off a mental list. 'Crops failing in certain fields. Water courses suddenly turning bad. Babies born dead. Folk dying of unrecognised and dreadful illnesses, and some of them youngsters, too. And apparent accidents which should never have happened, but happened nonetheless, to any who happened to cross Mad Alice.' He spat her name with venom, causing Jake to recoil from the apparent hatred in the elderly man's voice.

'Her appearance was as ghastly as her character,' Mr Brunton continued. 'A hag of a woman. Make a picture in your mind of a traditional witch, hooked nose, warts on her chin, wild hair and fingers like talons…' Here the landlord caricatured a very acceptable impersonation of a wizened crone, complete with clawed hands and grimace. '…and you'll probably be close to the description in the Witch Finder's documents.'

Anna, the suggestion of a smile twitching around her lips, made a point of not meeting her son's eyes. If he was as amused as she then there was a very real danger of both of them sliding over the edge of good manners and into outright mirth. Certainly Mr Brunton had not intended his yarn to be taken for comedy, and she didn't want to offend the friendly and forthcoming gentleman. His parody, though, had been unintentionally humorous.

She noticed that Jake, however, seemed to be torn between an amusement similar to her own, and anxiety. She recognised the signs. He felt uncomfortable, she was sure. Where the disquiet came from she couldn't tell, but he had a nervous habit of rubbing his palms together whenever unsettled or frightened. He was rubbing them absently now.

Mr Brunton pressed on. 'She had to be dragged from Damara, the story goes. Kicking, screaming and cursing the good folk of Welham all the way. Her path to the noose took her along that track of yours.' A nod in their direction. 'The one leading from the cottage to the village. It's said that she still revisits that last fearsome walk.'

The publican's voice quieted then, as if imparting a great secret, and Anna noticed that he was beginning to sweat slightly, that his jovial eyes had taken on a faraway sheen, lost in another time or place.

'Of a summer night when the moon is full, her screams can be heard. I've heard them myself. Most who live hereabouts have.'

Anna caught a glimpse of Jake reflected back from the long mirror behind the bar. Eyes wide, mouth slightly agape, and cheeks flushed as if fevered.

'There've even been locals who've sworn to having seen her, my son included, but I can't claim it myself and for that I'm thankful.'

Mr Brunton paused, now clearly distressed, a fine sheen of perspiration beading his forehead and upper lip. The atmosphere had darkened perceptibly and Anna no longer felt even a slight inclination towards hilarity.

The tale continued. 'The old Doc, Bert Grassington, who lived in Damara before you? Now there's a strangeness. Right as rain and fit as a flea, he was.' The publican shook his head, running the back of his hand across a moist forehead. 'They found him at the foot of the cellar stairs. Back broken. Face ruined. Must've hit the corner of a step on his way down. Carved out from cheek to crown on one side. His one remaining eye was wide open. Staring and full of fear. The locals around here still believe, almost to a man, that Mad Alice holds sway. And most put Doc Grassington's death down to her meddlings.'

Mr Brunton's eyes locked with Anna's, the questions placed to her directly. 'Did he see her in the cottage that once was hers? Could she have sent him down those stairs to his death? His last sight was certainly something that no rational man would want to bear witness to, judging by that awful staring eye. No one knows for certain, of course, but many will tell you that it's so.' He paused, his glance now darting and nervous. 'Damara stayed empty after that. No one round these parts cared to take on the wrath of the witch. It's been almost ten years now, since that night.' The tea-towel behind the bar was used to mop his face and balding pate again and again. His distress was palpable and Anna placed a reassuring hand upon his hairy forearm.

'Please, Mr Brunton, you don't have to share this with us. It's obviously upsetting for you…'

'No, no, it's started now, so might as well finish,' he exclaimed, his tone tetchy almost to the point of rudeness. He pointedly snatched his arm from beneath her hand and squared his ample shoulders.

'Luke – my lad – is a grown man now, educated and rational, but when he was a young'un, no more than ten or eleven, he caught a sight of her. It frightened him so badly we had to get help from the old Doc to sort him out. And there've been others too,' he nodded, as if to convince them of the fact, 'who will all swear to sight of the hideous and malevolent look on her face.

'It was the eyes, Luke kept saying. The look in those eyes which was the worst part. That was what haunted his dreams for the best part of a year. Nightmares, I should say, for that's what they were. A bad time for us.'

He shook his head, seemingly lost in his own thoughts. His eyes had again taken on a glazed and slightly vacant look, and it took him some moments to become aware of his silent audience once more.

Anna wondered now whether the old publican actually believed the story. His very obvious distress gave that impression, at least concerning sections of the tale. The doctor's death, the inclusion of his own son's ordeal and the apparent effect on the family, made it seem unlikely that this was merely a local legend, another tall tale to be spoken of around the fire on a winter's evening.

'If you'll excuse me a moment, I'll just grab myself a small snifter. I haven't spoken of those times for many years now, and it still has the power to unnerve me.' Mr Brunton turned from them, the colour almost gone from his usually ruddy cheeks, and helped himself to a double whisky from the optic behind him.

Jake raised his brows and blew out his cheeks, the glance he threw his mother showing that the story had certainly made an impression. He looked like his old self again, she thought thankfully, and she mouthed an 'are you okay?' in his direction. At his nod, she turned her attention to the elderly publican.

'Mr Brunton? Are you alright?'

The landlord had downed his spirit and was now leaning heavily against the back-bar, head and shoulders drooping once more. He visibly gathered himself and, turning back towards them, carved a forced smile onto his cherubic face.

'Fine and dandy, thank you,' he replied somewhat tersely. 'I felt just a tad light-headed for a moment.' He approached their end of the bar once more, the hollowness around his eyes diminishing, a rosiness returning to his cheeks again, no doubt helped along by the hefty shot of single malt.

Anna was keen to learn more, but even at her gentle promptings, the landlord would not speak further of Mad Alice or his son's sighting. It was a 'difficult time' he said, and dredging up old memories didn't make for a 'comfortable night's sleep'. Apparently eager to change the subject, Mr Brunton wondered aloud if Jake may be available to help out in the bar.

'Part-time only, lad. It's all I can offer as I do most of the shifts myself, but evenings and weekends can be busy. I already have a part-timer helping me out at those times, and I could do with another pair of hands if you're after making a bit of pocket money?'

The landlord seemed back to his jocular self. Jake had stopped the palm-rubbing. If she tried hard, Anna could almost convince herself that the apprehension she'd felt during the tale-telling had never happened. Almost.

A job was what Jake needed though, and Anna guessed that work of any description would be difficult to come by in Welham. She began to thank the publican, before a look of recognition in Mr Brunton's eyes, and a smile of genuine warmth aimed at a point just beyond her left shoulder, caused both Freers to follow his gaze.

She turned, still seated on her bar stool, to find herself looking into possibly the deepest blue eyes she had ever seen. To say this man was good-looking was an understatement. He was, quite simply, a physically beautiful specimen. She had to remind herself to exhale, having held her breath since their eyes had met… was it only seconds before?

He extended his hand.

'I'm Dr Brunton, George's son. Please, call me Luke. I insist. I'm so very pleased to meet you. Mrs Freer, I presume? And this must be Jake?' His voice had a resonance, a deep and pleasing timbre which reminded her of dark velvet or melted chocolate or… She found herself wishing that he would speak again just so that she could listen to that silky sound.

'Oh, you must call me Anna.' The words had formed and were past her lips almost before she'd had chance to think about them. Her voice didn't sound even slightly like her own. There was a certain girlish and breathy quality which, had Anna been a bystander, she would have called simpering. She didn't feel at all like herself, as if she were watching events unfolding from across the room. She was aware of a strange detachment, whilst in the same moment being drawn into the deep blue pools of Luke's incredible eyes.

Taking the proffered hand, her eyes remained locked with those of Luke – she already, unaccountably, felt comfortable with the familiarity – until he turned his attention to Jake, releasing her grip from his friendly handshake. At once she felt bereft. As if the sun had suddenly ceased to shine. Giving herself a mental shake and a very sharp internal scolding at her very obvious ogling, Anna noticed immediately that the atmosphere in the room seemed to have cooled considerably during her very one-sided appreciation of the younger Brunton. A shiver caused the small hairs on her arms to react and she rubbed some warmth into them, musing unconsciously that these country pubs could often be a stark contrast to temperatures outside.

That Jake was not as dazzled by the dashing doctor was all too clear, to her at least. Although his conversation was polite, and all responses made appropriately, Anna was aware that her son was trying hard to maintain a calm facade.

'I hear you're going to be working here, Jake?' The doctor's question seemed friendly enough, but she could sense her son's hackles rising, could see the effort it was taking him to preserve a normal visage.

'How do you know my name?' His voice was strangely clipped and curt, the question blunt.

The answer was, of course, simple. 'It's a small village, Jake.' Was it her imagination, or was there a slight emphasis on her son's name? That voice though – it was just divine. 'You'll get used to everybody knowing your business pretty quickly. At least, you will if you want to be happy here.' The words might have appeared hostile had not the beauty of his tone belied any threat.

Jake pointedly turned his back on the doctor. Unforgivably rude. 'I'll let you know about the job for certain later, Mr Brunton? I want to chat it through with my mother first.'

At a loss to understand the sudden change in her son's mood, and unwilling to allow the situation to deteriorate further so that the Messrs Brunton might challenge Jake's distinctly un-charming manner, Anna took control.

Thanking the elder Brunton for his company and conversation, and making all the right noises to Luke, she made a clearly feeble excuse about having errands to run, and dashed for the door, pushing Jake before her.

Steering her son deftly out of The Wishing Well and into the bright heat of the High Street, they set off, looking for all the world like a pair of power walkers, towards Mad Alice Lane, strides lengthening in an eagerness to put distance between themselves and the public house.

Explanations could wait until they were well away from the cause of their very different reactions.

Dr Luke Brunton.

His effect on her had been extreme to say the least but the reasons for their differing perceptions would be difficult to explain for some time to come.

To each other, and perhaps to herself.

THE PEEL PLOTS

The dappled shade beneath the ancient trees was welcome after the heat of the exposed High Street. Anna put a hand to flushed cheeks and wondered how much was due to the temperature, how much to her own embarrassment. And how much to the bewildering excitement she'd felt at meeting Luke Brunton.

Their experience in The Wishing Well, the publican's tall tale, and her own extraordinary reaction to his son, had certainly made for a morning to remember.

The Freers had deviated off the main road in an unspoken decision to cool down, both physically and metaphorically, the cool of the shadows drawing them away from the sun's glare. They found themselves by chance in the quietude of the cemetery.

That Jake was angry was very apparent, but what had caused that response, unexpected in one of his usually calm temperament, she was still at a loss to understand.

She chanced a glance at her son. He seemed lost in his own thoughts for the moment. Wandering between the gravestones, he paused now and then to read the inscriptions more closely before moving on again. A slight frown creased his otherwise unlined young face, and she tried once more to broach the difficult subject of their early, albeit very different, opinions of Dr Brunton.

'Jake?' she called.

He looked up. There were questions behind his eyes, none of which she could answer.

'Shall we sit, and cool down? There's a bench over near the wall.'

At his answering nod, they carried their grocery bags to the seat.

He sat hunched forward, elbows on knees and head down, as if studying the recently-mown grass beneath his trainers. His first words surprised her.

'Did you notice the graves, Mum?' At her raised brows, he went on. 'Everyone who died here was really, really old. Well, almost everyone. There are the odd ones who died in accidents and stuff, but most people had a pretty good innings.'

Anna hid a smile then, at his use of one of her favourite phrases. 'A good innings' – a long life, well-lived, and with no regrets. What more could anyone really ask for?

'Must be a good place to live...' she started to joke, but the words died on her lips at the look on his face.

'Aren't you getting this yet?' he interrupted, his voice sharp-edged with barely-controlled aggression. 'Weird stuff going on at the cottage? And then this.' He gestured vaguely in the direction of the headstones. 'It's just not normal.' He ended almost on a shout.

Clearly upset, Anna struggled to understand what had distressed her otherwise calm and placid son to this extent. And 'weird stuff'? What on earth was he talking about?

'But, isn't it a good thing? To have a long life?' She tried hard to maintain an appeasing tone. 'Perhaps we've just chosen a really happy and healthy place to settle down. Goodness knows, we deserve something good to happen, after...' She bit back the words, not wanting to bring back memories of Peter's death. Not now, when Jake was just beginning to move forward, to regain his enthusiasm and energy.

There had been times over the past months when she had worried that he may never find his way back to happiness. Losing his father had punched a hole in his world. There had been a real danger that the jagged rip in the fabric of his life was irreparable.

In a very short space of time, the move to Welham seemed to be working for both of them, although it was still early days, of course. She didn't want their encounter in the pub – the meeting with Luke Brunton, to be more precise – to drag Jake back into the half-light in which he had been living since his father's accident.

'Is this about what happened in the pub?' she started again. 'I don't know what has upset you, but it's clearly something to do with Dr Brunton. He seemed really nice to me.'

'Nice?' He almost spat the word. 'Oh, c'mon, Mum! Surely you didn't buy into it. You must be able to see what he's really like? It was obvious.'

She tried for conciliation. 'What though? What was obvious? Dr Brunton was just a very charming man who stopped to say hello, to welcome us to the village. I don't see what's upset you so much.'

Jake jumped to his feet and turned to face her, towering over her seated frame. He trembled visibly with emotion, his body tight as a coiled spring.

'He's *not* a good man.' The words hissed from between clenched teeth.

Their eyes held for what seemed an age, before Jake gave an exasperated snort. Throwing his arms in the air, the universal gesture of 'I give up', without another word, he grabbed the groceries from the bench, spun on his heel, and stalked away from her. Anna didn't even try to follow. He was young and fit, and could easily out-pace her. She watched his tall figure disappearing towards Mad Alice Lane and Damara Cottage.

But the venom in his voice had startled her. She had never heard her son sound like that. Not even at the worst times during his grief. There had been sadness, and a quiet solitude, but never anger. This was new, this aggression, and she found it frightening.

She sat back beneath the shade of the sighing trees, feeling the slats of the bench press through the thin fabric of her blouse, and tried to allow the peace of the cemetery to wash over her.

At a loss to understand what'd just happened, a snapshot of her son's flushed and angry face still clear in her mind, Anna felt the beginnings of fear nibbling into the deepest parts of her consciousness.

Something wasn't right. She couldn't pinpoint exactly what was off-kilter, but her son's reactions, his uncharacteristic rage, disturbed her. She drew in a ragged breath.

The huge gun with the ornately carved stock was passed around once more to be admired and praised. The collection was impressive, Jake had to admit, but he had seen all of the weapons now – more than once – and was keen to head home for his lunch; and to find his mother.

After his outburst in the graveyard, and his self-righteous and angry exit, Jake had stomped around for a while, working off his anger and allowing himself to calm a little.

His mother's behaviour had horrified him. Her simpering and fawning to the oily doctor had been horribly obvious. Jake had been embarrassed and uncomfortable. The fact that he'd taken a sudden and colossal dislike to the man hadn't helped the situation either, but he acknowledged now that his own behaviour had left a lot to be desired. He probably owed some apologies. As one of those whom he may have offended was possibly his new boss – and he hadn't even started working yet – he decided to do the honourable thing, and made his way back to The Wishing Well to build some bridges.

He noticed immediately that the younger Brunton had already left, thankfully saving him the discomfort of deciding whether to make amends in that direction. Jake's true feelings there were a mystery even to himself, although he knew for certain that what he'd shouted in the cemetery – 'he's not a good man' – had come from somewhere deep within, from a place of absolute truth. How he knew, though, he could not have explained.

He'd made his way through the pub to where Mr Brunton was still serving behind the bar and dumped the shopping bags at his feet. Hesitantly he attempted to atone. 'Mr Brunton, I'm so sorry...' he began, but the landlord immediately waved away his apology.

'Don't even mention it, lad,' he'd said cheerily. 'It's been a strange old morning, one way and another. How about you do a trial shift this Friday? Start at five o'clock and we'll see where we go from there. Smart casual. No jeans.'

'Thanks, Mr Brunton. I'll be there.'

Now, though, Jake had become embroiled in what was obviously one of the publican's favourite pastimes, showing off the historical weaponry which hung, all to best advantage, above the fireplace in The Wishing Well.

Jake smiled and nodded as the landlord pointed out again the polished wooden stock of what was, he was told, a blunderbuss. Or, more accurately, a dragon.

'A shorter barrel than its larger sister,' Mr Brunton explained proudly, 'and it gave name to the Dragoon Guards, so it's said.' He demonstrated once more, to the tiny audience of locals clustered around the table, the smoothness of the firing mechanism and the quietly impressive clicks of hammer and trigger, his great hands surprisingly gentle as he handled the medieval firearm.

Jake glanced around, the faces showing either a polite interest or, in the case of diminutive Fred Turnbull, an expression of sycophantic attention. At least this impromptu, if small, gathering meant that Jake was able to meet a couple of the regulars before starting work at the pub; and that should stand him in good stead for Friday evening when his first shift was scheduled.

Mr and Mrs Fowler, 'Brian and Linda, lad', were apparently related somehow to the Bruntons.

'Have you met your neighbours yet?' asked Brian quietly as Mr Brunton continued undisturbed with his lecture on the workings of ancient weaponry. At Jake's head shake and questioning look, he explained in a stage whisper. 'The Coopers at Welham Farm, just over the way from you. Steve and I go way back. He's a good chap, and near at hand if you need help with anything.'

Jake smiled his thanks. It was good to know names, at least, of the people living closest to them.

Mrs Fowler – whom Jake instantly labelled 'busybody' – was, she told him softly, the sister-in-law of Mr Brunton's 'poor wife, Helen; dead many years now'.

Then there was Mr Turnbull who, to all intents and purposes, seemed to spend most of his free time in The Wishing Well. He and Mr Brunton managed a very fine parody of Master and Servant, the 'ever so humble' Fred hanging on the publican's every uttering, and adding cringe-worthy words of encouragement with monotonous regularity.

Jake finally managed to extricate himself from the group without too much indecent haste, and set off for Damara Cottage – *home*, he reminded himself – and the very necessary task of talking things through with his mother.

He was prepared to meet her halfway, acknowledging his own failings in the events of the morning. But he also really needed her to see how her own behaviour had looked from his perspective. Witnessing her flirting had been mortifying, especially with such a slick and unpleasant man as Doctor Brunton. She had disappointed him. Hopefully she realised this, he thought, sounding a little pompous even to himself. Much more importantly though, in Jake's world anyway, was that she had let his father down.

Disturbingly too, he couldn't quite crush an unsettling sensation that there was more to Luke Brunton than met the eye, and not in a good way. He stored that thought in his internal filing cabinet for later perusal. Uppermost in his mind now was mending the quarrel with his mother. They worked well as a team, neither able to let any disputes, large or small, fester for long. He quickened his pace, keen to get started.

When he reached the cottage, however, she wasn't there. The discussion would have to wait.

The set of shoulders and tilt of head spoke of his anger where words had failed. Anna had watched her son's retreating back, his long strides putting much needed distance between them, and wondered how the situation could have deteriorated with such suddenness. Their relationship, usually based on mutual love, respect and, she hoped, liking, seemed to have hit a very high hurdle. The disappointment in his eyes had been all too easy to see.

A tell-tale lump started in her throat, a prickle behind the eyes, and she pushed the emotion down once more. Each one of those irksome little molehills had piled atop the next though, until a mountain now blocked her way. The events of the morning – she acknowledged that her fawning behaviour in front of Doctor Brunton had been, at best, unseemly – and the resultant argument with Jake, threatened to topple her hard-won control.

She'd heard people say that weeping was a release. That you always felt lighter, cleaner, afterwards, but she'd never experienced that luxury herself. Crying made her feel weak, desperate, and despondent in its wake. She knew from previously glimpsed reflections of herself in the aftermath of tears that she was not a pretty sight either. Her face became swollen with unsightly blotches, eyes red and puffy, and always she was left with a nagging headache afterwards. She rarely gave in to these emotions that, she felt, served her badly. This time, however, the choice was not hers.

A sob caught in her throat before she could stop it, quickly followed by another. Her hand flew to her mouth, as if to push back the unwelcome sound. The pressure of the past months had finally reached breaking point. The dam burst, and she was reduced in seconds to a moaning, snivelling shell of a woman.

Aware, almost as a passive observer, that of its own volition her body was moving into an embryonic curl, she allowed her arms to wrap around her middle, and head to rest on knees. Anna's frame heaved and wheezed like a pair of failing bellows, and she had no option now but to allow the tears their outlet until the worst of the eruption had passed.

The aftereffects, as always, left her weary and desolate, the ache of missing her husband a physical as well as emotional pain. She fished in her handbag for a tissue.

Another reason not to cry, she thought, a tiny spark of spirit returning. *The snotty nose.*

Easier said than done, though, and small hiccoughing sobs continued to plague her for several more minutes. Finally, the storm had run its course, and she sat for a while longer, blowing her nose, gathering strength and composing herself.

Those people, friends and family, the ones who told her that she was strong, or brave, or 'doing really well', ought to see her now. Although she knew that their intentions were pure, they truly had no idea. The daily struggle to maintain a semblance of control, to keep her world moving forwards, when often all she wanted to do was find a quiet corner, pull the duvet over her head, and sleep forever.

It had been a difficult decision to refuse sedatives offered by her GP back in Winchester. The thought of a continued numbness from the pain had been appealing.

Initially, of course, shock had ensured that she went through all the correct motions with robotic efficiency in the days following the accident. That anaesthetised feeling, recognised by all who suffer a sudden bereavement. An inability to believe the unthinkable. The body's protection against a hurt too great to process.

She had identified Peter's body, of course. Had organised the funeral and wake, and remained steadfast, strong and controlled in front of, not only her son, but everyone.

She didn't cry either. Not even when she was alone. Not then. Crying had seemed so useless, trite, in the face of such tragedy. Crying was something she did when watching a sad film, or for other people's misfortunes. Never for herself. Not when the hurt was her own.

She remembered now a moment of self-awareness, of clarity. One of those crystal clear memories when she'd realised that actually, despite all evidence to the contrary, she wasn't managing at all well with the loss of her husband.

She'd been sitting on the edge of their double-bed, thinking of him, of his death, and trying, really trying, to weep for him. For herself. For all that she'd lost. She couldn't. The tears wouldn't come. Instead was a vast and aching emptiness, a hurting void inside her which, it seemed, would never be filled, could never be healed.

That was when she'd considered the medication. Not immediately, but in the weeks following. That time when friends and family had seen that she was 'coping' and had stopped checking in for a cup of tea every other day. When the phone stopped ringing. They had moved on with their lives. They assumed that she had too.

Only one thing stopped her. A very real fear that if once she took the tempting option of tablets, she might never be free of them again. And so she'd weathered the storm, had supported her son – as he had supported her – and the two of them had pushed forward from that dark time as best they could.

North. To Welham.

Since the decision to move back to her roots, her beloved North Yorkshire, she noticed, though, that her emotions seemed closer to the surface, more easily stirred. Tears pricked her eyes often. That uncomfortable lump in the throat was an almost constant companion. And she was more easily wounded.

Today, following the strange morning in The Wishing Well and the resultant spat with Jake, the floodgates had well and truly opened. She hoped, with a spark of black humour, that this was not the next stage of the grieving process. To have uncontrollable bouts of unattractive weeping whenever a cross word was said.

Anna glanced around the quiet cemetery, hoping fervently that no one had witnessed her meltdown but the only onlooker was an enormous raven perched on the wall some distance away. It watched her with the attentiveness of all wild creatures when human interlopers trespass on their territory, but also without judgement of her noisy sobs, or opinion of her blotchy face and red-eyes. Thankfully, it seemed the bird was her only audience. She did feel a little better though and, gathering her bag and rumpled tissue, she rose to her feet.

In an effort to distract herself, she began to wander, haphazardly, through the gravestones.

Most were made of local sandstone, and were weathered and worn by the harsh North Yorkshire winters. Some stood at lopsided angles, and a few had actually fallen, their faces hidden from passing scrutiny. Granite marked the memorials of the wealthier folk of the parish. But Jake was absolutely right. Almost without interruption, the inscriptions showed that the villagers lying beneath had lived long, sometimes surprisingly so, lives.

She noticed also some familiar names, obviously local families who had remained in the area over many generations. Bruntons, Coopers and Longstaffs were numerous, with dates reaching back, in some cases, to the eighteenth century. The lack of any modern markers indicated that more recently-deceased residents must now be laid in another resting place. Or perhaps cremations had become the more popular option.

Anna's amblings had taken her to the boundary at the rear, separating the cemetery from the woodland beyond. She paused, leaning against the dry-stone wall, allowing her mind to still and her thoughts to quieten.

The peace of the place washed over her and, as she gazed over the wall towards the undergrowth beneath the trees, she noticed a small and unkempt plot on the far side. The grass remained uncut, and was long and lush. Detritus of many years' leaf-fall had accumulated around two small headstones, almost obliterating them from casual view. The grave-markers were unremarkable, each around a foot tall, and in a plain style of square cut sandstone. They were unmarked save for two words on each. Names, obviously, thought Anna, but they were almost unreadable. Lichen clung to the stone, and weathering had taken most of the depth from the inscriptions.

On further investigation, she discovered a small gap in the length of wall and, squeezing through – the space designed for a person of much smaller stature, although Anna was of a slight build herself – she found herself almost knee-high in damp and abundant grass. It seemed to cling around her legs as she pushed her way the short distance to the plot.

The closer she got, the calmer she felt, her earlier fear and worry dissipating, and a gentler emotion taking their place. She was intrigued to discover who lay beneath the fertile earth, and she knelt before the markers, noticing as she did a third stone, large and flat, lying to the far side of the graves.

Using fingernails to pick away the lichen, the first headstone quickly revealed its secret. Margaret Peel. No date, and no eulogy. The second was equally easy. Edith Peel. Again, no further facts. She moved around to the third stone. It was laid flat to the earth, and of a length and width to suggest it might cover another grave. This was even more worn, the sandstone pitted and rippled, but was clear of the moss which had obscured the first two markers.

A symbol of some sort had long since blurred beyond recognition, but Anna made out letters beneath. They had been crudely, but deeply, carved into the stone, as if gouged by a hand working in anger. A possible 'W' to begin, and with an ending letter of 'h'. Hard as she tried, though, the mid-section could not be read.

She sat back on her haunches, excitement pricking at her. Could the word spell 'witch'? Could this be 'Mad' Alice, legendary sorceress and subject of George Brunton's Halloween-style story? She couldn't be sure that the word on the stone was witch, and even if it was, whether the unfortunate woman's surname had been 'Peel', which would at least give her relationship to the other two plots. These three markers could belong to another family entirely. Anna felt an irresistible need to learn who lay beneath, but why, she could not have said. The discovery of this tiny plot seemed suddenly of utmost importance.

The atmosphere changed in an instant. The very air seemed charged with electricity and Anna felt the small hairs on her arms and neck tingle. The feeling was not one of fear, though, or of danger. Rather, it was one of expectancy. She stood slowly and peered into the gloom, searching the shadows, for what, she didn't know. There was nothing though. Just a feeling. This air of anticipation, of excitement.

Rubbing her arms lightly, she stood, quiet and alert, waiting and hoping for something – anything – to happen.

A stillness came. The trees ceased their whispering, birdsong quieted, and any slight breeze that had stirred the tall grass fell away, leaving a cocoon of silence around Anna. It seemed that the very earth held its breath.

The force of the emotion took her by surprise, a wave of supreme joy which entered and filled her. Her hair lifted as if in a strong wind, and she felt her legs brace as she took the impact. That her soul was touched by the intensity, by the crackling surge of sheer rapture, she had no doubt at all, and her eyes closed in the bliss of the moment. She welcomed it, allowing it to flow through and around her.

Eventually the strength of feeling faded, leaving in its wake a quiet serenity. She stayed a while longer, needing to spend more time in this magical place with the long-dead Peel women.

Kneeling once more before the forgotten graves, the word on the third marker, the flat stone, burned in her mind.

Witch! Anna was sure of that now.

Whatever had just happened, wherever this surge of feeling had come from, a fortitude had been borne within her, a seed of fresh resolve, of hope for the future.

Whether for good or ill, she vowed now to discover the truth of the quiet – or unquiet – dead who lay beyond the wall.

THE GUARDIAN

The house was empty when she returned, but there was a note on the mat, pushed through the letterbox while she and Jake were in the village. It was short and to the point, wasting no ink on trivialities, and said:

Steve, Maggie and Lottie Cooper,
Welham Farm (your next-door neighbours).
Come for a coffee anytime.
We'd love to meet you.

It also had a landline telephone number scribbled as an afterthought at the bottom.

After the peculiarity of the morning, and with renewed energy following the occurrence in the cemetery, Anna fished her mobile out of her bag. Perhaps these new neighbours may be able to shed some light on recent events, although, in all honesty, Anna wouldn't know where to start. How could she explain what she had just experienced? Now *there* was a challenge. She was still trying to come to terms with it herself. The joyful infusion had calmed within her to an extent, but there still remained a quiet happiness, a feeling of positivity and vitality.

Relishing the long-absent feeling of well-being which, after the uncharacteristic behaviour of Jake was bewildering in itself, and half-laughing to herself at life's absurdities, she dialled.

Early afternoon found her seated at the well-scrubbed pine table in Welham Farm, a bag of Maggie's kitchen-garden vegetables in a carrier bag by her feet, and a large mug of strong, steaming coffee before her. Anna sighed with pleasure. This was just what she needed.

The same Maggie was sitting across from her, an attractive woman with flashing hazel eyes and a head of lustrous dark-copper hair, pulled back into a sensible ponytail. She was what might, in a less politically-correct world, be described as buxom, but the hard work of a farmer's wife clearly kept her figure toned.

She had a vivacity about her which Anna both envied and admired. Maggie's vibrancy was magnetic, and Anna was enjoying herself immensely. The two women had been drawn to each other immediately, and chatted easily and comfortably. It had been a long time since Anna had found herself thus, in the kitchen of what she dearly hoped would be a good friend, sipping coffee and putting the world to rights. It all felt so normal, and normal was something to be craved, especially after this morning's strange happenings and Jake's very worrying behaviour.

She found herself opening up to this warm and friendly lady. Maggie's empathy enabled Anna to share what had been kept locked tightly away for many months now. She was so tired of always being strong, of keeping up the pretence that everything was fine. Everything had been very far from 'fine', at least until her experience in the cemetery this morning, and it felt good to be able to let down her guard for once.

She had already spoken of the reason for the move to Welham, the struggles that they had both encountered in dealing with their bereavement, and finally the oddness of both her own and Jake's behaviour that morning.

Anna chuckled as she recounted the episode in The Wishing Well, giving Luke Brunton's huge impact upon both herself and her son a humorous bent. Maggie, however, wasn't laughing along, and Anna felt herself stalling as the cheery atmosphere around the table seemed suddenly awkward.

Sitting back in the chair, her expression now serious and

questioning, Maggie asked quietly, 'And what did you make of the Brunton men, then? It sounds like they made quite an impression.' This last was a statement, and there was no mistaking the cooling of tone.

Unable to fathom what had cracked their comfortable tête-à-tête, Anna again tried for frivolity. 'What's not to like about Dr Brunton? He's absolutely gorgeous. And Mr Brunton – George – offered Jake a job this morning, so I've got to give him a tick in the box.' Sensing that she was gabbling, she willed her voice to still.

Maggie didn't answer immediately. Silence stretched. The tick of the mantle clock was abnormally loud. Feeling a need to fill the void, Anna nevertheless restrained herself, sensing that she should await a response from the other woman. The moment hung, suspended in time.

'You shouldn't take everyone at face value, Anna,' came at last. Much of Maggie's innate sparkle had evaporated and her face had paled markedly. She made a discernible effort to gather herself before continuing. 'Please excuse me. I won't say take no notice, because it's so important that you do, but I truly don't mean to upset you. It's just that…' She paused, searching for the right words. '…sometimes people aren't all that they seem. The Bruntons? Well, let's just say that they may appear hale and hearty, and Luke is certainly easy on the eye,' she allowed a trace of a smile, 'but there's history there, and I wouldn't want you to get hurt. Especially after…' Her voice trailed away.

'No, no. It's fine.' Anna was quick to respond, although she was more shaken by the conversation than she cared to admit. 'I'm definitely not interested in any relationship of that kind, if that's what you were saying?' She looked questioningly at her new friend. At the affirming nod, she continued. 'It's not something I can even think about at the moment. Much too soon for me. If ever. I don't know what came over me this morning.' She shrugged her shoulders helplessly. 'It's just not in my nature to be taken in by a pretty face. I feel a bit foolish to be honest.'

Maggie nodded her understanding. 'Luke Brunton has been

known to have that effect. He's got all the equipment to dazzle, but I'm afraid he's just not a nice man.'

The same words! Exactly what Jake had said this morning. Surely it was more than coincidence.

Suddenly, bizarrely, Anna felt on the verge of tears again. She looked up to find Maggie's eyes also brimming in a moment of shared understanding.

The sharp rap on the door startled them, both heads turning towards the sound in unison. An inkling of unease pricked at Anna.

'Steve's still at Thirsk, at the cattle auctions, and Lottie's not due home from college for another hour.' There was a definite edge to Maggie's voice – perhaps irritation, perhaps fear – Anna couldn't gauge which. Her new friend's face was still turned towards the door, but the safe bubble of the Coopers' kitchen had suddenly burst.

The knock came again, more insistent and sharper even than the first. Maggie rose to answer. Before she could reach it, however, the handle turned and the door swung inwards.

As if on cue, the impossibly handsome figure of Luke Brunton was revealed, a quirky grin causing those deep blue eyes to crinkle at the corners.

'Ladies!' he announced, inviting himself into Maggie's kitchen as if by divine right. 'How wonderful to find you here, Anna. I called at Damara Cottage. I have a rota for Jake's first few shifts. My father asked me to drop it off whilst out on my rounds.' His voice, as melodic and smooth as she remembered, washed over her like warm chocolate. It was not lost on her, however, that, other than the token joint greeting, he had completely ignored Maggie. She had moved to the door and now stood, hand on the handle, as if encouraging his exit, but neither had acknowledged the other in any way at all. The air prickled with mutual animosity.

'Well, thank you very much, Dr Brunton, but you could have saved the journey and pushed it through the letterbox. Or phoned, and Jake could've picked it up.'

'Luke, please,' he insisted, 'and I was passing this way anyway.'

Maggie's ill-disguised snort indicated her thoughts on the plausibility of that claim, but he ignored it with aplomb and carried on without pause. Placing the rota slip on the table in front of Anna, he half-turned to Maggie. It was barely discernible, the change in his tone. His next words bent towards insolence, although delivered in that same velvety voice which cleverly made the comment difficult to challenge.

'Is the kettle on, Farmer's Wife? I have things to discuss with Anna. A coffee, if you've time?' This last was phrased as a question, but delivered as an order.

Maggie, though, was having none of it. 'No, I'm afraid not.' Her tone was brisk. 'Anna was just leaving, and I'm on my way to pick up my daughter. If you don't mind…?' She gestured to the still open door, her manner verging on outright rudeness. Luke acknowledged her words only by the swift change in tack, and exaggeratedly turned his back on Maggie.

'May I offer you a lift home then? My car is just outside.' He leaned towards Anna, one hand on the table, the other on her chair-back. She could feel the pressure of his thumb behind her shoulder and, invisible to Maggie, he began a gentle circular rubbing against her back. The heat of his touch, the rhythm of the movement, combined to elicit an excitement deep in the pit of her stomach, and she struggled to maintain a calm demeanour.

'I think I'll walk. Thanks anyway,' she managed, although it had taken much willpower to resist his persuasive offer. 'I could do with some fresh air and exercise, and it's such a lovely day,' she finished weakly.

'Of course. Another time, perhaps? Or a drink in The Wishing Well later?' The question was posed to Anna and, not waiting for a reply, he breezed out, pushing past Maggie without another glance. She closed the door with a gentleness that belied the expression on her face. Anger. And fear.

Slowly, she returned and sat at the table, both palms flat to its surface.

'He doesn't come here often,' she said, by way of explanation.

'Knows he isn't welcome. He only came today because he knew you were here.'

'But why? I don't understand.' And genuinely she didn't, although she could see the animosity between the two and believed it to be deep and real. Her own reaction to him, only now beginning to fade, had been surprising and sudden. She felt flustered and foolish that she could be so affected by his presence, and more than a little shocked at his audacity.

Maggie went on. 'He has a history, and I think – no, I know – that he has his sights set on you. He'll be very persistent, I can guarantee it. And he can be so very charming when he has a mind.'

Although Anna tried to squash the feeling, knew that her friend's words were well-meant, she could not stop the excitement which coursed through her at the thought of being pursued by Luke Brunton.

'Okay. Just supposing,' she argued, 'that I can accept that a man like him would be interested in me – why not just wait until we met again? It surely wouldn't have been long in a small place like Welham. What's his hurry?'

'Oh, he has his motives, believe me. Suffice to say, I'd steer well clear if I were you.'

Maggie rose to put the kettle on again.

'I thought you had to pick up Lottie?'

'No, she gets the bus to the end of the lane. She's fairly independent. I wanted Luke Brunton out of my house though, and that was the first thing I could think of. He knew Steve was away, or he wouldn't have risked the visit. He knows, too, that it was an excuse – that Lottie doesn't need collecting from college.'

'Then, why?' asked Anna. 'Why didn't he challenge you?'

'I told you. He's a game-player. We've never been friends, have never even pretended to like each other, ever since childhood. He'll have loved the chance to score points. He'll probably save this up and try to use it to gain an advantage at some point.' Maggie sighed as she made them another coffee. 'It's always been like this, Anna. Call it "village politics" for want of anything better. It's always been there, simmering away just below the surface. Probably best if you avoid getting sucked into the middle of it – for as long as you can, anyway.'

She refused to be drawn any further on the subject, and their talk turned to more usual topics of conversation. Their children, the weather, and when to schedule another coffee.

The churning excitement remained with Anna though, and she found her thoughts turning with ridiculous regularity to when, and how, she might next meet the handsome, and so very charming, Dr Luke Brunton.

MANIPULATION

Maggie's advice shouldn't have been so easily ignored, and Anna knew instinctively that heeding it would have been the sensible option. Her new friend had offered it with the best of intentions. Yet here she was, hiding behind The Wishing Well, fidgeting with hair and lipstick and wondering why she couldn't pull herself together, make up her mind, and go inside.

Dr Brunton's invitation earlier in Maggie's kitchen had been concise – 'a drink later' – and like a moth to a flame she had found the thought of spending an evening in the company of the charming local doctor impossible to resist, even with warnings of his unsavoury character still ringing in her ears.

On returning home from her visit to Welham Farm, she was frustrated to find a note from Jake, saying he'd gone out with his camera and could they talk later. She'd then done more sorting and unpacking of the many boxes still waiting in the spare room. Doubts as to the wisdom of her proposed outing were shelved quickly, and very deftly, in the back of her mind and Anna had given herself permission to go for drinks with him. Just drinks, after all. Nothing to worry about, and nothing at all to feel guilty about.

Yet still there was a seed of doubt. An inkling that this was a bad idea. The fact that she was keeping the secret outing from her son sat badly with her. Deceit was not something she enjoyed.

She had admitted, in a moment of honesty, that the choice

had been made all along, however much she'd tried to convince herself that this was a last minute decision. The amount of time she had spent on hair and makeup, the care she had taken choosing her outfit, belied any thought of an evening in front of the TV.

And now here she was, loitering with intent in the shadows of The Wishing Well, plucking up courage to enter and wondering why on earth she was not at home watching some silly soap opera, or unpacking yet more of the endless boxes.

The low growl of an approaching sports car made up her mind for her. Unwilling to be caught hanging about in the pub car park, she began a brisk walk around the outside of The Wishing Well. Not quickly enough, unfortunately, to avoid being spotted by the driver of the car.

And it just had to be, she thought, as Dr Brunton's sleekly-sexy and highly-polished Audi TT purred past her. Parking almost exactly where she had so recently been standing, he seemed to uncurl from the low-slung machine, movements fluid and elegant. Anna felt gauche and flustered as he approached.

His smile was wide and warm though, and his words, that voice, again made her pulse quicken and her cheeks flush.

'Anna. What a lovely surprise. I'd hoped to see you here. Come inside and I'll get us a drink.'

She smiled agreement and, although he didn't touch her, she felt guided to the front door, could almost feel the warmth of his hand on the small of her back. He indicated a cosy seat in the corner of the pub rather than the high stools by the bar, leaving her for a moment to speak to his father who was serving alone tonight.

'Chianti?' Luke had suggested. 'A bottle to share?' and she had again smiled her pleasure. She did not drink often, had actually not touched a drop since the day of Peter's funeral. It had been an easy decision. Had she been alone, had she not had Jake to think of, then wine could very easily have become a crutch, something to numb the solitude of the long, cold evenings. Her son had been a reason – the only reason, in fact – to work her way through the months of misery without the aid of either pills or alcohol.

This was a social drink though. Completely different. She knew what she liked and Chianti was up there with her favourites. And why not let her hair down for once? Where was the harm in a couple of glasses of her favourite red? And what a lovely coincidence that his wine of choice was also hers. The thought of what else they might have in common coloured her face once more, and she scolded herself at these girlish fancies as she sank into a low and comfortable settee near to the hearth.

The pub was quiet, only a few Thursday night regulars sitting at tables to the far end of the room. The remaining drinkers were leaning against the bar, chatting softly. After a whispered word and a smile shared with his father, Luke collected their bottle and two glasses, and made his way towards her. Their eyes met and held as he took the adjoining seat beside her.

'Shall I?' He indicated the wine and, at her nod, poured for them both and handed her a glass.

'To new beginnings?' He raised his glass and they toasted.

'New beginnings,' she responded, and the words felt good. The liquid was thick and richly red, clinging to the glass as she took a sip. She felt decadent and daring, the gentle and almost forgotten sting of the alcohol chasing a path down her throat. She relaxed slightly, warming to him once more beneath the obvious admiration of his gaze.

They passed a pleasant hour or two chatting about inconsequential topics. Her move back to Yorkshire and the reason for it – he was surprisingly empathetic, encouraging her gently as she spoke falteringly of her husband's death for the first time, and of Jake and his somewhat vague plans for the future.

He responded in kind with information about The Wishing Well and his father, the area generally, the village specifically, and about his own work as village doctor.

Luke refilled her glass several times whilst ignoring his own. 'Driving,' he explained, 'but please don't worry. I'll make sure you get home safely.' His smile was open and honest.

The Chianti helped to unwind the tight knot of anxiety which had lain, coiled within her, since Peter's accident. Luke's quiet attention drew a response from her that she had not felt for many months now. That of a woman to a man. He was interested in getting to know her better – a lot better, judging by his body language. That knowledge, coupled with the heaviness of the wine, acted as a heady aphrodisiac, and Anna was aware of her body, of her heightened senses, as rarely before. It was many months since Peter's death, and she'd been left to cope with both her own grief, and Jake's, in the aftermath of losing him. A heavy load to bear. The appreciation Luke was showing her now, being in the company of an attractive man and having his full attention, was bringing out the wanton in her.

She tried to focus her mind on the conversation, to pay attention to his words, but the Chianti was working its magic, and she floated on a red cloud of relaxation and semi-arousal.

'I'm actually based in Northallerton on a daily basis. That's where the practice is. If there are any house calls here in the village, though, then I'm almost always the doctor you'd see arriving at your door.' He leaned towards her confidentially. 'Truth be told, Anna, I'm not kept terribly busy by the fine folk of Welham. They're a healthy bunch, almost to a man.'

He had turned towards her during their conversation, and his arm rested along the back of the settee behind her. He was close enough that she could feel the heat of him near her neck. Her thoughts wandered again as he continued.

'I have a flat in Northallerton, close to the practice, and rented, in case of a career move. It's fairly convenient for me…'

His voice seemed to fade and blur as he spoke of normal everyday matters, and as she drifted, she wondered what it would be like to really get to know this man, to spend time with him. She crossed her legs, rubbing her thighs tightly together, the friction causing that imp of desire within to open a sleepy eye. A picture formed in her mind of herself in his arms, of how it would feel to kiss him, to…

'…and so I lost my mother quite young. Since then it's been just my father and I.'

Anna snapped back into the room with a jolt, aware that she had missed what was probably a most important and revealing insight into Luke and his background. She took a large gulp of wine in an effort to cover her embarrassment, managing, in her haste, to spill a little down the front of her blouse.

'Oh.' The gasp of dismay brought Luke to her rescue. He grabbed a napkin from the table and began to pat gently around the front of her blouse, the small stain apparently covering a much larger area than she had originally thought. The flush was again back in her cheeks, his near-fondling of her breasts bringing blood rushing to more than just her face.

'Luke… please! I can manage…' But even as she said it, as her hand closed over his, she wished for him to continue, found herself reclining back into the softness of the cushions as he leaned in towards her, the napkin now still and his hand lying perilously close to the swell of her bosom.

The imp was wide awake now, and wanted more. Much more.

The intense blue of those azure eyes seemed bottomless, and she fell into the beguiling depths as their lips met in a grinding kiss. Her lips were forced apart by the welcome probing of his tongue, and she opened to him like a flower to sunshine, hands reaching to cup his head, fingers running through the silken blondness of his thick hair.

In a moment, it was over. He pulled back without warning, as if suddenly aware of the surroundings, of the inappropriateness of their actions, leaving her gasping and exposed – a fish floundering on the shore – at the abruptness of his retreat.

The smashing of a dropped glass behind the bar broke the tension and with a slight shake of the head, Luke turned from her, a rueful grin shaping his fine lips.

'Anna, I must apologise. Please forgive my crassness. What must you think of me?'

Still spread-eagled on the sofa, arms and legs akimbo, she struggled to recover her equilibrium and dignity. Snatching the wine-stained napkin from him, whilst at the same time straightening her skirt, which had somehow risen high on her thighs during the kiss, she made a play of dabbing the remainder of the tiny pink mark on her blouse. Avoiding any eye contact – for therein lay her downfall – she reassured him.

'Please… don't worry. It was just one of those things. If I hadn't spilled the wine…' Her voice trailed off again as the implication of what had almost happened hit her full force. If Luke hadn't stopped that kiss when he had, she would, she admitted to herself, have been swept away by the moment. May well have actually made love to a man of very short acquaintance, in a village pub, in front of the landlord and all its customers.

Her actions shocked her to the core. Yet she couldn't forget the pressure of his mouth on hers, his hands on her body, of how she had felt, rather than heard, the groan of pleasure escape him as his tongue found hers.

Picking up her glass, she took another shaky gulp. This Chianti was remarkably good. She chanced another glance at him from beneath her lashes, and found that he was watching her mouth as she drank. A bolt of excitement, of pure sexual chemistry, shot through her. Unable to stop herself, she allowed her tongue to lick the taste from her lips, watching for his reaction as she did so.

Slowly, and with a sardonic grin, he mirrored her movements. Re-filling his own glass with the ruby liquid, he sipped. Powerless to look away, she found herself spellbound by those perfect lips as his tongue traced a pathway around their pink edges. She held her breath as he leaned towards her once more.

'This is going very well, Anna.'

A cough designed to draw attention broke the spell, and Anna raised her eyes to meet those of a tall, rangy man, kindness and strength obvious in his beaky face.

'I'm sorry to intrude, but are you Mrs Freer?' The nod and acknowledgement he gave to Luke was cursory – 'Doctor' – and Anna was aware without explanation of the animosity between the two men.

'Maggie told me all about you and Jake, and you fitted the picture.' The stranger smiled, and his weathered face creased in all the right places, the sign of a humour not yet displayed.

'Steve Cooper,' he explained. 'Your next door neighbour, and Maggie's other half.' He stretched across the low table and his grip was firm and warm as they shook hands.

Anna's first rational thought as she'd torn her attention from Luke was how much had he seen, and her cheeks burned in embarrassment at the display the two of them had been putting on in this quiet corner.

Her stammered reply and flustered fidgeting did little to disguise her discomfort and she was grateful when the offer of a lift home was suggested.

'I'm going your way now, and it'll save you the walk. The track can be a bit uneven in the dark.'

'Cooper, it's fine,' Luke interrupted. 'I'm perfectly capable of seeing Anna home safely. And she's not ready yet anyway.'

At this assumption, at his peevish dismissal of Steve, Anna bridled. She was not yet ready to be part of a couple, decisions made for her without discussion. The whole situation suddenly seemed wrong, humiliating, and she longed to escape from The Wishing Well with whatever shreds of her dignity were still intact. A few minutes earlier, it would have been a whole different story. An unconscious decision, she realised, had already been made. Without doubt, she would have ended the evening in Luke's bed, and the thought shocked and disappointed her.

'Actually, I am ready. Thank you, Steve. A lift home would be great. Luke,' she turned to him as she stood, 'this was a lovely evening.' She couldn't bear to meet his eyes, her embarrassment in front of both men, and for very different reasons, intense. 'But it's late, and time for me to leave.'

He too stood, a picture of flawless civility and suavity.

'Of course, Anna. We'll no doubt continue this another time?' His hands on her shoulders, the kiss on her cheek, seemed strangely cool now, all heat gone from the passion of previous embraces.

As she walked towards the door, away from Luke, away from what would have undoubtedly happened without the timely intervention of Steve Cooper, a shudder of disgust took her. At her own shameless behaviour? Certainly. But there was more. Something dark and unnamed that she couldn't quite grasp.

As she left The Wishing Well, she knew, could feel, that his eyes were still on her.

Steve dropped her at the end of Damara's pathway. She was grateful that he made no mention of The Wishing Well, and maintained a gentle flow of light conversation for the short journey home. How were they finding the cottage, the village, the area? If they needed anything, to just shout. If they had any problems, 'you know where I am. Just down the track or on the end of the phone.' This last was delivered in a much more serious tone, and Anna wondered at his change of mood. She had bigger fish to fry, though, than analyse her neighbour's conversational skills. After tonight's embarrassment, she wanted to shut the front door and never show her face again. She could hardly wait to get out of the car.

'Thanks so much, Steve. For the lift home, I mean.' Anna felt intensely awkward.

'No problem,' he smiled, previously mellow humour apparently restored. 'It was on my way, after all.'

She got out of the car quickly, and gave him a wave as he pulled away. The tail lights winked along the track until they disappeared into the darkness of the copse.

She turned and went inside. It was a relief to be home. Thankfully Jake was waiting up for her, with the kettle on, his intention to make amends for their earlier disagreement. It would be good to talk and regain her equilibrium. But memories of the evening, of what could have happened had not Steve Cooper so fortuitously appeared, haunted her thoughts. She shook her head. How could she have done it? What had she been thinking?

It was with worries aplenty that Anna finally slipped between her sheets. She felt drained and exhausted, and more than a little anxious. Sleep, she thought, would be a long time coming.

DREAM TIME

She walked along the familiar yet altered track, feet weighted and dragging. A vague sense of danger nibbled at the edges of her mind. It was dark. The mist was all around, thick and swirling. It eddied and moved, forming half-seen figures or faces, gone before they could be distinguished.

She knew that somewhere just ahead was safety – Damara – but the path was shrouded by the curtain of grey, unclear, the ground beneath her feet now pitted and rock-strewn. Each step forward took all her effort, both physical and mental. Her nerves were tightened and fragile.

From somewhere close came sounds of movement. Skitterings and scrabblings, like long claws on scree. And the sounds terrified her.

Her eyes strained against the fog, searching for whatever shadowed her progress, arms outstretched both for balance and for protection. Seeking, always seeking. For home. For safety.

Yet she knew that she was not safe. Knew that within the hidden spaces of her dream, danger lurked. She tried again to push forward, to reach the light and security of Damara, unsure of who, or what, walked with her, unable to breach the misty curtains swirling around her.

A light touch on her shoulder caused her to spin around in fright. No one was there. Yet the fog swirled more quickly here, as if disturbed by sudden movement. An indistinct shape, of a person perhaps, quickly disappeared before she could be certain.

Anna knew that she was dreaming, and tried to force herself to waken, only to find that with each conscious effort, the mist thickened further. She wore only a short satin nightdress, and coldness stroked where moist air touched skin. She turned for home once more, the way known to her, although the path was different and more rugged than the true approach to Damara Cottage.

He was in front of her then, on her turning. There had been no sound, no warning of his presence. Even the dreadful scurrying noises had ceased, leaving a profound silence wherein nothing moved, or breathed, or lived. She was alone in this place, with him. And the knowledge was fear.

His beauty was undiminished in this world, but the eyes were pools of madness, black and glinting, with green depths of jackal or wolf. She tried to back away, but her feet were caught, stuck fast in an unseen trap. He stretched a hand towards her, long, claw-nailed fingers reaching to touch. Lips peeled back from teeth made sharp and wickedly pointed in a grin of hideous welcome.

'Anna, my darling.' Again, the voice was known to her, yet beneath the smooth and sensual tone there vibrated an edge. Of corruption. Of malevolence. 'I knew you would come to me here. That you would recognise my call.'

His fingers brushed her cheek and she recoiled in horror at the ice-coldness of that touch. She was frozen, fear rendering her helpless against the control and power of the creature before her. Her feet were horribly immobile, as if sucked down into thick mud. The harder she tried to lift them, the heavier they became.

He stepped forward, hand now cupping her chin, the terrible eyes only inches from her.

'Kiss me, sweet Anna, and seal our pact.' He bent towards her, head lowering, sharpened teeth visible behind his perfect lips. She found herself leaning in, reaching for his embrace, yearning for his caress even while the horror grew within her.

Another voice. 'Mum. No! Run. Run now.' Jake was very close, somewhere just beyond the mist, his tone urgent, yet quiet. 'Get away from him.'

The Brunton-thing paused, head cocked dog-like, a snarl showing yet more of those ice-white fangs.

'Ah, the upstart. But you're too late. I have her now.' He slowly returned his gaze to Anna, languid in his movement, eyes now completely and horribly black. He grinned in the sure knowledge of victory. Anna could see herself reflected in the awful depths of those eyes, a cringing, sorry creature, beaten by a force greater than herself. She gave herself up to debasement.

Again, closer now. A light in the darkness. Her son's voice.

'Now, Mum. It has to be now. Follow my voice.'

Within the dream, trusting, following her intuition as never before, Anna closed her eyes, stopped trying to fight against the feelings, and let her arms drop to her sides. Concentrating every fibre on Jake's words, putting all of her physical energy into just one action, she moved first one foot, then the other. Gingerly at first, and then with more confidence as she felt something slacken, the hold on her somehow weakening.

Taking no account of where Luke might be, whether before or behind her, she forced her feet loose from whatever held them captive, and began to walk, baby steps at first, then strides, then running full pelt towards Damara Cottage and the voice of her son.

'Forwards, Mum. Keep moving forwards.' Jake's voice was fading now behind her, yet she raced onwards, eyes kept tightly closed, fearing neither obstacles nor pitfalls. She trusted that Jake would guide her to safety.

She met no resistance. The expected barrier of Luke in front of her had not impeded her flight, although she'd felt the coldness of the grave touch her soul as she passed the point where he should have been standing. She pressed her eyelids down tighter in an effort to remain blind to her surroundings. Her son's voice, calm, encouraging, again sounded faintly as she ran.

'Go, Mum. Keep going.'

She awoke with a gasp, the dream still fresh and clear in her mind. If she had expected to find Jake by her bedside, then she was mistaken. The room was dark and quiet, and there was no sound of movement from across the landing where her son slept.

Anna swung her legs over the side of the bed, and reached for the table-lamp. The illumination did much to calm her tattered nerves, as did the knowledge that she was indeed safe and secure within Damara Cottage.

She'd had nightmares before, of course, and her fair share of truly awful ones over the months since Peter's death. Ghastly and horrifying dreams of his accident, the aftermath. Worst of all, of a horribly-damaged, yet living, parody of her husband who walked and talked, but carried the dreadful injuries which had ended his life. Anna had learned to deal with them, to let the memories drift away with the dawn of each new day, leaving behind them only a dragging sadness of what might have been if fate had been more forgiving.

But this nightmare had seemed so real. And still, now, she could remember every detail. Could feel the touch of his icy fingers on her cheek. Could see the inhuman pools of madness that were his eyes. And could feel the terror as she realised that she was powerless to resist him. How could any ordinary dream remain as clearly remembered? How could her senses replay to her now what she had felt in that other world?

And why should Luke Brunton, village doctor and respected paragon of virtue, appear to her as a monster?

At breakfast, Jake was playing the grumpy teenager to a tee. Head down as if to avoid eye contact, a grunt the most communication she had managed to elicit from him so far. She had tried to bring up the subject uppermost in her mind a couple of times, but at each tentative approach Jake had effectively side-stepped the conversation, firstly clattering around in the cupboard – apparently searching for an elusive plate – and then, when she tried again to engage in discussion, by disappearing to collect his mobile phone.

The message was clear. If Anna had hoped to question him about her night-time experience, then she was to be disappointed. And honestly she wasn't even sure where to start. How to ask one's son whether he had travelled into a dream to rescue her was not the easiest of openers, and with a sigh, she shelved the conversation for another time. If ever, she acknowledged inwardly.

For the first time that morning, Anna looked at Jake properly. Even distracted as she was, she couldn't fail to notice how pale and tired her son appeared this morning, and she wondered whether he might be sickening for something. Either that, she thought, or he'd had a disturbed night of weird and frightening dreams like his mother.

With a sideways glance from under his lashes, and a sudden, 'I'll eat this on the way,' Jake grabbed his trusty mobile, a slice of dry toast, and headed for the door.

'Will you be in for lunch?' was met with a bang as the front door closed behind him.

Another apology for rudeness owed to his mother. Jake shrugged ruefully. This was becoming a habit. But he couldn't have discussed it with her. Not at this point. Truthfully, he wasn't even sure what had changed last night. Nothing like this had ever happened before.

Although he had, for most of his life, been able to gatecrash other people's dreams, always in past experiences he had been a spectator, watching from the sidelines while the sequence played out before him. In his earliest ventures, he had tried to participate, to speak or to interact, but it appeared that he was invisible and voiceless within this ability to travel through the unconscious minds of others.

From a young age, he had become aware that, although everyone had dreams, they seemed unable to control either the content or the outcome. Most certainly, he had never heard of anyone who could visit in the way that he could.

He had finally done some research and had settled on either

lucid dreaming or astral projection. He couldn't decide which description best suited what happened with him. Perhaps a combination of both? Whatever the label, though, he had always been able to control his own dreams, and to visit others whenever he wished.

His mother's nightmare had been different though. Previously he had made decisions about who and when he would visit during dream time. Never, for obvious reasons, had he chosen his parents' night-time excursions to observe.

There had been no choice to be a part of this nightmare. He was suddenly there, watching, just beyond the curtain of mist, apparently hidden from them, but able, himself, to see through the shrouding greyness with the clarity of a sunlit day.

He had known immediately that there was danger, that he must act quickly or risk losing her. When he spoke for that first time, in fear and horror of the drama unfolding before him, when she heard his voice and responded with a slight turn towards where he stood, his relief was immense. He had feared that it would be as before in dream time. That he would be mute, would be unable to help. Would be forced to watch this dreadful scene unfolding, unable to stop his mother's degradation, her capitulation. That the creature would be victorious.

At his voice, the monster had raised its head also, had acknowledged him, was most assuredly aware of who he was. A fear had gripped Jake then, so great in its intensity that he was momentarily stunned.

What was this thing?

Grotesque in its ghastly depravity, he shrank from the evil it exuded. Although vaguely male in shape, the clawed talons and hideous visage belied any humanity. Never had he seen anything like this, not even when visiting the worst of childhood night terrors.

He had called again to his mother, and this time she seemed able to break the hold of the creature upon her. Jake had seen her close her eyes, saw the monster's snarl as it lost control of its prey, and looked on in horror as its attention turned now towards him.

Then she was moving forwards, passing through the monster's form as though without substance, gaining speed, away from them, towards safety. He had encouraged her with his words one last time before she disappeared into the mist.

The creature's bottomless eyes met his, and Jake had stepped forward to meet his adversary for the first time.

He shook his head at the memory now. The night's events had certainly taken a toll on him and he felt bone-weary, his energy depleted and weakened. But he had won. Had vanquished the creature, their battle a meeting of minds rather than fists. It had retreated in howling vexation at being thwarted.

Since the day in The Wishing Well, that first meeting with Luke Brunton, Jake had been dimly aware that he had met his nemesis, had known that a time of confrontation would arise.

His connection with Alice on the first night in Damara had furnished him with a knowledge of past events, and also a vague insight into the battle ahead. But how, or when, he had not known. The speed with which this first challenge had occurred was a shock. He felt unprepared and vulnerable in the face of it.

Jake had also expected that they would meet in the physical world, rather than the tenuous unpredictability of the unconscious mind. His lips twitched in a wry half-smile at this thought. The creature had, he felt, made its first mistake. It had underestimated him as an adversary – or perhaps was unaware of his prowess and confidence gathered over years of visiting in the metaphysical realm. This was a level playing field of dreams, if not tipped slightly to Jake's advantage.

He knew, though, that this was only the beginning. That whatever he had met in the mists around Damara was merely thwarted, not conquered. Not yet.

There was much work now to be done, and his first visit would be to the library in Northallerton. He needed to know more about his opponent before they met again.

Next time, the Brunton-creature would be better prepared. And for that challenge, it was crucial to recognise the foe.

THE RAVEN

It was huge. He'd remembered seeing them before, on a visit to the Tower of London with his parents as a child, but had never come across any in the wild before. Probably suburban Winchester wasn't an ideal habitat for them, he thought. The wilds of North Yorkshire definitely seemed a more appropriate setting.

It was unusual too because of the permanent milky-white of its left eye, giving it a strange expression, almost as though it were winking at him.

Jake put the food in the dish and took a step back, waiting.

He'd first seen the raven two days after they'd moved in, from the sitting room window. Quite a distance away, it was standing in the middle of the footpath that led to Welham Farm.

He'd noticed it initially, of course, because of its size – even from afar it was obviously a huge and impressive bird – but also because of its stillness. It didn't seem concerned with searching for food, or looking for a mate, or any of the other bird-like activities Jake would have expected to see. It merely stood, looking towards the cottage, for all the world as though waiting for somebody to emerge.

Intrigued, Jake had quietly opened the patio doors and, cautiously and slowly, made his way down the garden towards the magnificent creature. It seemed unperturbed by his presence, his nearness, and cocking its head to the right to reveal a beady and knowing eye, it returned his gaze. He got to within a few feet of it, close enough to see clearly the veil of its blind eye as it turned its head, and the sleek gloss of black plumage, before it took to the wing, soaring majestically over his head. He resisted an urge to duck as he felt the downdraught. It circled in an effortless arc, skimming Damara's roof, before disappearing over the tree tops.

Since that first sighting, the raven had become a regular visitor around the cottage, both of them spotting it at numerous times during any given day. His mother had mentioned seeing a similar bird in the cemetery on their first visit into Welham, and he had to assume that it was the same one. Ravens, however rural the setting, were not a common sight, and a bird this large would presumably have its own territory.

Initially it would stand in the same place on the track, but as time progressed, it began to move gradually nearer. The past few visits had seen the bird adopt a perch on the wooden bench at the end of the garden, and here it would stay, sometimes for hours at a time.

Jake named it Albert, after Albert Einstein, because of the prominent black eyebrows which reminded him of a halo of hair, and also because it seemed to suit the creature's intelligent yet humorous expression.

Doing online research, and finding that ravens are 'omnivorous and opportunistic', Jake had hitched a lift with his mother and visited the supermarket in Northallerton where he purchased several of the cheapest tins of dog food. Each morning, he scooped a portion into a wide dish, supplementing the fare with leftovers and vegetable peelings for variety, and placed the dish on the ground outside, a few feet from the patio doors.

Neither of them had seen Albert eating the food, or indeed even approach the cottage, but Jake's offerings disappeared nonetheless.

He was not a noisy bird. A throaty cawing could be heard occasionally, mostly at dusk. A farewell for the night? Or when the food had disappeared in the morning, perhaps a 'thank you for breakfast', Jake thought.

The residents of Damara Cottage and their visitor became

used to each other as the days progressed, and easy in one another's company. Jake heard his mother wish Albert 'good morning' as she hung out washing, and he would make a small noise of recognition in the back of his throat. Jake passed by the bench-perch regularly on his various explorations of the nearby countryside, and the bird would nod his great head sagely, eyebrows twitching as if in amusement, as their eyes met.

As Jake stood in the garden, waiting and wondering what the bird would do next, Albert approached the dish with apparent unconcern. It was the closest they'd been thus far, and Jake watched quietly as the raven devoured every scrap of the unappetising mess. The clattering of his massive beak against the metal bowl sounded harsh in the stillness of their surroundings. Finally finished, he looked up, his one beady black eye glinting with intelligence.

Jake took a tentative step forward. Albert didn't retreat. Slowly, Jake bent into a squat and reached out to touch the glossy plumage. Evidently though, the bird was averse to being handled, taking a massive and ungainly leap backwards and emitting a strident croak of obvious rebuke. He didn't go far though, merely resuming his favourite perch on the bench in a few unhurried strokes of his great wings, seeming content to be on the periphery of the daytime activities going on around Damara.

He had an agenda, it would seem.

GUARDIAN-ELECT

His first glimpse of her was through a sea of faces, auburn head moving in and out of his line of vision as he tried for a better, a longer, look. She was busy, customers calling for her attention in a good-natured but demanding fashion.

'Lottie, here, I was next' or 'Over here, Lottie, regulars first.'

So there it was. Lottie was her name, and he was here presumably to relieve some of the obvious pressure and to serve the crowds of drinkers who spent their weekends and evenings in The Wishing Well.

She was tall and slim, glossy chestnut hair pulled into an untidy but fetching knot on the top of her dainty head. Despite the demands from the other side of the bar, she seemed completely unfazed, and continued pulling pints, filling wine glasses and measuring spirits with good humour and a ready smile.

Mr Brunton, burly arm around Jake's shoulders, now gave him a reassuring pat on the back.

'Bit of a baptism of fire, lad. Fridays are always busy, Saturdays busier still, and Sunday lunch is like a free-for-all. All good news for me.' He laughed loudly, reminding Jake of the laughing policeman, head back and rounded belly shaking. 'It's all money in the bank.' He rubbed fingers and thumb together in the age-old gesture of coinage.

Guided tour of The Wishing Well complete and hugely inadequate training session under his belt, it was time now,

Jake guessed, to start his first official shift serving at the bar. Alongside Lottie, it would seem. The thought filled him with both trepidation and excitement and he hoped he would measure up, especially in front of this extremely pretty girl.

If he had a type, then she was most definitely it.

That first evening passed in a bit of a blur for Jake, and afterwards he wondered how and at what point they began treating each other like old friends, as if they had known each other for years. The chemistry didn't diminish with the easiness he felt in her company though. Not in the slightest. In fact, by the time the last customer left The Wishing Well he'd made up his mind that he would be asking Lottie out on a date. And hoping against all hope that she felt the same way and would say 'yes'.

The moon was huge and golden, its glow gentle but easily sufficient to light the rough track as they made their way home. A light breeze rustled the hedgerows occasionally, noticeable only when their conversation quieted. Their talk had an easiness to it, a flow, which would have been more expected had they known each other for longer than just this evening.

Jake thanked his lucky stars once more that Lottie lived at Welham Farm – nearest neighbour to Damara Cottage, and just down the right-hand fork of their shared access – enabling him to walk her home without the need for questions or formality.

He learned that her parents were farmers. 'These are my dad's beasts. The sheep in the next field too.' He loved that she spoke like a farmer. Loved her voice, full stop. Soft and gentle yet with the unapologetic accent of a Yorkshire lass. 'I was born and bred here,' she went on. 'Don't you feel blessed to live in such a beautiful part of the world?'

He smiled, making an agreeable noise in his throat. He didn't want to interrupt. Wanted to listen to her speaking forever. Her voice captivated him. She attended college in nearby Northallerton, she told him, studying history, art and psychology,

'…and I catch the bus at the end of the lane three mornings each week. It takes me practically door to door. Really convenient.'

Her hours at The Wishing Well were part-time, Friday evening through the weekend, as and when required.

'Mine, too,' he chipped in. 'Yours sound really similar to those Mr Brunton offered to me.' Fate, he thought, was certainly smiling on him tonight.

At first they had walked without touching, side by side but separately. Occasionally and accidentally their hands brushed, and a frisson of electricity passed between them, unspoken but acknowledged by both. It seemed a natural progression that when Lottie stumbled, and Jake caught her elbow, their homeward journey continued with hands entwined.

Lottie's whole persona, her character and attitude, enchanted him. Her openness and ability to share of herself pulled him like a magnet. He found that he could talk about himself with equal candour, holding almost nothing back, laying himself bare to her scrutiny.

He was surprised by his reaction to her, was a little shaken at how very easy he felt in her company. At her gentle prompting, he spoke aloud for the first time of recent months – unconsciously acknowledging a massive personal progression in the sharing of such hurtful times – of the death of his father and his own difficulty in coming to terms with the loss. Of the move to Welham and leaving his past life behind.

'It was an accident,' he said. 'Could've happened to anyone. But when it happens to someone you love, when there's no warning, it's hard to take.'

She squeezed his hand, offering silent encouragement.

'Moving here, a new start, was probably the best thing for me and Mum,' he went on, 'although I'll admit I wasn't that interested when she started making plans for us. I felt a bit lost, to be honest. I could've been living anywhere. It didn't matter to me.'

'And now?' she prompted.

'Well,' he paused, 'it's early days yet, but so far so good,' and as he smiled down at her, their eyes met and held. He felt his stomach do a double flip.

As yet too unsure to share, he kept back only his newly discovered feelings regarding Damara Cottage. Of the way the energies swirled and eddied. The constant feeling of being watched. About the cellar. And about the dreams.

He wished that he could speak to her of these thoughts and experiences which, thus far, he had locked tightly away within himself. It felt natural and right, and he sensed that she would understand. That, had he chosen to speak of these things – of the woman and her messages, of the monster in the mist – Lottie would squeeze his hand and lay her head against his shoulder, as she was doing now, and that he would feel that this solitary knowledge was one that he could now bring out into the light.

They reached the fork in the track far too quickly, neither of them ready for the evening to end. Eyes met again, and when he bent towards her, she raised on her toes to meet his tentative approach. Their kiss was gentle and almost chaste. A soft touching of lips, their young bodies remaining apart. Yet there was a confidence too. A knowing of more to come, of a road ahead which they could travel together. As they pulled away, their eyes locked once more, darkened now with a passion they would learn more of soon.

She touched his cheek briefly with warm fingertips, lips curved in a soft smile, before turning towards her side of the path.

'See you tomorrow, Jake.'

The moonlight briefly marked her passage before dense shadows beneath the copse swallowed her slight figure as completely as if she had never been.

'Yeah, tomorrow.' His reply was late, an afterthought. She took his breath away. He stood for a moment on the path. He could still taste the sweetness of her kiss, feel her touch on his cheek.

That something huge had just happened for them both, he was certain. That their future lay together, he was equally sure. Love at first sight was not something that he had previously given any credence, but he had known almost immediately that Lottie was for him.

Somehow he knew without the need for words that she felt exactly the same way about him.

With a last look at the darkened Welham Farm fork, he turned left, towards Damara Cottage and home.

Lottie watched from the dense shadow of the copse as Jake paused on the path. He seemed lost in thought for a moment before spinning on his heels, a small smile playing about his lips. Making a sudden decision, he jogged, light-footed, beneath his own over-hanging foliage and was swallowed by the darkness beneath. The beat of his footsteps faded to nothing.

Her own feelings were tinged with regret. That they were not, could never be, just another young couple meeting for the first time. That theirs was not to be a usual courtship, one filled with laughter and fun. Decisions about the future, their future, would never be wholly their own.

Fate had decreed that Jake was the one. Her mother had explained clearly and in depth. Lottie had accepted long ago, although not without many heartfelt and bitter rebellions along the way, that in the battle ahead they were destined to fight together.

She had tried to dodge her fate, to sidestep this duty that was undoubtedly hers, several times, only to be guided back gently and with sympathy by a mother who understood only too well the weight of their mutual responsibility. And still, at times, the burden of it pressed heavily upon her young shoulders. Yet meeting Jake tonight, seeing him in the flesh for the first time, a real person and not some far off, nameless stranger, had quieted many of her anxieties.

That the young couple had sensed a bond immediately was indisputable, and Lottie was relieved and grateful that Jake was the chosen, the catalyst sent by Fate to stand by her side for the coming conflict.

She had been prepared from a young age for what was to

come and knew that the path ahead was a perilous one. Jake, for all his intuitive knowledge, had not the slightest idea of the dangers which lay just around the corner. Or that he, himself, was the trigger, the finger on the switch, which was about to set everything in motion. Events must now happen as preordained. And what lay ahead of them scared her.

With a sigh, she finally turned for home. There was much to be spoken about, and her mother would be waiting.

The cards fanned out before her, face down, waiting to deliver their differing messages. Maggie closed her eyes, allowing her hands to hover above them, drifting, moving slowly, feeling the diverse energies flowing. Every so often, a further card was selected and placed within the pattern forming on the table before her.

Seated opposite, eyes also closed, Lottie placed her palms on the scrubbed pine surface. Immediately Maggie felt the faint vibrations, the power of the Tarot, in the wood beneath her hands.

The last card finally added, both women now opened their eyes, mirroring each other as their concentration centred upon the nine couriers before them.

Maggie reached forward and revealed the face of each, one at a time, taking but moments to absorb and understand meaning; messages overlapping and influencing others. Singularly the cards could, at times, be obtuse, but always reached a clarity when taken as a whole.

So many major Arcana in this spread though. The reading thus far was clear, easy to decipher. Maggie didn't think she had ever seen so few minor cards appearing. Only three. The Page of Swords, and two others, both of them also swords.

The Three. Strife and opposition.

The Five. A cruel card. Defeat, degradation, infamy and dishonour. An indication of their adversaries, and the severity of the challenge they faced. Looming confrontation, and the changes which they would all have to deal with in the fullness of time.

All of the main protagonists were clearly revealed within the spread.

The Empress represented all three of the affected Guardians. Past, present and future. Alice, Maggie and Lottie.

The Lovers. Lottie had tried, and failed, to hide a blush on its turning, assuming ownership for herself and Jake, but Maggie merely nodded absently in her concentration, continuing with the reading undisturbed.

Death. Anna. To an extent, Jake too. A fresh start for them here in Yorkshire. The end of an old life, with the loss of Peter, and the beginning of a new one.

The Page of Swords. Obviously Jake. She was relieved to see him appear as a warrior, well equipped, prepared to take on his foe.

The Devil lay across The Page of Swords. No surprises. Luke and George Brunton. Possibly James Brunton too. Their evil intentions, the conflict to come, revealed. No room for doubt.

The Tower, of course, had a two-fold message. That of past loss and grief – complete destruction of previous lives – and obviously relating to Anna and Jake. Perhaps reflecting Alice's murder too. The placing of the card, however, also indicated that The Tower's influence still held sway. That more devastation was to come.

The Wheel of Fortune was the final card of the spread. The outcome. No help there then. A state of flux, with fate falling as it would. The answer was still undecided, the victor yet to be determined.

Maggie, brow furrowed in concentration and frustration, drew another card in an effort to gain more clarity, a hint at what the path ahead might hold. For although the spread showed everything she had expected – the main players clearly outlined, and the forthcoming battle which they would face – the future was still shrouded in mystery. She turned the card.

Ten of Wands. The card was upside down, its meaning inverted. A pause in the current struggle, but then deception and hidden enemies.

'Who, Mum? Who don't we know about?'

Maggie could only shake her head.

'This is the future, Lottie. What will come afterwards…?' She shrugged. 'We haven't even got a clear answer about this conflict, let alone anything beyond it.'

She tried again. The final card of the day, for to press any further would be to question what had already been divulged.

In truth, Maggie had never before taken the step of turning more than one extra card at the end of a reading, had always previously been able to glean at least some clarity by this stage.

The Moon. Again inverted. Lottie gasped. It emphasised and reiterated the message of the Ten of Wands. Deception and danger. Falsehood and disillusionment. A concealing veil masking truth and honesty. And again, unknown enemies.

Maggie was still, head bowed over the deck, thoughts centred on the cards before her. The lack of clear guidance was disturbing. No apparent answers with regard to who might win the fight for Damara, and The Chronicle.

That the book was safe for the moment was a blessing. Protected for centuries by elemental magic, it remained hidden from sight from any but the Guardians. Only retraction of the ancient words could render it visible once more.

More frightening still was what lay beyond the battle. For, even if they were victorious in this conflict, the cards pointed towards yet more strife. A brief lull before it all began again. Another adversary, it seemed, beyond Luke Brunton and his kin, pressing to take control of The Source.

Maggie was scared, for she knew the consequences of their defeat. Luke Brunton, or another following him, wouldn't stop merely at killing the Guardian and taking The Chronicle. That would only be a means to an end. Control of The Source was merely a first step.

There were many more such forces, both nationally and globally. The fall of just one into evil hands could be the start of a domino effect. More would be lost, and wickedness would rise.

As she looked across the table at her daughter's pale face, she saw an understanding. The same fear reflected back from Lottie's amber eyes.

In truth, the battle ahead may not be the closing of a chapter, or a conclusion. It may, in fact, be the beginning of something much greater than either of them had expected, or were prepared for.

THE WELL

The light was inadequate, the stone steps slippery with damp and a slimy green moss. Jake had felt his feet sliding on a couple of occasions, making him catch his breath. The lack of a handrail or, in fact, any protection to the drop on his left side was making him doubt the wisdom of attempting this chore alone, and the fact that he could see nothing in front or below him was not helping at all. The thought had occurred to him more than once this morning that perhaps he should have prioritised scrubbing the stairs with bleach and a sturdy brush before starting this present task.

The large cardboard boxes, although uniform in shape, differed greatly in weight dependent upon what was stored within. None of them afforded views of his feet when in transit.

This was his last load, however, and the thought of a cold drink and one of his own amazing sandwich creations was spurring him on to finish the chore. He could picture himself picking his way gingerly up the death-trap steps, clicking off the ancient light-switch, and closing the tiny door for the last time – at least for today – on the dank and foisty cellar.

This 'Labour of Hercules' had been on his to-do list for the last few days, and only his mother's nagging had finally pushed him into starting what he had been trying to avoid since waking on that first morning in Damara.

His initial compulsion to explore the cellar on moving in

had faded with the arrival of dawn. The strange dream-like experiences – the vision of the woman, followed soon after by his meeting with the Luke-thing in the mists outside the cottage – had unnerved him more than he cared to admit. As had the very tall tale told by the elder Brunton at The Wishing Well.

He shook his head. Unbelievable!

Since then he had been conscientiously avoiding both the task and, more importantly, even thinking about the possibility of secrets lying hidden within the foundations of his home. Almost convincing himself that it was all just local legend, his dreams a result of stress and tiredness, still there remained the puzzling fact that he had been very consciously putting distance between himself and the cellar.

There was the other stuff too. The figure never quite there. He kept catching sight of her just out of the corner of his eye but when he turned his head, she was gone. And the unexplained footsteps. He heard them downstairs when he was up, and always when his mother was out of the house. Then there was the watching, the endless feeling of being observed. Everything seemed to be on the lower floor of the cottage.

Except the dreams, he amended. *They were upstairs.*

Prevarication was merely postponing the inevitable though. He had known, had always known, that he would have to venture downwards at some point.

So, finally, here he was. Almost done. He had strategically piled the boxes in the far right corner where the floor seemed drier. Light from a weak bulb managed to penetrate this area too, making it the most sensible option. Much of the remainder of the cellar, which ran for the whole length of the cottage above, remained in near-darkness. Jake felt disinclined to splodge about in the puddles which he was sure were lurking just beyond the pool of light. Perhaps when he had a flashlight, or the present bulb was replaced with a 100 watter, he would feel more enthusiastic about exploring the shadowy depths.

Maybe then he would discover what, if anything, the dream-woman was hiding. He gave an internal shrug at his musings.

Wild dreams, tall stories and hidden treasures? Bah, humbug! But try as he would to disbelieve, still his own eyes, his own senses, were telling him otherwise.

His feet disappeared from beneath him in but a moment. There was no warning. Both soles slipped at once and he saw himself, as if in slow motion, begin to topple from his mid-point step, the box bouncing away into the gloom in front of him.

He landed hard on his hip before gracefully, and still in slo-mo, slithering off the open edge of the sandstone staircase and nosediving towards the floor beneath.

The throbbing in his temple woke him. Lying face down, his cheek pressing into damp earth, he opened his eyes slowly and carefully. The dim glow from the overhead bulb made him wince slightly. He could feel cool dampness now, soaking through his clothing and pressing against his skin, causing an involuntary shiver.

Pushing gingerly into a sitting position, and leaning back against the rough wall of the stairs, Jake took stock. The hip would have an impressive bruise for certain. Cautious exploration of his throbbing head revealed an egg-sized lump which, when fingered, made him hastily draw back his hand with a grimace. He felt spacey and slightly dizzy. Sitting still for a few more minutes seemed like a very good idea.

Jake was unsure when he became aware that he was not alone.

He must have dozed, or perhaps the head injury was distorting his senses, because he was conscious that some time had passed. His clothing, where it touched the damp earth, was uncomfortably wet, and he felt chilled from inactivity. He checked his watch, confirming that he'd been drifting for almost half an hour.

The feeling of being watched wormed its way gradually into his consciousness. He raised his eyes and searched the shadows.

She was there. In the far, darkest corner of the cellar. Illumined in her own clear aura, she gently smiled as their eyes met once more.

The pain of body, and mistiness of mind, slipped away as if

imagined. Jake rose easily to meet her, the vision of his dream, excitement infusing him, coursing through his veins.

How had he forgotten this feeling? Why had he pushed her away? He knew now and in an instant why she was here, why he was chosen, and he embraced the knowledge.

She was lovely, as he remembered, but her true beauty shone from within, was almost tangible. With purpose in his stride, he approached, his steps now confident on the treacherous ground beneath, and she held out a hand in greeting.

The cellar was now illuminated by the soft glow radiating from her, moist walls and ancient floor revealed for his scrutiny.

At her voiceless direction, he stopped, awaiting further instruction.

'Beneath. Look beneath.' The sweet voice, audible only in his mind, was clear and pure, and he immediately bent to the ground.

Initially there seemed no disparity to the hard-packed earth before him, but at her bidding, he began to probe, to dig, using his hands to move the soil. It came away easily, less dense than he'd expected, and after working for some time he felt his fingers touch the hardness of something covered. Something concealed many years before.

Made from ancient wood, now split and rotten from its time within the ground, his labours revealed finally a large square of oak. Jake felt around the perimeter and discovered edges of around an inch thick. At her behest, he continued to work, to release the cover from its earthy prison, finally freeing all sides and sitting back on his haunches to survey his handy-work.

Raising his eyes, he saw her nod her encouragement. He knelt to remove the oaken lid from its resting place, noticing as he did, a carved emblem on its surface.

'Hulinjalmur.' The word whispered in his head. 'The Helm of Disguise.' He understood. Whatever was beneath the cover had been hidden, protected, by this symbol.

Again her voice murmured unfamiliar words, beyond his comprehension but beautiful in their rhythm and cadence. He bent to his task.

It came away more easily than he had expected. Immense age had lightened the ancient timber, even sodden as it was. As he lifted, it released with a suddenness and speed that surprised him. The cover flipped over, coming to rest against the far wall, and Jake was thrown backwards with the force of his own momentum.

Before him was a hole.

The Well!

He knew that now. Alice – he acknowledged her name – had told him, many times, but he had chosen to block her, to ignore his dreams and to pretend an ignorance of what he had really known all along. Clarity and knowledge came suddenly, a clearing of mists and cobwebs, revealing what had been there within him since that first night.

At her continued instruction, he crawled to the edge and peered downwards.

The darkness was impenetrable. Even Alice's auric glow could not pierce the blackness. Jake strained his eyes, but only the first few inches were visible, these lined with what looked like ancient stonework. Cool air eddied around the top of the well, released finally from long years of confinement, but despite the temperature, Jake was suffused with a feeling of hope and well-being.

He inhaled and was surprised at the freshness. It brought to mind spring meadows, or the sea on a stormy day, or summer blooms – all things good and pure suffused the breath. Jake blinked in surprise and sucked in once more, trying to fill his lungs to their full extent. A huge surge of energy and joy took him by surprise, as though every cell in his body was rejoicing in the healing breath.

She spoke in his mind then. A warning.

'The Well is potent, Jake. Have a care.'

Again raising his eyes, he asked the question, 'Where?'

She answered distinctly.

Lying flat on his stomach, head and shoulders over-hanging the lip, he reached downwards. His hand disappeared into the darkness, as if swallowed by a giant's mouth. The blackness within seemed to swell, to accept his intrusion and absorb the extra mass, aware of his intent. A rush of warmth travelled up his arm as his fingers touched the curved walls beneath him.

Easily locating the loosened stones, he removed them carefully one by one, placing each gently by his side before returning to his task. Six bricks came away, revealing, to his touch behind them, a space. He hitched forward still further, needing that extra length of limb to penetrate the hiding place.

His fingers finally touched it. Carefully, he inched it from the space and raised it into the lilac light.

It was swaddled in leather cloths and pieces of linen, still surprisingly pliant after their time in hiding. Again, the emblem, still visible on the bindings. Again the whispered word, 'Hulinjalmur'. At her bidding, he carefully unwrapped the layers, revealing, finally, the huge and ancient tome.

Bound in tan leather, and with symbols and patterns carved into its face, it appeared as fresh as if only placed in The Well yesterday. He made to open the book, but Alice stilled his hand. Her instructions were clear.

'We can abide no mishap. All must be done as The Source ordains.'

Jake nodded his understanding. He knew where he must take The Chronicle. It must be returned, and quickly, to the one to whom it belonged. Before the forces of evil gathering strength nearby gained knowledge of its finding.

THE GLADE

While Jake was moving boxes and meeting Alice at Damara, Anna had returned to the cemetery again. She was undeniably disappointed when all was quiet and still. No inrush of energy. No unexplained wind to fill her with joy. Just another plot, peaceful and calming. Instead, she allowed the serenity of the place to wash over her again.

Since that first time, though, she had continued to feel an ongoing sense of wellbeing, of vitality. If for no other reason, the tranquillity of the quiet spot would draw her back time after time. It was a balm to the spirit in itself.

She knelt for some time by the plots, hand resting unconsciously upon Alice's grave marker. She still felt acutely the embarrassment and shame of the evening in The Wishing Well. Being rescued from such a scene, and by a neighbour she had not even yet been introduced to, did little for her self-esteem. Gradually, knotted muscles relaxed and released, and her tumbling thoughts quietened. Finally, she rose again to continue on her way, surprisingly rested yet energised in equal measure.

Today, she had decided, she would venture further, passing the graveyard and onwards into the woodland beyond. There was no plan, no reason for her exploration, other than a need to be outside, to enjoy the peace and beauty of the countryside around Welham.

There was a path of sorts, beyond the Peel graves, which led away into the shadowy coolness of the trees. Anna had already promised herself that she would investigate this track when time allowed, and now she turned and wandered beneath the dense shade of the overhead foliage, her aim merely to enjoy the fresh air, get some gentle exercise, and learn more about her new surroundings.

She walked for some time, a circuitous and meandering route, enjoying the solitude and the birdsong from the canopy overhead. Occasionally she caught sight of some wild creature scurrying for cover at the sound of her approach.

These woods extended much further than she had originally thought. The dense undergrowth still showed no signs of thinning after a quarter of an hour walk and she was considering re-tracing her footsteps when she was, surprisingly and suddenly, out of the trees.

Before her was a glade almost perfect in its beauty. She drew in her breath sharply in appreciation of the sight.

At the point furthest from her, the ground began to slope upwards steeply. Towards the moors, Anna surmised, for more trees masked from view what lay beyond. A fast-flowing stream broke the surface of the incline just clear of the treeline from its earlier passage beneath the earth, travelling barely a few feet more before tumbling into a tiny waterfall. The movement of water over pebbles made for an enchanting sound, the babbling brook of countless fairy tales. The stream then disappeared below ground again a few feet from where she stood.

Constant movement of water had caused a pool to form at the base of the fall, and beside it – as if placed by design – was a large, flat rock, its surface smooth and appealing. Anna smiled to herself. Accepting the mute invitation, she strolled forwards, at first sitting and then stretching out along the surprisingly comfortable surface of sun-warmed sandstone. What luck to discover a spot of such tranquillity, and on such a wonderful day.

Her eyelids closed against the glare of the summer sun, and she relished the heat of its kiss against her skin after the coolness of the woods. The trees moved and sighed in a gentle rhythm, and the brook continued its busy journey back to the darkness of Mother Earth, its time above ground all too brief. Anna relaxed into the serenity of her own private paradise.

It could have been the passage of an age, or but a moment. Time had ceased to have meaning. She drifted at first in the eternal space, hovering in a netherworld just above sleep, before allowing herself to sink, almost intentionally, down into a deep and impenetrable slumber.

Peter came to her then. Was with her in the glade. Lay beside her on the rock. He was strong and whole, as he had been in life, unbroken and unmarked by the violence of death. The man she had loved. Still loved. Her husband and soulmate.

Within the dream, her eyes remained closed, as if she knew any sight would render void their meeting. Her hands, too, were still, unwilling or unable to risk breaking the spell.

His fingers caressed her temples, wound through her hair, a touch so well-remembered that her body responded instantly to that longed-for contact. Her lips parted in a sigh as she abandoned herself to the joy of reunion.

A whisper of pressure against her mouth as his thumb stroked the fleshy centre of her lower-lip, the message recognised and welcomed. Always a prelude to their love-making, a gesture so personal, and of such intensity, that a coil of longing tugged immediately within her. Her body rose in recognition of her mate, moving to accommodate his weight above her, tongue reaching to taste him. His hand caressed her breast, thumb now stroking her nipple, this intimate touch lifting her still higher. And then they were one again, the barrier of her flimsy panties no hindrance, easily tugged aside, as she felt once more the welcome push of his entry.

But this was wrong. The feel and taste of him was wrong. There was sourness, a bitter and acrid hint of something corrupted, and she recoiled within the dream.

A voice close beside her – a woman's voice – whispered with urgency.

'Wake up, Anna. There is danger here. Awaken now.'

Upwards she swam. Through the mists of sleep, straining to break the surface of consciousness once more. It seemed that forces beyond her control were pulling her back towards darkness though, a blackness beneath, and she struggled against their unseen fetters, pushing ever upwards towards the light of warmth and sunshine.

A groan escaped her as she awoke, the dream blowing away like petals on a breeze, forgotten before she could remember. She raised hand to forehead in an effort to dispel the haze of confusion still clouding her mind.

A snap of twigs close-by forced her eyes to open and she raised onto her elbows, frowning into the sun's glare, bewildered at the silhouette approaching from the edge of the clearing.

'Anna?' The voice seemed vaguely familiar, a deep, velvety smoothness. 'Can I help? Are you hurt?'

'I… No, I'm not hurt. I fell asleep, I think.' She pulled herself to a sitting position and rubbed her eyes in an effort to clear the last of the fog from her sluggish mind. 'Too much sun, probably. I feel a little faint.'

Luke Brunton bent towards her, an expression of friendly concern etched on his handsome features.

'Here, let me help you.' He leant downwards. 'I'm a doctor, you know.' The teasing smile in his voice immediately calmed and settled her. One knee bent to the rock, his arm around her shoulders, the other supporting beneath her elbow. 'Can you walk, do you think, or shall we stay here for a while longer?'

That honeyed voice, the heat of his skin on hers, caused a frisson of desire to shoot through her. Dream now all but forgotten, the undeniable excitement it had aroused nevertheless remained. Anna wondered vaguely at her reaction yet again to this man, at his ability to affect her this way. Their last meeting had ended in humiliation, at least on her part. He was barely even a friend, let alone a lover, and yet it seemed right, and completely normal, to open herself up to him. She turned to him as if in a trance.

'Luke…?'

Their eyes met, his a deep, azure-blue, darkening with desire. He bent towards her, lowering his head slowly, cradling her in his arms. Their lips met in a crushing kiss, blistering in its passion and intensity.

Peter's voice then, within her, but seemingly all around too. An anguished cry of desperation, diminishing quickly and fading out of her ability to hear in but a moment.

Anna's eyes snapped open and she pulled away with a force borne of deep shame, jumping up and away from him in one lithe movement.

'I… I'm so sorry.' Arms hung loosely by her sides, feet planted wide as if to steady herself, she shook her head to clear the last vestiges of confusion from her mind. 'I just don't know what to say, Luke. Please forgive me. I think I must have a touch of sunstroke or something…' She trailed off in confusion.

What on earth was she thinking? This was not the sensible, in control, always reliable Anna of the past, but a wanton woman of low morals who bore no resemblance to her true self. She felt mortified by her behaviour. The perceived betrayal of Peter wounded her still more deeply.

He sat easily upon the rock, leaning back on his hands, apparently completely unaffected by their recent encounter.

'Well,' he laughed, 'if that's what the sun can do, let's hope for more fine weather. Come here, Anna, and let's get even better acquainted.' He patted his stony seat, the invitation impossible to ignore.

'I…' She looked from side to side in confusion, arms wrapping around her body in an unconsciously protective gesture. 'No. I can't. I'm so sorry, but I just can't.'

The tears were falling now, unnoticed by one, and ignored by the other.

'Come. Come here, Anna.' The tone had changed, was now more order than request. 'We're both adults, and we both know what we want.' His face hardened with the words, and she felt a first prickling of unease at her isolation and vulnerability.

No one knew she was here.

She backed away a step, and then another.

'No. It's not what I want,' a sob threatened to choke her words but she squashed it down with difficulty, 'and I must go now. I'm so sorry,' she said again, as she turned and bolted for the path through the woods.

His laughter, mockingly loud and without restraint, followed her passage as her feet gained momentum. She ran as a child will run from danger. Without thought of hurdles or mishap.

The root caught her ankle, bringing her down with force amplified by speed, as his laughter continued to echo through the trees. Her forehead connected with a resounding smack against the nearest trunk, and she blacked into unconsciousness immediately.

When she awoke, the sun had lowered in the sky. The rock beneath her back had cooled, and trees shaded the glade now, making shadows where once was sunshine.

She sat, puzzled and afraid. The kiss. Peter's scream. Luke's malevolent laughter, and her own headlong flight still seemed fresh in her mind. She reached to her head, searching for a tell-tale bump or bruise to give proof to her memories, but there was nothing. She was back in the glade, not lost in the woods.

And she was alone. Of that she was certain.

Anna rose unsteadily to her feet, unsure and confused by what had or, more probably, what had not happened that afternoon. She felt violated, dirty, and as though she had let Peter down very badly. Her body told her the same story, the ache in her groin very real; and yet it would seem that nothing had actually occurred.

Time had passed, certainly, but a gentle breeze still stirred the trees, birds still sang from the greenwood, and there was no sign at all that another person had ever been there with her.

Feeling exhausted, drained, and unaccountably sad, Anna set off along the path towards Welham, and Damara Cottage, head down and footsteps dragging. All of her previous energy, the vitality given to her during her visit to the Peel women's graves, had retreated like an ebbing tide.

Home! Suddenly, all she wanted was to be back within the sturdy walls of her cottage. Safe and protected, as she always felt when in Damara.

She squared her shoulders and lifted her chin. Whatever had occurred today, dream or no dream, she would not allow it to reclaim the gift offered to her in the cemetery. That of joy, and hope, and wellness. A belief in the future once more.

In the same thought, she resolved to find out whatever she could about Dr Luke Brunton. Something was very wrong.

A worm of desire again snaked through her at the memory of their dream kiss, but there was also an underlying hint of something bad, something rotten. A shiver took her, and she quickened her pace towards Damara Cottage and safety.

Lottie had felt a need all day to visit the glade, to spend some time alone and in her favourite spot. It happened fairly regularly, this necessity to be by herself, and she always listened to, and acted upon, her internal voice. Today, though, felt more urgent, more powerful.

Something was amiss.

From an early age, she had considered the clearing in the woods her own private sanctuary, a haven from the stresses and strains of the everyday. A place where she could recharge her batteries, calm tattered nerves, and ponder on aspects of her life which she couldn't share with friends. Things that were decidedly outside the remit of normal teenage angst.

The glade was one of those places that all locals knew of, but most rarely ventured, the two approaches from the village being meandering, under-used and overgrown. The majority of dog-walkers headed in the opposite direction, away from the moors, where fields and bridleways offered less challenging terrain. Hikers and ramblers tended to bypass the wood completely. The relatively short and circuitous route through the trees was of no interest to them, and they usually struck out straight for the higher heathlands.

The track from Welham Farm, however, was well-worn, mostly

by her own footfalls, but also by those of her mother who visited occasionally, and for much the same reason as Lottie. Maggie had once told her daughter that past Guardians had used the clearing as a place to meditate, to reconnect with nature. She had no reason to doubt it, had always felt their closeness and kinship as she did the same.

Today, though, was different. There was an urgency somehow. As soon as her errands in town were finished and the bus had dropped her at the end of the lane, she had hurried home, grabbed a quick bite to eat, and completed her usual tasks with efficiency and haste, her eagerness to set off speeding the chores along.

She was now heading towards her glade with some trepidation, rather than her usual lightness of tread. The day had seemed endless, and she longed to sit upon her rock, to feel the earth vibrations moving beneath her. Perhaps then she would regain her equilibrium, some peace of mind.

Such a disparity this time though. The serenity of the woods was unsettled, the atmosphere, as she approached the glade, fragmented. The nearer she drew, the more the sensation amplified, and her steps slowed as she recognised disturbances in the usually serene energies of the copse.

At the edge of the clearing, she stopped, her presence masked from casual glance by the density of trees and vegetation, wary of moving further, awaiting some sign that progressing to her usual spot by the waterfall was safe. Or otherwise.

A dart of colour to the right caught her eye. The retreating form of someone she recognised leaving the glade by way of the cemetery path. Jake's mother. Lottie had only met her twice so far, and briefly, but the figure was unmistakeable.

Head down, strides heavy, Anna was quickly swallowed by the early evening gloom of the woods. A frown of confusion furrowed Lottie's brow. Could the unsettled energies be anything to do with Jake's mum? Every instinct cried out in the affirmative.

In truth, though, Lottie would not have dared to call out. What could she say to the mother of her very-newly-acquired boyfriend? *'Have you noticed anything strange and disturbing in the woods today, Mrs Freer?'* Probably not the best way to make a good impression.

There was no one else around. Lottie was certain. Yet still the energies swirled and eddied, their vibrations jagged and edgy. Something had happened here, something wrong and unnatural, and whatever it was, it had been sufficient to damage, at least temporarily, the tranquillity of the immediate surroundings. She sensed destructive influences, but was unable to identify the cause.

Stepping carefully from the cover of the trees, she moved slowly forwards. Perceptions heightened, she was alert for any small sounds or movements, but there was nothing. Nothing but the spoiled quietude of the dell, and a churning aftermath of grief, anger... and fear? She was sure now that whatever had happened here, dread and panic had been at play.

That Anna was involved was now obvious, but why had she been here, and what could have happened to distress her so badly? The turmoil had been severe enough to infect everything around her.

A sensible option, of course, would be to run for home and let her mother decide what the next step should be. Whether to let matters lie, or to question Anna about the happenings of the afternoon. They were friends, after all, albeit of short acquaintance.

She knew though that the damage to the energies in the glade would begin to heal itself very soon, and that any information to be gleaned from Mother Nature would then be diluted, if not lost altogether. She needed at least to try to find out what had upset Anna so severely that it had polluted and corrupted the surrounding atmosphere.

Resolutely bracing herself, and purposefully allowing all vibrations to wash over and around her, messages of pain and anguish pushing against her the closer she got, she approached and sat upon the rock.

Lottie removed her sandals and planted her bare feet firmly

on the soft turf, feeling the delicate grasses caress her skin. She placed her hands, palms down, against the cooling surface of the slab. Breathing deeply, she allowed trivial tensions of the day, memories of happy times with her family, the joy of her blossoming relationship with Jake, to slide away, muscles relaxing and lengthening.

Her mind cleared, allowing only the here and now, the shifting and uneasy atmosphere of the glade, to hold sway. She closed her eyes and waited.

The pictures within formed slowly, faint and blurry outlines, as if observed through chiffon. Two figures. Both, she thought, recognisable even through the mist. Entwined in passion on this very spot, upon the rock on which she now sat. Lottie frowned and tried to push the images away. Observing this private moment was not what she had expected, and she felt like a voyeur, witnessing a scene so personal.

The shadow couple faded then, to be replaced immediately by starkly etched freeze-frames of horror. The girl gasped as she was bombarded with a slideshow of misery. Of Anna standing before Dr Brunton, confusion and dismay contorting her pretty face. Her headlong flight into the woods. Him carrying her inert body back to the rock; and lastly – and most dreadful of all – of the pair coupling, Anna's oblivion apparent by the sagging of limbs and tilt of her head.

Then it was gone. All that was left was an aftermath of desolation, experienced by proxy by Lottie. She wished fervently then that her gifts did not include empathy, this ability to sense the emotions of others, to tap into energies and auras both past and present. She drew in a ragged breath, more than a little frightened by what she had seen. Yet at once she felt a change in the atmosphere, an easing of tension, a lifting of despair. She filled her lungs again and again, allowing all negativity to flow away with each exhalation. The glade was beginning its healing.

She opened her eyes.

A woman was before her now, facing Lottie from a short distance away, in the centre of the clearing. Beautiful, ethereal, she was surrounded by a fluid aura of violet and lilac light. Lottie knew instantly that it was Alice. They had met many times before, although previously only in thought. This was the first time that an image had been allowed to Lottie, and she smiled her thanks.

As she watched, the flawless purple radiance around Alice began to expand, to move outwards towards the trees, pushing back the evening gloom and flooding the clearing with a luminous beauty. Shadows, both physical and emotional, retreated before the light, and Mother Nature bathed in its restoring warmth.

Lottie, too, welcomed the healing as it worked its magic on all around. She felt a vitality and hope rising within her as she inhaled the purity of its embrace.

Alice approached now, bare feet leaving the delicate grasses beneath unmarked. Her smile was tender as she stood before Lottie, hands outspread, palms upwards, as the restoration of natural balance continued.

There was more to be shared between them, this much Lottie knew, and she opened herself still further, a flower opening to sunlight, allowing Alice access to her higher self.

A new vision. The future now. What was yet to come. Images, both moving and still, paraded before her, some clear, others hazy and more difficult to discern, but all recognisable. All people and places that were familiar to her. Except for the two little ones. The children. Her brow furrowed.

'I don't understand,' she whispered. 'How can this be?' But in an instant there was no more. Alice could disclose nothing further.

The light began to draw back, leaving the glade to shadows, and Alice's figure grew misty and insubstantial as she diminished and faded. The healing was completed and her message delivered. The glow, the figure of The Guardian, finally paled into darkness, and Lottie was left alone in the clearing once more.

Some time had passed since she'd arrived, and the gloom beneath the trees was now deep. Yet the atmosphere had calmed, and the girl felt safe within the circle of trees. She could not linger though. She had to get home, to her mother, to deliver the message shared by Alice.

Lottie hoped that she had misinterpreted the meaning, that her mother would have a reasonable explanation for the images she had been shown. For if what she had seen were to come to pass, then their impending fight would not be a conclusion, and may not see an end to the struggle. The Tarot had spoken true. There would be a brief lull, a cessation of hostilities for a short while, but then the battle for control of Damara would resume.

This new adversary, if she'd understood Alice's message, would have the potential to be more formidable, more powerful, than any so far.

SCRYING

As Anna pulled the carefully-wrapped parcel from the last of the packing boxes and gently removed the bubble-wrap that had ensured its safe journey to their new home, she recognised an unwelcome tightening of emotion within her throat.

The mirror had been in the family for years, at least as far back as her great-great-grandmother, and was unusual in its simplicity. Care over many generations had ensured that the dark oak frame remained unblemished, and the glass itself was free from mottling or silvering. It was small, about a foot in diameter, and round, which Anna knew was unusual for a mirror of this age. The frame had been made from a single piece of oak and was smooth and warm to the touch. The very fact that Anna's mother had cherished it would have given the mirror some emotive meaning, but also, and very simply, she loved it for itself.

Over the days since their arrival at Damara Cottage, and especially since her experience beside Alice's grave, she had noticed a return of her strength, an ability to cope with life generally.

Emotions, both positive and negative, seemed much closer to the surface now, much easier to access. Apart from her encounters with Luke Brunton – for these meetings always seemed to end in her own embarrassment or shame – she found herself smiling more regularly, even laughing at times. Occasionally, too, sometimes for minutes at a time, she almost forgot why they had made the journey to Welham at all. Almost forgot that Peter was no longer with her.

The mirror lay in her hands, the glass reflecting a woman she could hardly recognise as herself anymore, so much had she changed. She rubbed its smooth wooden surround as memories crowded back.

Each time that a much-loved object surfaced from its box, an object which took her back into her past – back to Peter – her resilience wavered and those squashed down feelings came flooding back. Tears pricked once more and she pushed both them, and the knot of grief, down; to be dealt with later, no doubt. Briskly she stood, using the back of one hand to clear her misty vision.

She had already screwed a hook into the wall in readiness for the mirror. It was to hang, as always, above her dressing table, and she carried it through now to the bedroom. The sturdy chain across its back caught securely as she stretched to place the much-loved heirloom in its new home, the hook holding the solid weight with ease.

The room was gloomy now as evening began the slow merge into night. Jake was working at The Wishing Well, not due home for a while yet, and she had been busy with small renovations, and unpacking the last of the remaining boxes, since early afternoon, stopping only once for a quick snack and a coffee a couple of hours earlier.

This was the final crate, and she had forced herself onwards, wanting at least to complete this chore before the day's end. Suddenly bone-weary, she allowed what she told herself would be a five-minute sit-down on the velvet-covered bedroom chair.

A few stray clouds pushed across an otherwise clear summer sky and obscured the lowering sun, the last vestiges of late evening light becoming still weaker. Anna's reflection returned her gaze from the mirror, hazy in the failing day. The stress of the past few months had definitely taken a toll on her appearance, but the gloom made a beauty of her shadow-self. She found herself becoming lost in her own eyes and the darkness of the room beyond.

Memories took her and she allowed herself, just this once, the luxury of remembering. Tears surfaced once more, making her image shimmer and blur. Her memories of Peter had changed, become more positive over the time spent in Damara, but still, occasionally, the hurt would catch her unawares.

In the weeks immediately following his death, he had haunted her dreams. At times, still and unreachable, a lifeless statue on the mortuary slab. At others, she found herself entering the undertaker's parlour to find her husband waiting for her, a rictus grin stretching his vacant features, and death-injuries horrifically apparent. She would jerk awake from these nightmares shaken and sweating, the images taking too long to fade.

The passage of months, though, had turned her gradually towards happier times. The nightly terrors faded, and her dreams were more usually filled with laughter, love and the memory of their joy in each other. Only occasionally did the spectre of Peter's death return, and each time Anna found the strength to move forward, to force the nightmare down.

How long she remained seated, she couldn't say for sure, but her cheeks had long since dried when she became aware that the reflection in the depths of the mirror was no longer entirely her own.

Intuitively, and as yet unsure where the knowledge came from, she allowed her gaze to remain relaxed and looked through the reflection to a point behind herself. Both images, her own and the mirror face, merged briefly before the new visage gained strength and cleared.

Deep blue replaced the hazel-green of her own eyes, and her dark bob was now a lustrous mane of ebony. The woman's beauty was angelic in its purity, and Anna knew that she should feel shock, or perhaps fear, at seeing another image replacing her own. Yet the feeling was neither of these, because the woman was familiar. Fragments of forgotten dreams, the woman always there. Instead of fear, a calmness, a serenity, slipped over her like a healing balm, her whole body relaxing as she felt herself held by the steady gaze of the mirror-woman.

The eyes welcomed her, pulled her. Misty pictures formed within her mind. Still the woman held her a willing captive, lips curving into a smile as she guided Anna inside herself, to a knowledge, a sharing, between them.

The images within Anna's head took more solid shape as she allowed the stranger entry into her deepest unconscious. A shabby wooden door leading to steps – stone steps – going down to a gloomy space. The woman was before her in this place, holding a guiding hand up from the dark beneath. Damp. Earth. A feeling of moisture, and the need to go down still further. Down into the very heart of Damara. There was something, waiting, in those depths…

Anna snapped back to her darkened bedroom, the connection broken as completely as if it had never existed. The reflection was now hers alone, the mirror-woman gone without a trace. The feeling of peace, however, remained, as did the image of the doorway, stairs – and movement, ever downwards.

The face of the vision was now as familiar to her as her own, imprinted in her mind. Anna accepted unquestioningly their entwined destiny, a gift shared between them, without demur.

Strangely too, she accepted the experience, her 'voyage through the glass', as though a normal and everyday part of her life. She knew that a change had occurred within her, and that it was irrevocable and eternal. This newly-acquired knowledge, although outside of anything she had encountered before, settled easily and comfortably, and she wondered how she could have existed before this 'knowing' became hers.

A weight had been lifted, a dark curtain pulled back, and the horror of the day in the glade, which had preyed on her mind since that time, became muted and diluted. She revelled in a new freedom, a peacefulness of spirit, which had been missing from her life for so very long now.

The door, the stairs, she had recognised. The message had been clear and unmistakable.

The location was merely the first step though. The mirror-woman's instructions had been clear. She must speak to Jake.

The air was charged with tension as the Freers shared breakfast in the sunny kitchen of Damara Cottage. It was obvious to Jake that something had happened, something that had affected his mother. She seemed edgy and nervous, and yet had a luminosity about her that gave her a ready smile and made her eyes sparkle. It fairly shone from her.

He bided his time though, waiting for her to share, convinced that whatever had happened must be to do with Alice, or The Chronicle, or both. Perhaps the time had finally come for them to be honest with each other, after too long spent treading on eggshells for fear of seeming foolish – at least on his part. He hoped so, but didn't want to push. Didn't want to misjudge and force the situation before the time was right.

She sat down opposite him again, bringing them each a tea, and looked at him directly. Her eyes were clear and calm, her manner steadier now, although there was still a look of excitement, of energy, about her.

'I need to talk to you. About something that happened to me. And it's going to seem a little strange.' She wrapped her hands around the warmth of her mug, and took a deep breath.

Jake waited, saying nothing, but nodded briefly his encouragement. This could be it. This could the turning point.

Anna didn't know how to start. 'While you were out yesterday and I was doing the last of the unpacking, something happened.' She hesitated again, unsure how to proceed or how to explain. Again, the sigh. Anna tried again. 'Jake, you know that mirror of Grandma's? The one that I love and that always hung in my bedroom? Well, I was looking into it yesterday, and drifting off a little, into memories...'

She omitted almost nothing, told him nearly everything. Her meeting with the beautiful lady in the mirror, the wisdom they had shared. The knowledge of The Chronicle. She spoke too of her experience in the cemetery at Alice's grave. The infusion of positivity she had felt flow through her, and which had stayed with her since, only dented by her experience in the glade. She couldn't bring herself to tell him of that though. Not yet. Perhaps never. It was enough to share what was here, what was real.

Eventually she sat back in her chair, words spent, and awaited a reaction from her son.

'You're talking about Alice, Mum.' He spoke quietly. 'She's the woman in the mirror. She's a Guardian of the Source, one of the writers of The Chronicle. Although there were other Guardians before her, of course – and after.' He paused at Anna's intake of breath.

'But… you know, then? About all of this? How long?'

'Since just after we moved in.' He shrugged. 'There were all sorts of energies and strange things happening when we first came here. I was a bit freaked out, if I'm honest. I met Alice in a dream that first night. But I only found The Chronicle two days ago.'

She gasped again. This was all too much, and moving a little too quickly for her to keep up.

'You've *found* The Chronicle?'

'I took it to Maggie straight away, like Alice told me. It's important to keep it safe now, and Maggie knew what to do, of course, being the present Guardian.'

This was all running away from her, and Anna shook her head.

'But… what…' she finally managed, 'Maggie?'

Jake grinned. 'She'd want me to take you to her now. Shall I give her a call?'

THE CHRONICLE

As they'd done so many times over the past days, Anna found herself seated at the large oak table at Welham Farm sharing a coffee with Maggie. This time, however, her son was beside her, and a large, leather-bound tome took centre-stage before them. She couldn't take her eyes off it.

That she was taking all of this in her stride was probably the most surprising, within a day filled with the unexpected, but Anna had a feeling that she had been well prepared by her meeting with Alice the previous evening. That all of this was meant to happen. The knowledge was unsettling, but uppermost was the desire to learn more. To find out what her own part was – and that of her son – in the bigger picture of Alice, Damara Cottage and The Chronicle.

Maggie gave her a reassuring half-smile before she began.

'I know this is a lot to take in, Anna, and you'll have to take a deep breath and a leap of faith, but I've a feeling that you're halfway there already after meeting Alice last night.'

'How did you know that?' Anna was shocked to the core. She had been there in the kitchen when Jake had phoned, and he had certainly not mentioned it then. He'd merely said that they were 'coming for a coffee' and 'it's time'. Since their arrival at Welham Farm, there had been much bustling to fetch The Chronicle and to make drinks, but nothing had been said about the mirror, or Alice, or Damara Cottage.

'I've been waiting,' said Maggie gently, 'for Alice to decide that the time is right, and to speak to you personally. Think of yourself as the last cog being fitted into a clock, and now the hands can start to turn again.'

'I don't understand, I really don't.' Anna felt out of her depth again, struggling to keep pace with the speed of developments and the enormity of what was now being shared with her. 'I know of Alice, obviously. That she is 'The Witch of Welham', 'Mad Alice', and now the lady in my mirror. But...'

'Don't worry. I'll tell you all that you need to know.' Maggie patted, then squeezed, her hand, a gesture designed to calm and comfort. It did, at least in part, but Anna needed to understand the rest. Her son was obviously in possession of all the facts, and she desperately wanted that same knowledge. To be fully aware of exactly what was going on around them.

Maggie placed her hand reverently atop The Chronicle.

'This,' she said, 'is the journal of events – both positive and negative – of healings, and of magic, concerning the well in the cellar of Damara Cottage.' Anna's head snapped up at the use of the word 'magic', but Maggie continued without pause. 'Its true name is The Source. And it is a source – of energy from the earth, from nature. Its purpose is ultimately for good, but as with all forces, those of evil intent can corrupt the power. They can use it for their own causes, can harness its strength and channel it towards darkness. That's where I come in.' She looked up, confirming their understanding thus far and, at their nods, continued.

'The Well must have a Guardian, to protect against those of ill-will, and to channel the power of The Source for the benefit of Welham and its people. I'm the present Guardian.' She paused and took a deep breath. 'Damara Cottage houses The Source, but I am – have always been – forbidden entry unless Damara falls back into my hands through natural means. All I can do presently is try to protect from afar. The Guardians following Alice's murder were evicted, and cannot now regain control until Fate provides a way of gifting Damara back. Money cannot change hands. The Source is not for sale.'

Anna was at a loss. Jake, however, seemed to be following without any problems.

'Why can't you get to The Well? What stops you?'

'We, the Guardians, permitted Damara to fall into the hands of bad souls. However innocently lost, whatever the crimes committed by enemies, and even though taken by force and without permission, it means that it can now only be returned through natural progression.'

'But what does that mean... 'natural progression'?' Jake was leaning forward in his chair, every fibre of his being attuned to Maggie's words. Anna wondered at the change in her son. That he truly understood what was being said was not in doubt, but more than that. Anna could now see a strength and resilience in him that had grown over the time spent in Welham. He had always been a kind boy, gentle and sensitive, but now she could see the beginnings of the man he could become. A combination of steely determination and a beauty of spirit. A genuine goodness that would stand him well in the trials of life yet to be faced.

Her understanding, though, seemed to be progressing a little more slowly than her son's, and she was struggling to keep pace with Maggie's words. Alice's knowledge, the 'sharing' of last evening, had settled easily within her, but the grass roots practicalities were what Anna was struggling with now. The very fact that she accepted without question what was being told to her, however, showed how much she herself had grown since their arrival.

'Natural progression,' answered Maggie, 'means that Damara Cottage can only be returned to The Guardian by destiny, rather than by the hand of man. It can never be bought back – finance is a tool made by people. Damara can be inherited, or shared. Never purchased – at least by The Guardian.'

'That will be why my solicitor took such a long time looking through the Deeds perhaps?' asked Anna. 'He said that there were 'historical clauses' which had to be adhered to before he could let us proceed with the purchase.'

Maggie nodded. 'That's why Damara stood empty for so long,

too. Since the death of Doctor Grassington. The cottage can only be bought by someone without any previous familial attachment. Your ancestry was probably being checked.'

Anna blew out her cheeks. *Unbelievable!*

'What's in The Chronicle?' she asked quietly. 'May we see inside?'

'The last page – the page which concerns the two of you – is all that I can show you. The rest I can explain another time.' She laughed. 'It's filled mostly with potions and poultices. Ways of healing using natural methods. The last entry, though,' her voice dropped, 'is very different.'

Maggie pulled the huge tome towards her and opened it around halfway through, gently turning the parchment pages, searching for the final entry. The Freers had inverted glimpses of ornate and scrolling calligraphy, some pages embellished with colourful borders, others with well-drawn pictures of flowers, leaves or vegetables.

Stopping at last, The Guardian turned the book towards them. The writing here was without decoration, was less legible and more cramped, as if written in haste and urgency.

June 18th, 1616

My sister, Alice, did on this day leave natural life at the wish and behest of Mister James Brunton; she, hanged by the neck and given not chance of trial or discourse. She, accussed of witchcraft, with defence offered not by friends nor either neighbours, all whom did previously take succour by way of healing or poultice.

Mister Brunton did incite the parish to remove my sister with force from her home of Damara, within the hamlet of Welham. He was occasioned not otherwise, despite plea by myself and a very few more on the behalf of my sister.

Alice did conduct herself of great courage and was decorous unto the end. May her spirit rest in the peace granted those of good and pure intent.

She, as Guardian of the Source now removed, needs must be replaced. I, Edith, take this charge to my own with a willing heart albeit burdened by bereavement and grief.

There be such few parishioners do give fair and honest warning that Mister James Brunton does intend to make good his right under the law of our good King James to take Damara to his own. As befits the order of his office to take the life of any presumed or proven of witchcraft.

This may be challenged not under restraint of his lawful office. His judgement, I must trust, will come to that of a higher order on account of murder this day of his professed bride.

My daughter, Margaret, with me to abide as can be found within this parish, at the goodwill of those of faith and stout heart.

Little is left of time to make good. I do try. The Chronicle in which I now scribe I will cover within Damara. It there to remain within the boundary until time as such is nigh to make right the wrongs of this day.

Rest peacefully gracious sister, Alice, true Guardian of The Source. The time of reckoning will summon you once more.

They sat back in unison, both with a myriad of questions and yet at a loss to know where to begin. Jake rallied first.

'Brunton! Then Alice's murderer, her betrayer, was an ancestor of George and Luke?' He phrased it as a question although truthfully the answer was already apparent. 'That's how Damara was lost, why The Chronicle was hidden, and why The Guardians were exiled.' He had a dawning of recognition. 'They're the ones of 'evil intent', aren't they, Maggie? Just as you're the Guardian, they've inherited a wickedness from their ancestor, James – Witch Finder and murderer.' He had never felt so coldly furious.

'What happened after Alice's murder?' his mother asked.

Maggie explained that Alice's sister, Edith, and her daughter had been forced to live on the charity of neighbours sympathetic to their plight until Margaret's marriage many years later. The Guardianship had been passed from Margaret's hand forwards, ending with Maggie herself.

'This Chronicle – the original – was lost to us. We knew it was within Damara but we couldn't regain it. We also knew that it was protected by ancient magic. That it was invisible to any but the Guardian until the spell was lifted. That is what Alice did – she lifted the spell – to enable Jake to recover and bring it to me. A new Chronicle was started by Margaret, soon after her mother, Edith's, death. The one in use now. But the most precious information, the early knowledge, remained hidden for all those years.'

'Why do the Bruntons want it so badly? What kind of power can they take from it?' Jake felt the first stirrings of a deep and real fear as he voiced the question uppermost in his mind.

'The Source enhances natural forces, whether good or bad,' explained Maggie. 'Whatever the truth of a person's soul, the energy of The Well will strengthen it. As the Guardians use the power for healing, so one of evil intent can use to corrupt, to spoil, to manipulate – or to destroy.' Maggie paused, obviously gauging how to phrase her next words. 'He'll try to destroy us – to kill us – so that he can control The Source. If he then gains the power of one such natural force, he can move on to take others. His strength would grow proportionately.' All around the table were silent, the enormity of her words only now beginning to register. She went on. 'History has given us names, although in truth they are only labels, and we are just people. It is the soul inside which decides the path.'

'Names?' asked his mother, her voice sounding thin and reedy.

'I am what would be called a 'witch'. As was Alice. To be branded such was her downfall. Her gift was used only for goodness though, as is mine. You'll have heard of the name by which the Brunton men go, too. They are warlocks. Their interest in The Source is, always, for their own gain, and for their own power.'

His mother, Jake saw, paled noticeably, before voicing her next question. 'Luke's gift, his 'power'? What is it, Maggie?'

The Guardian raised her head and her words were gentle. Yet their content filled Jake with dread.

'We all have different strengths. His are mind manipulation. Hypnosis. Astral projection too, I'd presume. Anything that involves controlling others, or bending to his will. He's a dangerous man, a strong warlock, and gifted at his craft.'

'There's a lot at stake here, isn't there, Maggie? Our lives, for starters.' Jake's voice was quiet now. 'If he wants to control The Source, my mum, as owner of Damara Cottage, is a way to gain that control? That's right, isn't it?'

Maggie nodded, meeting his eyes.

Jake's understanding of the situation was a surprise even to her. That he was destined to be the catalyst was now not in any doubt. Any lingering misgivings that she had about his youth or inexperience were replaced in an instant by a calm acceptance.

The Source had called out for a champion, and Fate had provided Jake. There could be no question. The battle for control of Damara Cottage was about to begin. The hands of the clock were once again turning, and the countdown had begun.

MAGICAL MOORS

He could feel the movement of the leaves overhead, could see their outlines on the inside of his eyelids as the breeze made them dance and whisper. Heaving a contented sigh, he allowed himself the luxury of enjoying the final part of this perfect day. Lottie, her head resting on his shoulder, stirred slightly and he revelled in their intimacy, their togetherness.

It had been just over a week now, since their first meeting, and each time he saw her his stomach still did that double-flip and his palms grew moist. Yet, it was as though he had always known her too, so easy was their relationship.

They had spent most of the day in talk, of things personal and mystical, of The Chronicle and Alice, and it was a joy to be able to finally speak freely of things kept hidden within him for so long.

They spoke of their past relationships, of fun they had enjoyed with other partners, both agreeing though, with candour and no embarrassment, that what they had together now felt deeper, special. They spoke too of the energy of the earth around them, of ley lines, dowsing and healing waters.

'That's what gives this area such magic,' she smiled. 'There are lots of underground springs and they all converge around Damara. That's a part of the strength of where we live. We're so lucky.'

She seemed excited by his depth of knowledge too, encouraging him to share with her what he already knew. His innate abilities had provided him with both practical experience, and also the book-reading which accompanied a need to understand his childhood feelings of isolation, of being somehow different from his peer group.

'I started seeing things when I was very young,' he began. 'Stuff that I thought everyone else could see too. It was a shock when they laughed, or called me names. Kids can be pretty cruel to anyone who is a bit different. I learned quickly to keep it to myself.' He was looking inwards now, the remembering raising a swift shadow of remembered childhood pain.

Lottie touched his hand, encouraging him. 'What things, Jake? What did you see?'

He glanced up at her, sensing her empathy. With a small shake of the head, he continued. 'At first I thought they were just regular people. A bit like the kid in the film. You know, the one who 'sees dead people'? When I realised that they weren't flesh and blood, and that no one else was aware of them, then I guess I started to ignore them.' He rubbed his forehead. 'But it's always been there... in the background. Things moving out of the corner of my eye. And I've always been conscious of atmospheres. A couple of times, I caught someone standing behind me when I looked in the mirror, but they always disappeared as soon as I looked directly.' He laughed self-consciously. 'Pretty weird, huh?'

'But you know almost as much as me about earth energy,' Lottie said. 'How did you find all this out, if you were squashing down your gift?'

'It didn't feel much like a gift back then.' He snorted. 'But I did always know that there was something more. Something that most people can't see. Or maybe... choose not to?' He raised questioning eyes to her face. 'That's it, isn't it, Lottie? Can everyone see this stuff but, for whatever reason, they block it out? A bit like I did?'

Her answer was measured. 'You're right. Of course, you're right. But not many have a psychic ability as strong as yours. That's probably why you couldn't completely close it off.'

He nodded. 'I used to read books when I was small, about UFOs, or unexplained phenomena. Mysteries of the earth, like stone circles or the pyramids. Then I moved on to the internet. Stuff about energy, ley lines, crop circles and dowsing.' He glanced at her. 'I never told anyone though. Not even Mum, although I know she saw the books sometimes. But she never gave me the third degree. She always called me an imaginative child.' He laughed self-consciously.

They spoke then of Damara. Of the vibrations ebbing and flowing within.

'I've seen more, heard more stuff since coming to Welham than in all of my life before,' he said. 'Like the peripheral vision stuff. And when I'm in the cottage alone, and always upstairs, I can hear someone moving about in the kitchen.' He shrugged. 'It doesn't seem creepy though.' He tried to explain. 'Everything in Damara feels sort of…' He searched for a word. '…gentle. The only bad things have been when he puts in an appearance.'

The talked of Alice too, and Jake's experiences with her. Lottie listened, contributing when necessary, but mainly just giving him the freedom to allow it all into the open. He held nothing back, trusting her with his secrets, his innermost feelings.

'She was so beautiful, Lottie,' he finished. 'So lovely. Have you seen her too?'

She nodded. 'Just the once, and in a place very special to me. I'll take you there sometime.'

He asked her about George Brunton, and his tall-tales of a hideous, mad woman.

'That just doesn't fit, though. Not with what I've felt, and what I've seen. There's only good stuff in Damara. And why, Lottie, with all the history between your family and the Bruntons, did you ever go to work there… in The Wishing Well, with him as your boss?' His brow was furrowed but the answer, when it came, was obvious.

'It worked for both sides, I think. Mr Brunton offered me the job earlier this year, probably thinking to pick my brains about my mother's work, and to try to find a way of locating

The Chronicle.' She smiled ruefully. 'I accepted for much the same reason – to spy on Luke and his antics, although there's not been much, to be honest. At least until you arrived.' He slowly nodded his understanding. She continued. 'We were watching them, watching us, watching them. We all knew the game we were playing. It would be funny if it weren't so serious.'

He raised his eyes to hers. There were still more questions.

'But Alice?' Jake was genuinely puzzled by the disparate personas of the myth of local legend and his visions. 'I haven't got it wrong about her. I know it was Alice, and I know that there's nothing ugly or bad about her.'

'No, you haven't got it wrong. Not at all. If you accept the power of Damara, can just *believe*, then everything else falls into place.' Her fingers toyed with the soft grasses beneath them as she seemed to strive for the words to make him understand.

'Damara – or the energy within and around Damara – enhances the natural world.' She paused again, glancing at Jake to gauge his reaction. 'It's like Mum said. If a person is mean or horrid, then they will become *more* mean and horrid. If they have a beautiful spirit, it will become more so. Your gifts, your physic awareness,' she reached out and touched his temple, a gesture of such affection that he was moved, 'has also taken a boost, making it easier for you to see beyond the curtain between the two worlds. Making it impossible for you to ignore it anymore.' She grinned, giving him a soft punch on the shoulder. 'Your mum? She has an enormous capacity for love – especially for you. She also has an emotional strength that she's not even aware of yet. But she's hurting too, and before the hurt can heal, it must run its course. That will also amplify because of Damara, but the energy will help her to get through it, to mend properly.'

'But, I still don't understand. Why has the story of Alice become so negative when she was a healer? Why is she described as hideous and evil, when we know she's truly beautiful? It doesn't make sense.'

'Haven't you ever heard that history is always written by the victors?' She smiled, but it didn't reach her eyes. 'And because George Brunton sees what he expects to see,' she explained. 'He's not a good man. His power is weaker than his son, but it goes way back over generations, this evil seed. I know you've realised it over your time at The Wishing Well. Mr Brunton covers it well, but his negative perception of life – of everything, really – colours the energy he picks up from living near to Damara. He's what my mum calls 'a corruptible vessel'. And he's a pawn to his son's ambition, to Dr Brunton's need to control The Source.'

Jake nodded, accepting the truth of her comments and allowing himself a moment to organise his thoughts.

'The cemetery!' It was also starting to fall into place. 'Is that why everyone in Welham lives for such a long time? Does the magic of Damara make people healthier?'

'You've got it,' she laughed.

Lottie told him then of auras, the natural force given off by all living things, and then showed him how to see. First, a tree, she said – the massive oak beneath which they now lay.

They strolled away from their picnic site to a grassy knoll a short distance away. Sitting down, legs crossed in front of them, they looked towards the oak.

'Relax your eyes,' she said. 'Look at a point beyond the tree and let your vision blur just a little.'

He was amazed when a shining arc of light suddenly became clearly visible around the canopy, only for it to vanish just as quickly as he tried to focus upon it. Many minutes were spent with Jake screwing up his face as he tried to perfect his 'aura-vision', as Lottie called it, and with both of them laughing at his efforts.

'Trees have much stronger energy during the spring and summer months,' she said. 'Their auras are wider and brighter then. During the winter, it's much more difficult to see. They pull almost all of their energy within while they're sleeping and regenerating. Plants and flowers, too. 'Some people see only light. Others can see colours.'

She told him that, for her, perception of auras was through her

Third Eye; that she had to actually close her physical eyes before she could see the energy before her.

'Almost like a photographic negative. I don't see colours – only light and shade – but I can spot where there's physical, mental, or emotional damage. If the spirit, the soul, is wounded, it shows at the outer edges of the aura – much harder to spot, and much more difficult to heal. It's taken a bit of practice, but it's something that I'm really good at now.' She sat back then, leaning on her hands, and Jake thought that he had never seen anyone so at peace with her surroundings, so relaxed within her own skin.

'Try *me* now,' she challenged.

Jake, turning to face her, did as she had taught him. At first, nothing, and he was a little disappointed that he may have taken a step backwards from his success with the oak. Taking a deep breath, he relaxed even further. The colours appeared immediately, surprising him in their intensity. Clear, bright and beautiful, Lottie's aura was a glorious mix of yellows, pinks, and a beautiful pale lilac. Just to the left of her throat, there was a small patch of green which, when he described it, Lottie explained was 'probably that argument I had with Mum last night. Green is the colour of healing, and the throat is about communication, so it would make sense.'

Jake was overwhelmed. Amazed and awe-struck at the beauty around him, and at his own ability to be a part of it. They came together then, their excited embraces beginning as a celebration of his success, and of all around them, but becoming something much more personal and sensual as passion overtook them.

Moving back beneath the sheltering canopy of the oak, they made love together for the first time, the soft earth cushioning them. It, too, was perfect. Intimate, intense and tender. He wanted her so badly. Yet somehow their physical union did not need to be rushed, as had happened in all of his limited experiences of the past. He found that they could share this unique pleasure together. He felt himself a part of her, and of all of nature around them. He lost himself in the moment, yet felt a completeness as never before.

They were caught in the afterglow, relaxing and dozing beneath the shade of the ancient tree, the moors stretching upwards and away beyond the fields, sunlight dappling the soft grass on which they lay. The detritus of their picnic lay near his backpack, waiting to be gathered away before the half-hour walk back down the incline towards the farm and Damara Cottage.

He sighed, a smile of contentment curling his lips. It had been a day of wonder and of beauty, and he would remember this time for the rest of his life.

Earlier in the day he had even managed to capture the exceptional landscape with his camera which he had brought along too – the excuse the young couple had given to escape on their own for the day – and felt sure that some of his shots, taken when the light was beyond perfect, would be of a standard to begin his portfolio. He sighed again. It would be time to start back soon, and he was reluctant to see an end to this magical day.

The scream took him by surprise, bringing him to a sitting position, the speed of his movement shocking Lottie still dozing by his side. She sat up also, rubbing her eyes, a puzzled frown hovering on her brow.

'Jake? What is it? What's wrong?'

He was on his feet now, turning, searching for the source of the sound. For the person who, he felt sure, must be either in danger or in pain.

There was nothing. The soft breeze continued to move the leaves above them. Occasionally, the bleating of sheep carried from the fields.

Lottie stood too, laying a hand upon his arm.

'Tell me. What did you hear?'

He looked down into her eyes, confused and unnerved by the silent scream.

'You have to trust yourself, Jake. Trust your instinct. What did you hear?' she said again. 'Could you tell?'

'I think…' He paused, closing his eyes and trying to go inside himself, to hear again the sound that had echoed within. '…it might have been my mum.'

'We have to get back, Jake. Right now.'

Jake grabbed his camera and they set off at a run down the incline towards Damara.

TRUE COLOURS

The knock on the front door made her jump. She wasn't expecting anyone, and had been looking forward, finally, to a quiet day to call her own.

Not that she could relax, of course. Decisions and events of the recent past weighed heavily upon her. But the ancient Aga was almost begging her to try out some home baking, and the fine weather was urging her to tackle the colourful but weed-choked back garden. Some physical activity after all of the emotional and – she forced herself again to say the word – *magical* events of days passed, would be just what she needed. Activities without the need for thought. She smiled.

Jake was out with Lottie, picnic lunch packed, and camera securely stowed in his rucksack. Anna had watched the two of them from the sitting room window, heading hand-in-hand towards the summer splendour of Welham Moor that morning. Things were definitely going well there and she was sure that Lottie had played a large part in helping Jake to move forwards, to leave the pain of the past behind.

Leaving her coffee on the table, she was half way across the kitchen when the knock came again, just a little louder and more insistent. Through the side window of the porch, the back of Dr Brunton's blond head and tailored jacket was instantly recognisable.

She hadn't seen him since the afternoon in the glade, had

avoided any occasions when she might run in to him accidentally, and had stayed well away from The Wishing Well.

Her initial thoughts that day, of wickedness and corruption, of searching for skeletons in Luke Brunton's closet, had seemed ridiculous after a good night's sleep and in the cold light of day. Events since then, however, had proved her initial assessment correct. Alice, The Chronicle, and the conversations around the table at Welham Farm had all confirmed that she should trust her intuition. And she knew from personal experience of his ability to control.

His unexpected appearance on her doorstep today was a shock.

The humiliating episode in The Wishing Well, which still made her cringe, had been explained by Maggie as a product of the doctor's manipulation skills; that Anna had very likely been in a trance for the majority of the time spent with him. Steve Cooper's fortuitous arrival that night had definitely been the saving of her tattered modesty. Embarrassment and shame flooded back in an instant at the memory.

The bewilderingly erotic dreams about Luke were mortifying too. Again, she had shared with Maggie the intensity of these dreams, each exceptionally real in its own right, each leaving her feeling aroused yet sullied on waking. Her friend had gently explained to her the principles of astral projection. An ability to leave one's physical body and travel through space. The idea that their dream time couplings, herself and Luke entwined in passion, may have been more than just the product of her over-active imagination was still something that she was struggling to come to terms with. The dreams had stopped immediately upon her speaking about them.

Anna now toyed with the thought of 'hiding behind the sofa'. She hadn't yet been seen, and facing him on her own, in Damara, filled her with a very real sense of dread. Not answering the door would be the sensible thing to do.

What Anna knew for certain was that she felt out of control when in Luke's company, as if he were a puppet master and she the plaything dancing to his tune. She didn't trust herself to behave appropriately in his company. That was the bottom line, and she admitted it to herself. Even after everything that had happened, everything she knew, he still had a power over her.

Now, bizarrely, and warring with all her better judgement and opposing emotions, she couldn't quite quash the tiny imp of excitement at seeing him again.

But surely, her internal voice whispered slyly, *now that you know the truth, he can't control you anymore.*

Making a decision and mainly, she justified, because the front door was unlocked and he may just try the handle and walk in uninvited, Anna opened the door. He turned, a dashing smile lighting his face. She felt immediately the pull of his undoubted charisma.

'Too early for a coffee?' Not waiting for her response, he was through the door and into her kitchen before she had time to formulate an excuse.

She turned and followed, the same sense of dread, and of being manipulated, rising once more.

''Fraid not. I'm just dashing out. Lots to do, and not enough hours in the day.' Her tone was light, belying the anxiety she was already beginning to feel in his presence.

This would have to be nipped in the bud. She couldn't keep up the avoidance tactics any longer. Nor could she go through this each and every time she saw him. The truth – of his real character, of his dark gifts, – must not be spoken of, but she could at least tell him that his attentions were unwelcome and unwanted.

Anna had played this particular scene in her head over the past few days, and especially after her talk with Maggie. She had known the time to confront him would come, had practised the skills – again taught by Maggie – with which she could at once remain in control of herself and her behaviour, and at the same time tactfully diffuse the situation without alienating him and putting herself in potential danger.

The thought of the conversation frightened her more than a little – she was unsure of his reaction – which made it all the easier to know for certain that this needed doing sooner rather than later.

He sat at her table now, impossibly handsome, deep blue eyes following her movements – and with the hide of a rhinoceros. She would have to be blunter than blunt, unfortunately, as Luke seemed completely unable to take any hint.

'Ah, but you've always time for me, surely.'

His smirk had an edge of condescension to it and Anna felt faintly patronised. The confidence in his ability to manipulate alarmed her. And manipulated she was. Once more. Most certainly.

As if of its own volition she felt her hand begin to reach for the kettle, an answering reply in the positive forming behind her lips. She wondered hazily if all women of Luke's acquaintance fell under his spell so easily. His magnetism was nearly impossible to resist.

Not Maggie though. Never Maggie. Remembering her friend's wise words, an image of Jake's face in her mind – and with enormous self-will and a very real reluctance – she forcibly pulled herself back and turned to face him. Her arms crossed her midriff in an unconsciously protective gesture. The need to make him that unoffered cup of coffee was strong, and her head felt sluggish and muddy.

The thought crossed her mind that she might be sickening for something. She concentrated hard to ensure that what she said next were the words that she wanted – needed – to tell him. With difficulty, a frown creasing her forehead, Anna pulled her thoughts together and backed a couple of steps towards the door.

'Luke, I'm so sorry, but another time. I really do have to run.'

His friendly expression seemed to slip, just for an instant, revealing something unpleasant and ugly beneath. She stifled a gasp at what she could swear she had just seen. A sneer, almost a snarl, distorted his features into a mask of anger, gone before she could be sure and replaced almost immediately by his suave default mode of rakish half-smile.

Yet in that instant of *his* extreme emotion, *her* thoughts had cleared and clarified, as if the one was affected by the other. As if his power over her had loosened momentarily.

Rising from his seat, he approached, his movements elegant, almost feline, in their grace.

'Later then. Perhaps a drink at the pub tonight?'

'Actually, I needed to have a chat, Luke.' The words seemed to be sticking in her throat. Her head was again losing fluidity, but she ploughed on anyway. 'Just so that we both know where we stand. You're a lovely man and I really value your friendship, but…'

His face was changing again, smile gone, replaced by an expression almost of contempt. Anna backed another step towards the door. His whole body had taken the lines of a predator, menacing, looming, and she had to fight the urge to cower from him.

'…but it's really too soon for me. I'm so sorry if I've given you the wrong idea.' Her words dried and died, but at least she had forced them into the open.

'What do you think is going on here, Anna?' The use of her name made her skin crawl, but his voice, silky-smooth, had a purring quality which seemed to hold her, prevent all thought of escape. 'Are you suggesting something more than friendship… that I could ever be interested in *that* way?'

The lines between fear and anger, repugnance and desire, melded and merged within her. She struggled to retain a grip on truth or fantasy.

Suddenly aware that she had backed herself against the wall, and that Luke now was blocking her way to the door, to freedom, Anna felt truly frightened for the first time. He was close to her, had moved without her noticing.

'Because if that's the case… His arms came up and braced the wall on either side of her face. '…then I must tell you that you're very wrong. You were only ever a pretty distraction, my dear.'

The piercing blue of his eyes bored into hers and she felt resistance, freewill, slipping away from her.

'Oh, but so very pretty, Anna,' he murmured. 'I can satisfy

those hungers, can make those dreams reality.' His face came closer still and she was held, a chainless prisoner, as he lowered his lips to hers. His kiss was unexpectedly soft, probing, but even so, fear and repulsion rose like a wave within her at his touch.

The internal scream, sounding too loud, too strident within her mind, released from her lips as barely more than a whimper, but the intensity of emotion provided her with the power needed to break free of the silken and invisible bonds. If she didn't move now, she may never have the chance again.

A frantic and high-pitched scree-screeching from outside caused Luke to turn his head towards the noise. The raven must be very close, Anna thought illogically, for the sound to be so loud. The cry continued unabated, to be cut short abruptly as something impacted with force against the window. The distraction gave Anna the chance she needed.

With all her strength, both physical and emotional, she planted her hands against his chest and pushed. Caught off-balance by the suddenness, he staggered back, clearly shocked at the challenge. An expression of surprise quickly changed to anger, brow lowering over eyes of ice, a snarl once more starting around his mouth. Anna's strength was returning though.

'How dare you!' Her voice was strong, clear. 'Get out.'

He gathered himself, the suave mask once more in place, but an underlying suggestion of violence simmered beneath the veneer. She was aware that something had changed between them. As if a mirror had cracked and a true image of the man was now visible. What she saw frightened her.

Making a play of straightening his still-perfect tie, he moved casually towards her.

'How dare I?' Silken-voiced once more, but all the more disturbing in its quietness, face now inches from hers again. 'You will have a chance to see very soon how much I dare, little Anna. Very soon.'

Turning his back with a disdainful sneer, he walked calmly and slowly from Damara, closing the door softly behind him. She remained rooted to the spot until she heard the throaty cough of his black Audi and the crunch of tyres on her driveway.

The trembling started immediately, and she reached to the table for support, her legs unable to hold any weight. Nausea washed over her in waves while trickles of perspiration carved tiny pathways down her back. Taking deep breaths, she slumped in the chair so recently vacated by Luke and allowed the feelings of panic and sickness to subside.

Recognition had come almost too late, she realised. Maggie's warnings returned now, making her all too aware of her own foolishness, pride and vanity. How could she think to confront this man alone? Luke's true colours were flying, and Anna wondered helplessly how she could possibly be any help in the conflict ahead. He was so very strong.

She felt the impending approach of something only yet whispered about. Something terrible, for which she was all-too-aware she was ill-prepared and ill-equipped to handle… on her own, at least. That was the mistake she had made this time. She would not make it again.

She raised frightened eyes to the window. A ghostly outline of magnificent wings, their span covering the whole of the double frame, was imprinted on the glass. Hoping for the best, fearing the worst, Anna dashed from the cottage and round to where the raven should have fallen. No sign. She scanned the garden for clues as to Albert's whereabouts. Still nothing.

A faint rustling from an overhanging rhododendron bush drew her attention and she bent to look beneath. The huge bird huddled, his body at an odd angle as he tried, and failed, to support himself on one side. A broken and ruined wing lay splayed on the earth, and Anna could hear a laboured rattle as he struggled to draw breath into lungs swollen and bruised by the impact. In his one good eye, she could see pain reflected back at her. She knelt, reaching out, and laid a gentle hand on the broad back. He allowed her touch without flinching.

'Mum!' With relief, she heard her son's call from behind the cottage, his voice sharp, edgy with worry.

'Here. Quickly. At the front.' Beneath her hand, the bird didn't react to the voices.

Jake and Lottie appeared at a run around the side of Damara, out of breath from their headlong sprint down the moor, but recovering quickly with the resilience of youth on their side.

'Are you okay? We came as fast as we could.' At his mother's nod, he came to her side and dropped to his knees.

'What's happened? I heard a scream. Was *he* here?' As always, when mentioning Luke Brunton, Jake's voice hardened and his eyes glinted ice. There was no doubting the enmity already apparent, or the feelings attached.

'He was. He's gone now. But Jake... look.' He followed her gaze. As she pushed back the dense foliage of the bush, the flight feathers at the tip of the wing came into view.

Jake gasped.

'What happened? Did he...?' His voice trailed off, but Anna shook her head.

'The raven was trying to protect me. Help me get him inside, poor thing.' Her voice caught on a sob.

Lottie knelt too and, between the three of them, they began to manoeuvre the giant bird from beneath his hiding place. He offered no resistance, merely allowing their gentle tugging and pulling as, little by little, he was edged into the open.

Once exposed, the severity of the injury became apparent. A fine line of blood showed in the corners of his beak, and the one good eye was half closed as he struggled with pain. The creature was horribly maimed. Probably dying.

With the help of Lottie's hands beneath the broken body, silent tears now streaming down her face, Jake lifted Albert into his arms, taking care not to touch the injured leg. Anna supported the wing as best she could, and between the three of them they moved the bird into the cottage.

'Lottie, here, cradle this wing while I find a blanket. Jake, take him over near to the Aga. There's enough space there, and he'll be warm during the night.' Anna's voice was calm and authoritative.

She was in what Jake always called 'Mother-in-Control mode', dealing with the situation deftly, and in a sensible, logical way.

As always in times of crises, her inner strength came to the fore. Afterwards would be time enough to worry about the events of the day and her confrontation with Luke. What was more important now was whether the raven could survive his terrible injuries. Although no one voiced their fear, none of them thought Albert would make it through the night. His breathing was laboured and rattling, becoming louder with the exertions of the move from the garden, and his healthy eye was now fully closed.

The blanket in place, Jake gently lowered the huge bird, taking care to lay him on to his uninjured side. The damaged leg and wing hung uselessly, and he seemed to have dropped into unconsciousness.

After filling a bowl with water and putting the usual meal of dog food close by in the vain hope of the creature reviving enough to need sustenance, the three of them left him in the kitchen to sleep. Although rest can be a great healer, it was obvious to everyone that a miracle would be needed to mend these injuries.

Lottie hadn't spoken since her first view of the great bird, although tears had started immediately. As she left the cottage, emotion overwhelmed her, and she sank into the garden seat, reaching to her pocket for a tissue. Anna took the vacant space beside her and placed a comforting arm around her shoulder, giving it a motherly squeeze.

'Why're *you* crying? I know it's upsetting, but you've never met Albert before.' Jake sounded almost indignant in his own worry for the raven.

At his look, between sobs, and in a halting voice, Lottie apologised and tried to explain. 'I'm so sorry.' She glanced at Anna from beneath lashes spikey with tears. '…but birds can carry spirits of relatives or friends. Sometimes our ancestors. This could be somebody special to any one of us, or someone from long ago. Either way, though, he's been keeping watch over Damara. Over you.'

131

At one time, not so very long ago, both Jake and Anna would have scoffed at such a claim. No longer though. Their time in Welham had taught them otherwise; that not everything can be explained with logic or science. That sometimes acceptance of the impossible, a suspension of disbelief, is the only way to make sense of the strange and unusual.

'Could it be my dad?' Jake's voice was quiet, and Anna understood his hesitancy. He, like her, wished with all his heart that it could be. But then, the raven lay horribly wounded. Would very likely die. He obviously couldn't bear to think of his father in pain once again. Thankfully, Lottie shook her head.

'I don't think so. It's way too soon for that.' She glanced up, her expression concerned, but both Jake and Anna sighed in relief.

'My mum's the one to talk to, though. She'll probably know.'

'Well, we can't do anything else here at the moment.' Anna's voice was brisk. She felt the need for action. To sit still would mean to think. Far better to talk things through than to dwell in solitary recriminations about what she could have done differently. She had lost control of the situation with Luke Brunton. Again. Helping Albert, or at least trying, would give her something else to focus upon.

'We could walk you home. Perhaps have a chat with your mum and get some of her good advice?' she suggested.

'Is your dad at home?' At Jake's question, Lottie nodded and he took her hand, pulling her to her feet. 'Maybe he can help Albert.' Looking to Anna, he said, 'You talk to Maggie, Mum. Tell her what's happened. We'll run ahead and find Steve.'

THE PANTRY

'Come with me.' Maggie walked towards the rear of the kitchen. 'We can talk in the pantry as I work.'

Anna had already spoken of all that had happened during that long day, beginning with her confrontation with Luke Brunton, and ending with the raven and its life-threatening injuries. Maggie had contributed little, merely nodding or encouraging quietly whenever her friend's words faltered.

Now Anna followed Maggie through a rough door and into a small, windowless room, shelved on both sides from floor to ceiling. A pine table stood at the far end, smaller than the one in the kitchen but equally sturdy. Two wooden stools crouched before it. Above, attached to the wall, was a star; a 'pentacle', Maggie explained at Anna's gaze, made from rowan twigs and bound together with red cord.

'Every witch must have one.' She smiled but it didn't reach her eyes.

The room was not large, but a far bigger space than the walk-in cupboard Anna had expected at the word 'pantry'.

'My office.' Maggie indicated the rows of bottles, jars and pots, all carefully labelled and containing an assortment of ingredients, some recognised, others unfamiliar to Anna. Mixing bowls of all sizes were stacked neatly to the far end, and on the table stood a mortar and pestle. An ornate dagger, its blade gleaming quietly, lay on a plush cloth of midnight blue. Raised above the rest, to the centre rear of the counter, a lectern supported The Chronicle.

Maggie perched on one stool, indicating the other for Anna with a nod of her head.

'Let's see if we can come up with something to help that poor bird,' she said, as gently she opened The Chronicle's heavy cover.

At the same moment as his mother was awaiting sight of The Chronicle's heart, Jake and Lottie found Steve on his knees in the barn tinkering with his pride and joy, an old, pre-war tractor.

'We need your held, Dad,' Lottie said without preamble, reaching to take a spanner from her father's hand as he rose to greet them. At Steve's raised eyebrows, Jake explained.

'It's a wounded raven. He flew into our kitchen window.' He tried hard to keep the catch from his voice. 'I think he's too badly wounded, but would you mind taking a look?'

'No problem, lad. Is the bird conscious?' Steve rubbed oily hands on an even oilier cloth, yet somehow his hands came away cleaner for the wiping. Jake shook his head, a lump in his throat.

'Then we'd better be quick about it.' Steve grabbed a jacket and was out of the barn in three quick strides.

As they followed at a jog, Jake caught the words 'take a gander at the wounded warrior'.

What they found on arrival did not fill them with hope. Albert hadn't moved in their absence, was motionless apart from the shallow fall of his chest as wounded lungs struggled to perform. His breathing had worsened, rasping irregularly on each exhale, although more softly than earlier as the volume of air he managed to process had lessened considerably.

Jake looked to Steve, the question on his face drawing a definitive head shake.

'I'm sorry, lad, but the best I can do for this chap is to end his suffering. It'll be over in but a moment,' and he stepped forward to carry out the unpleasant task.

'No! Please, don't.' Jake grabbed the older man's arm. At Steve's questioning look, he continued, 'He deserves a chance. At least until the morning. If he's no better by then...' The words tailed off as he pushed the unthinkable away.

'Right you are, lad, if you're sure. It's your call. But chances are I'll be making another journey over here tomorrow, one way or another. If it were one of my birds, I'd not let it see another sunrise, that's for sure.'

'You don't think he might improve with sleep and quiet, then?' Lottie was grasping at straws – they all knew it – and her father shook his head again.

'I know it means a lot to the both of you, but I'm pretty sure this is a lost cause. These injuries,' he looked again at Albert, 'are just too much for any creature to survive.'

Anna held her breath. She wasn't sure what to expect at first sight of the book's mysteries and she turned eager eyes to the exposed secrets. Maggie flicked through, her fingers moving at speed. But, was she mistaken? It appeared to Anna that her friend's fingers hovered just beyond touch of the pages, The Chronicle seemingly searching itself for the remedies sought, the answers needed. As pages flicked past, Anna glimpsed drawings, some crudely sketched, others colourfully ornate, along with charcoal diagrams and the curled lettering of handwritten script. Finally, the moving leaves settled, apparently having located the formula required.

Being able to understand what lay before her, at least to some small extent, she'd taken for granted, but it was not to be. As the pages came to rest and the chosen chapter lay uncovered, pictures and charts immediately began to blur and distort, becoming little more than vague parodies of what they had originally depicted. Script swam on the page, letters becoming jumbled and confused, and she raised bewildered eyes to meet the amused and knowing gaze opposite.

'Call it a security system,' Maggie explained. 'The Chronicle's failsafe. It will only reveal what the reader needs at any given time. What is clear and legible to me, I'm guessing looks like gibberish to you?'

Anna nodded, but her head had begun to swim, and she

was feeling decidedly nauseous. 'Wow.' Anything more seemed inadequate, and beyond her ability to vocalise. Anna looked again to the book. Nothing had changed. All remained undecipherable, shrouded in mystery. It might as well have been Egyptian hieroglyphs for all the insight she could garner. Overwhelmed, and beginning to sweat a little, she struggled to understand. She'd now seen, first-hand, magic at work – for what else could it be? – and the magnitude was mystifying. But also being permitted to share that knowledge, to be party to this secret, felt very special. She did not underestimate the trust Maggie placed in her, but right now she was very afraid that she might embarrass herself and faint.

'I'm so sorry, Maggie, but I feel a bit sick. Do you have a glass of water, please?' She lowered her head onto arms crossed before her on the table, beyond being able to cover up her distress. The shock of the day was obviously catching up with her.

'I've something much better. Hold on a minute.' Anna could hear Maggie moving behind her, but the sounds seemed to fade in and out of focus. 'Drink this, down in one, and quickly.' Maggie's voice was brisk, and Anna raised her head and did as she was told without question. The liquid was darkly coloured, and with a bitter taste, but she began to revive almost as soon as she swallowed.

'When's the baby due?'

The question hit like a bolt from the blue.

'Oh… but… I'm not pregnant, Maggie.' An image of the glade filled her mind. 'I can't be.'

Maggie remained quiet for what seemed an age. 'My mistake then. Just a touch of summer flu, maybe.' Her eyes were full of knowing and sympathy.

By mutual consent, they turned to the task at hand and busied themselves with the potion, but Anna could barely concentrate on the job in hand. She pulled her thoughts back to the present with effort.

'Will this help the raven? Can it? His injures were so awful, Maggie, I don't see how anything can save him.'

'Probably not,' her friend replied honestly, as she added a

miniscule spatula of pale powder from one of the chosen pots to a small bowl selected from the shelf. 'The Source is powerful, and the knowledge within The Chronicle is tried and tested. It's been handed down for many centuries, but if the hurt is too severe, then even this intervention can't reverse Fate. Perhaps it's just his time to die.' She shrugged her shoulders. 'We can only try, and know that we did our best.'

It wasn't the answer that Anna wanted, but she acknowledged the truth of the words. Albert's chances of survival were remote. Maggie was right though. They had to try.

'What can I do to help?' Again, her innate resilience, an ability to remain focused until any given crisis was dealt with, came to the fore, and Maggie nodded approval. She handed Anna the mortar and pestle, placing within it a sad-looking dried leaf from the second pot.

'The finer you can grind it, the better. I'll start over here,' she indicated the bowl, 'and then you can take the potion back with you to add to the bird's food and water. If nothing else, it'll ease his suffering.'

The two women worked in silence, intent on their work, Maggie adding a measure of emerald liquid to the powder and blending it thoroughly before finally taking the well-ground leaf from Anna. Referring again to The Chronicle, and using the tip of the dagger to measure and separate the fine particles, she scraped a tiny amount into the bowl, adding it to the green concoction. More mixing, before a small amount of the brew was syphoned into a glass phial and sealed with a tiny cork stopper.

'There.' Maggie sat back. 'That's the best we can do.' She handed the potion to Anna. 'Only three drops, mind. Four at a push.' Her instructions were specific. 'One drop – just the one, though – into his beak when you get back. Too much and it'll do more harm than good,' she warned. 'Less is more. It's strong stuff. If Albert survives the night, you can add a little more in his food tomorrow.'

Anna nodded, and their eyes met briefly. Neither expected a positive outcome.

Maggie reached over and closed The Chronicle gently, hand lingering on its carved binding. Its work for the evening was complete.

'If you want to talk about it, you know where I am.' Maggie's voice was gentle.

'There's nothing to talk about. Honestly. I just felt a bit queasy.' Anna was trying to convince herself as much as Maggie. 'Probably the stress of the day. I'll be fine.'

'The offer's there, Anna. I'm here if you need me.'

Anna nodded her thanks, and her thoughts whirled and tumbled. The two women left the pantry, closing the door softly behind them.

Jake had walked back to Welham Farm with Lottie and Steve to collect Anna. When they returned to Damara, cautiously and quietly opening the front and then the inner porch doors, both were expecting to find that the creature had died in their absence, so dreadful had his injuries been.

With small relief, they found Albert still sleeping. His breathing seemed gentler and more regular than when they had left, although a soft tell-tale rasp persisted on every exhale.

The wing and leg remained splayed along the blanket in the same position as when they had left. Food and water remained untouched. Albert hadn't roused or moved at all in their absence, and it seemed the best they could hope for was that he passed away quietly and painlessly without ever regaining consciousness.

Anna retrieved the medicine from her pocket, the tiny phial housing a vivid green concoction. Potion seemed a much better word, she thought, having seen its preparation just an hour earlier at Welham Farm.

To the raven's water-bowl, she added just one drop, as directed by Maggie. Into the food, she mixed three drops. Then she gently opened the huge beak with her fingers and allowed another single bead of emerald liquid to slide down his throat. There was no response from Albert. As she replaced the stopper, she recognised the futility of their hopes. Any intervention now probably was too little, too late.

With heavy hearts, they mounted the staircase, leaving the raven to its fate by the Aga below.

Anna slept badly that night, even exhausted as she was in the aftermath of a tiring and worrying day. Uppermost in her mind was, of course, her shocking encounter with Luke Brunton, and Maggie's comment.

Pregnant! How could it be? That would mean that her dream, the afternoon in the glade, had been real. It would make Luke Brunton a rapist. Her thoughts rattled and clattered around her head, and the more she thought, the more frightened she grew. Although she spared more than a few prayers on the raven fighting for survival downstairs in Damara's kitchen, still her mind kept returning to a snapshot of the glade, its beauty and horror forever frozen in her mind.

Finally, she slept.

Her dreams were filled with azure-blue eyes and long-fingered hands, and with the huge bird lying broken and vulnerable on the blanket, its screeching cry sounding again and again. A cry which had given her that moment of sanity and courage, and had very probably tipped the outcome in her favour. And always the sound was followed by the sickening thump as soft flesh hit the window with force.

Jake fared no better. His initial inclination had been to spend a night on the kitchen floor in his sleeping bag, keeping watch over Albert. Yet instinct warned against it. Whether to spare him witnessing the bird's final moments, or for some other reason entirely, he could not tell, and didn't spend too long analysing. He was learning to trust his inner voice.

Instead he lay sleepless in his bed for what felt like the entire night, listening for sounds of movement from the kitchen below. Remembering how Albert would mock-wink that milky eye, giving a shrewd nod of the head on every meeting, for all the world as though imparting sage advice. And how majestic those great wings had looked in flight as Albert circled above Damara.

Eventually, sleep took him.

THE MESSAGE

His mother's cry woke him early the next morning.
'Jake. Jake, wake up. Come and see.'

Bleary at the abrupt awakening and his night of endless clock-watching, he rubbed his eyes with the heel of his hands. Thoughts clarified suddenly.

Albert!

Dragging on some joggers and a handy t-shirt, he hurried barefoot downstairs, not at all sure what would greet him. He couldn't believe that he had actually slept at all, but clearly exhaustion had won out at some point during that eternal night. Her voice, he thought, had sounded excited, but he didn't want to pin too much faith on that, or even allow himself to hope.

She met him at the foot of the stairs, jigging from one foot to the other like a cat on hot bricks, eyes surprisingly bright after the stress of the past twenty-four hours.

'You won't believe it.' Her head nodded at variance to the words. 'It's just not possible.' She grabbed his arm and began to drag him towards the kitchen.

'I couldn't stay in bed any longer,' she babbled on, fingers digging into his wrist as she pulled him along behind her. 'Just had to come down and see…'

A croaky caw-caw from beyond the door interrupted her non-stop chatter, and stopped him in his tracks.

Surely it couldn't be… how could it… Albert?

Jake pushed by his mother and dashed the final few feet into the kitchen. Anna followed, a wide smile spreading across her face.

The raven stood on the blanket, both legs supporting the weight of his sturdy body, head cocked to one side, and beady black eye meeting Jake's gaze with vitality and acuity. The food was all but gone, only a few smears remaining in the dish. The only sign of yesterday's accident was the wing. It hung low against the body, Albert unable to fold it away correctly yet, but nevertheless without any other outward sign of distortion or injury.

'But… how?' He turned to his mother. 'I was so sure.'

'Me too,' she replied. 'But it must be something to do with Damara, with the potion. The healing powers that Maggie's told us about? I can't explain it any other way.'

'Albert was dying.' Jake shook his head, eyes glued to the great bird. 'Those injuries…' His voice tailed off in confusion as he approached and squatted on his haunches before him. Albert returned his gaze and, as he stretched out a hand hesitantly, took a single hop towards him.

'That leg, Albert. You shouldn't be able to use that leg.' Jake spoke quietly so as not to alarm the raven, but also trying to rationalise, within himself, the unexplainable. The bird cocked its head as if in agreement and hopped forward once more, now within easy reach of Jake's fingers. He raised his hand slowly, still further, and placed it gently against the raven's shoulder, allowing fingers to travel softly down the sleek plumage. The life-force, the energy of the creature, seemed to vibrate against his skin, and he turned to look at his mother. She shrugged and shook her head, the smile threatening to break into an unashamed grin.

'It's unbelievable.' Her voice was edgy with excitement. 'Early as it is, Jake, I'm going to phone Maggie. I can't wait any longer to tell her.'

'Tell Lottie I'll phone later?' Jake asked.

Still smiling, Anna nodded and retreated to the sitting room to make the call. Jake turned back to Albert.

Sitting himself comfortably cross-legged in front of the bird, their heads now on a level because of the creature's great size, he continued to stroke the silken feathers, his mind a patchwork of thoughts. Albert appeared content at the contact. His good eye half closed, he dozed in the shaft of early sunlight slanting through the window, warming the dark flags of the kitchen floor.

'It's a mystery, Albert. You shouldn't still be here.' Jake kept his voice soft, his hand now resting lightly on the raven's broad back.

As though events were not already strange and inexplicable enough, an unbelievable thing happened then, in the kitchen of Damara Cottage. Even taking into account his injuries, and the night spent in Damara, the raven was still a wild creature. Some fear or apprehension would be expected in the presence of his human carers. But Albert stretched forward suddenly, lowering his head to rest lightly on Jake's shoulder; a gesture of such faith that he was stunned and moved in equal measure.

Anna had made up her mind to speak to Maggie. She needed to be sure, and Maggie was the only person who might understand, would offer a sympathetic ear. She would buy a pregnancy test later today, get the result, and then decide what to do. In her heart, though, she already knew, and the knowledge was both terrifying and exciting in equal measure. She and Peter had always wanted another child. Had longed for it, but it had never happened. And now… this. A child conceived in hate. The product of rape. This was too much to keep to herself. And she couldn't speak to Jake about it.

A few minutes later, she returned from her call and gasped at the sight before her, mouth agape in wonder. It was a freeze-framed image that would never leave her. The giant bird, his great head resting easily against Jake's neck, her son's arms wrapped around the creature's girth, enfolding it protectively. They seemed unaware of her presence, eyes closed, motionless in the moment. A building of trust that would remain always. An unbreakable bond. She could not have guessed that, although both were physically present in the sunlit kitchen, they were, in fact, far away. In another time.

Jake opened his eyes slowly. A sound had awoken him. He was in a rocking chair in the sitting room of Damara. Although the dimensions remained unchanged, the décor was different. The curtains were open, night had fallen, and soft light from a standard lamp near the door showed him that he was alone in the room.

He pulled himself from the comfort of the chair, noting with some surprise the slight stiffness of his limbs and back. Catching sight of his reflection in the darkened glass of the window, he caught his breath. An old man returned his gaze. Kindly, intelligent eyes, a mane of tousled white hair framing a receding hairline, and a dapper dressing gown in red paisley-print completed the look. Jake's brow lowered in confusion, and he raised his hand towards the glass. The gentleman in the window frowned back and mirrored his movement.

Another slight noise beyond the doorway drew his attention. Feeling an overpowering need to investigate, knowing that he should follow his instinct and allow events to unfold before him, he turned towards the sound.

That he was within the mind of another soul, he realised, but why – or indeed who – was still unclear.

He made his way towards the kitchen. All was darkness beyond the portal, an inky blackness, and he clicked on the switch as he entered, throwing the room into instant relief. Again, the furniture was wrong, and placed differently. He scanned quickly, searching, but there was nobody. Yet the feeling of being watched was strong. His gaze was drawn to the far corner, beside the Aga.

The door – the cellar door in the corner – stood open. Just a crack, but open nonetheless.

He approached carefully, his slippers silent on the flag-stoned floor. The bulb in the cellar had been turned on, was leeching a faint glow around the opening. He knew at that moment, without doubt, that someone was inside the cottage with him.

A frying pan hanging beside the Aga became his weapon of choice, its weight feeling comfortable in his hand. From the top of the stairs, he reasoned, he would always have the advantage over an enemy approaching from beneath. And he had the element of surprise, for now there came another small noise from the cellar. The intruder was most certainly below.

The door opened quietly beneath his hand. No squeaking of hinges or rattling of doorknobs to betray his presence, and he stepped carefully through to the head of the steps. Another soundless pace forward, the descent stretched down before him. He raised the pan high, ready for action.

There was no warning from behind, no portent of a second foe. The forceful shove to his shoulders caught him unawares, and he felt his balance tilt. The pan fell away, echoing noisily as it collided with stone, and then spiralled away into the cellar. He made a grab for the wall but only grazed flat brickwork, hands flailing in a futile effort to grasp salvation. Feet finding no purchase on the damp moss, they slipped from under him on the slick surface.

A second and equally powerful shunt connected with force against his waist. A booted foot, he thought lucidly. His body twisted, back arching unnaturally, and he began to fall. Time slowed.

Jake became the unwilling spectator of the old man's demise.

He tumbled down the steps for eternity, seeing all through the eyes of the dying man. Every nuance was captured in exquisite, detailed clarity, a kaleidoscope of horror. The mossy green of the stairs, every crack in the wall, the earthen cellar floor rising to meet him. As he somersaulted once more, the frame of his attacker was silhouetted above, blackened by light from the kitchen. Then rotating again to glimpse the one cowering below, a miserable, snivelling creature. The decoy.

The steps rose up, and he sensed his face connect with stone, the left side decimated by the impact. There was no more pain.

He jerked back into the kitchen, sunlight streaming through the window, the raven's head still resting on his shoulder. At the movement, Albert raised himself away from Jake, and took a short hop backwards. Their eyes met in a moment of understanding.

Jake now recognised whose death he had witnessed. Sharp

in his mind were the last moments of Bert Grassington's life. Unfortunately, neither the old doctor, or Jake by proxy, had managed to identify the murderers. It had been a planned and strategic attack though, the deliberate removal of an innocent.

The first step of a journey to gain control of Damara.

THE DRAGON

The rain had been relentless since mid-afternoon and the shift had started quietly. Had it not been for the presence of Lottie, Jake might even have been a little bored. The rain had kept all but the most intrepid drinkers indoors, customers comprising all of the usual suspects. Locals who spent most evenings propping up the bar and chatting in The Wishing Well.

Mr Brunton was holding court, as usual, at the far end of the bar leaving most, if not all, of the service to his two young employees. Even they, though, were far from busy, and Jake was half-expecting the landlord to give them a flyer, the chance to get away early. A chance to walk Lottie home under the shelter of the huge golfing umbrella which he had brought with him with just this thought in mind.

The foolish grin of a young man in love again curved his lips and, catching sight of himself in the optics mirror, he straightened his face quickly. He had been the butt of good-natured ribbing by the regulars on more than one occasion over the past couple of weeks.

Lottie wandered up behind him, sliding an arm around his waist and stretching to rest her chin on his shoulder. Since the day of the picnic, they now enjoyed the intimacy and affection of a demonstrative relationship, although finding time and space for much-needed privacy they both longed for was always a difficulty.

'I think we might get away early tonight,' she whispered, her breath warm against his ear. She cast a sideways glance at Mr Brunton to ensure his attention was elsewhere. 'You could come to mine for a coffee if you like. Warm you up before you do the last leg home?' She moved around in front of him, maintaining a professional distance between them now for the benefit of any watching customers, but giving his bottom a playful squeeze under cover of the bar. She looked up at him from beneath dark lashes, her expression serious but huge amber eyes filled with laughter.

'I know how much you love my coffees.' Her suggestive wink drew a bark of laughter from him, causing heads to turn.

She moved away from him then, pert as a pixie, drawing knowing nods and smirks from the far end of the bar. He groaned inwardly knowing that, again, he would be the whipping-boy for more good-natured banter. 'Love's Young Dream' and 'Puppy Love' were the particular favourites at the moment, and even though the teasing was starting to wear a little thin, Jake still could not prevent the happiness brought by this fledgling relationship from showing on his face.

During the young couple's quiet flirtation, Mr Brunton and his usual drinking buddy, Fred Turnbull, had moved over to the fireplace, above which hung the much-lauded collection. The two men were in the process of debating, loudly and cheerfully, the virtues of pistol versus sword. The weapons were gently lifted down from their positions of display on the chimney breast, one by one, to be examined and exclaimed over. Mr Brunton, revelling in his supposed expertise, postured with the ancient weaponry, swishing rapiers and mock-aiming rifles, while Fred asked inane and slightly slurry questions which even a schoolboy would have been able to answer without trouble.

Why the situation between the two friends deteriorated so quickly, Jake had no idea. The problem seemed to come when Fred inadvertently picked up the blunderbuss which Mr Brunton had placed carefully behind him, out of harm's way. It was his favourite – even Jake knew that – and no one was supposed to touch. Ever.

The dragon, however, was suddenly in Fred's grasp. How he managed the manoeuvre, let alone so quickly, was a mystery. Why he would even attempt such a thing, bearing in mind the unwritten rule – Look But Don't Touch – was even more puzzling. Any other weapon in the collection could be handled, but never the blunderbuss.

Mr Brunton's shriek of rage filled the darkest corners of The Wishing Well, the sound producing the same toe-curling effect as fingernails screeching down a board, and causing the hairs on the back of Jake's neck to prickle in premonition. Every head turned towards the sound.

The landlord laid his hand over the stock, the intention obviously to regain custody of his prized possession but, whether in fear or foolishness, Fred's grip merely tightened.

'You will hand it back, or know the depth of my displeasure.' The voice ground from Mr Brunton's mouth as if dragged by force, but the tone and timbre had changed, deepened. The words, too, seemed strangely outdated. He towered over the diminutive figure of Mr Turnbull, forcing the smaller man to topple backwards into a well-placed settee behind him, his face a mask of abject fear.

Apart from Fred's whimpers and the guttural, ragged breathing of Mr Brunton, the pub had fallen silent. The two men seemed frozen in a snapshot of conqueror and victim, a snarl beginning to form on the landlord's face.

Unsure of what he was doing or why, Jake vaulted over the bar and ran the few feet towards the two men, arms outstretched, palms downwards, in the age-old gesture of placation.

'Mr Brunton… please.' Jake wondered briefly what had possessed him to put himself in the firing line – literally. The flared muzzle of the blunderbuss, by accident or design, now pointed directly at him, and he hoped wildly that the ancient gun had long-since been decommissioned.

Mr Brunton turned to face his young barman, expression dazed and vacant, his movements grindingly slow yet jerky, as if controlled by the crippled hands of an inept puppet-master.

His eyes, though. Jake almost recoiled from the madness therein. They were ablaze, shining with rage and – Jake was not certain – glee?

'Ah, and as predicted. Our hero to the rescue.' In a voice which dripped with a snide sarcasm, the caricature of George Brunton smirked nastily. Mr Turnbull continued to sob quietly, his fingers falling away from the weapon limply as a tell-tale patch darkened on the front of his trousers where fear had caused his drink-laden bladder to release.

'And what can a stripling youth, barely off his mother's teat, do to resolve this situation, do you think?' Quietly threatening now, the eyes were pools of insanity.

Jake was shaken to the core. There was no mistaking the implied threat. Or who was the target. He was somewhat reassured to note that a couple of the pub's regulars had joined him, were standing to either side giving him unspoken support. The talking though, he realised, they were leaving to him. He tried again, unsure with whom, or what, he was dealing.

'Mr Brunton, I'm sure Fred didn't mean to offend you. It's such a beautiful gun. I think he just got carried away.'

Mr Brunton's whole demeanour changed in an instant. Shoulders slumped, and his body seemed to deflate, to lose vigour and vitality.

'She'll come for you.' His voice, thankfully now sounding more like his own once more, took on a wheedling quality. 'You'll pay for the impertinence. It was his, you see.' He lifted the dragon, placing the flared barrel against his cheek, and stroking it reverently. Fred flinched at the movement, mouth agape and cheeks slick with tears. He burrowed his wet face into his arms, a snivelling embryonic curl of a man.

'And no one's allowed to touch The Book, save for the chosen. Mad Alice won't stand for it.' This last was delivered so quietly that Jake struggled to hear. Mr Brunton shook his head. There were tears on his face now, and a pleading expression. The regulars backed away, embarrassed at the show of emotion by their hitherto hearty landlord.

The Book! Jake was sure that he'd said 'The Book'. He just couldn't be certain – perhaps that whispered word had been 'gun' – but the possibility caused his stomach to flip.

'Why don't you put it back where it belongs, back up on the wall?' Jake began quietly. 'That way, nobody can touch it by accident, or without you knowing about it.' His tone was gentle, the words steering Mr Brunton towards his next move, and away from this awful situation. Whatever had momentarily taken hold of his body, controlled his words, had left now. The landlord nodded gratefully, his features mirroring that of a small child in need of guidance. He hugged the ancient weapon to his chest lovingly, before turning to the fireplace and lifting it to its usual place in the centre of the chimney breast.

Linda Fowler appeared then, as if by magic, placing a comforting arm around the publican's shoulder. She had been in the pub the whole time, Jake remembered, but had kept well back during the angry and disturbing scene. Her husband, Brian, had been one of the men standing at Jake's side. Now she bustled forward like a mother hen, clucking over Mr Brunton in his confusion. His manner was now that of an over-tired toddler, grumpy and fretful, and the locals averted their eyes in an effort to avoid witnessing the publican's humiliation.

At Linda's 'don't worry, love. I'll see to him now,' Jake stepped back. She half-coaxed, half-led Mr Brunton away into the back of the pub, and up the stairs to his living quarters above.

Lottie was into Jake's arms before he had time to turn, and he held on to her like a drowning man will cling to a raft, the shock of the past few minutes hitting like a sledgehammer. Her hands stroked his hair, his face, his neck, wanting to reassure herself that he was safe and uninjured. He raised his head and blew out his cheeks, a release of tension, before her lips stopped his breath once more with a quick, hard kiss.

The sound of slow hand-claps, applause from the remaining regulars, and words of support, filled the air. Another voice, from behind, one he recognised, said, 'You did exactly the right thing, lad. Well done.'

As Jake turned, he felt a firm pat of approval on his shoulder.

It was Lottie's dad, Steve. At his daughter's look of surprise, he explained. 'The rain, love. It's tipping down out there, and I thought to give the two of you a ride home. Save you both getting a soaking. Didn't think to catch George having another of his 'moments'.' He shook his head. 'This seemed worse than usual though, and I only caught the tail-end of it.' He looked questioningly at the few regulars remaining in The Wishing Well. Most had bolted for home during their landlord's moment of madness. The remainder nodded confirmation, and Steve sighed. 'It doesn't happen often, and mostly he's managed to keep it private, but every now and again something triggers him and he has a 'funny turn'.'

A movement caught Jake's eye. Fred Turnbull slinking through the outer door and into the night, shoulders stooped and head bent to take the lashing of the downpour outside.

Poor guy, he thought. *Horrible situation.* His heart went out to the small man whose friend had turned into a monster before him, had threatened and humiliated him, before being led away like a petulant child. It would obviously take Fred some time to recover his equilibrium.

'Poor Mr Turnbull.' Lottie shook her head and moved back towards the bar. 'Do you think it'd be okay to close up, Dad? It doesn't feel right to keep serving now, after what just happened.' She was putting on a brave front, but the slight tremor in her voice betrayed the shock that she, that all of them, had just experienced.

'I'm sure it would, love.' Steve looked to the remaining locals and most, taking the hint, began to gather coats and head for the door. There was little in the way of conversation, their silence indicating a shared horror of the way the evening had unfolded before them.

Brian Fowler gestured that he wanted a word with Steve, and the two men walked away to chat quietly in private. Jake and Lottie quickly tidied, making the till and bar area secure. As Steve returned to the young couple, Brian disappeared behind the bar to join his wife upstairs.

'The Fowlers are going to stay with him until Luke can be found,' explained Lottie's dad. 'Apparently his phone is going straight to voicemail at the moment, and it's not wise to leave George alone. Probably out on a call.' Steve's voice, try as he might to disguise it, had taken on a hardness as he spoke of the local doctor, and Jake surmised that, apart from the family problems, there wasn't much love lost between the two men either.

'Let's get you two home. We've all had enough fun and games for one evening. Have you got the keys, Lottie?'

She jingled them aloft in confirmation, and the three closed the door of The Wishing Well firmly, and thankfully, behind them for the night.

Maggie fussed and bustled around them, steaming cups of hot chocolate 'with a tot of brandy for the shock' placed before them, along with one of her celebrated fruit loaves in case they 'felt peckish'. Jake wished she would sit down with them – he had questions aplenty to ask – but realised that she needed, firstly, to take care of them. She was probably equally, if not more, disturbed by the events of the evening than those who had witnessed it.

The complete and sudden disintegration of Mr Brunton's mental faculties was somehow linked to The Chronicle, to Damara – that much was obvious – but how it impacted upon the bigger picture, Jake was at a loss to understand.

He also needed to tell Maggie about the way Mr Brunton had changed. His expression, his tone, had been frighteningly threatening. The difference had been so very marked, both facially and in that of his very posture, that he was surprised there had not been more talk of it afterwards. Surely he could not be the only one to have noticed? Even Lottie hadn't mentioned it.

'The Book'. Away from the situation, from the stress, he was becoming more rather than less certain that Mr Brunton had actually mentioned The Chronicle. That the words had been aimed at him, were *for* him. The situation with the blunderbuss was a ruse, he felt, and poor Mr Turnbull the hapless pawn used to gain his attention. The real target, the person who needed to hear, was himself.

Maggie finally settled. Steve had left again to do the rounds of the cattle sheds in the downpour, giving his wife a discreet peck on the temple and a quiet word of support on his way out. The three of them now remained in the warmth and safety of the farmhouse kitchen.

'So,' began Maggie and clasped her hands before her, as if to prevent them from more fussing. 'Tell me everything, Jake.'

He did, omitting nothing. Eventually he described the complete and utter loss of George Brunton beneath the persona of whatever had been speaking during, what Jake thought of as, The Scary Stage.

At this point, Lottie's head snapped up, her brow furrowing.

'I didn't see that. Didn't *hear* it. I heard the words, I mean, but honestly, it just looked like Mr Brunton having a bit of a meltdown about the gun.'

It was Jake's turn to look puzzled.

'But,' he shook his head, 'you must've heard the change in his voice? And he was speaking to me. About The Chronicle. Even his face looked different, somehow…' His voice tailed off in confusion.

Maggie patted his hand before giving it a squeeze.

'I absolutely believe you. There's still more that you need to know, Jake, and most of it will be a bit difficult to swallow.'

She rose again from her chair, unable to stay seated any longer, and began to pace the distance between door and table, head bowed and hands wringing.

Making a decision, she turned to them. 'Okay, kids, this is what I know for certain…'

With elbows on the table, she rested her forehead against clasped hands. Where to start. With a slight shake of the head, she chastised herself. Where to start? At the beginning, of course. Always.

Raising her eyes, she looked directly at the young couple seated across from her. They returned her gaze unflinchingly, prepared, and apparently eager, to hear it all. They were about to learn the crux, the heart, of their situation, and both knew it.

'The Source,' she began, 'isn't unique. There are many such places across our planet. Sites where lines of energy converge, and the Earth's power is at its strongest. Many are known – have been worshipped for centuries – and have been claimed by one religious cause or another.' A half-smile. 'Apparent miracles attributed to whichever god was being worshipped at the time. You've heard of Lourdes? And Bath, of course.' At Jake's nod, she continued. 'The healing waters there were recognised by our ancient tribes well before the Romans decided to make use of their restorative properties, and to build monuments around them.

'The great rivers – the Nile, the Ganges, and many others – have long been believed to have curative abilities, before they were contaminated by the carelessness of man, at least. But the truth of their power lies at source. Where the rivers begin, far up in the mountains.

'Stone and wooden circles – the henges – where ancient civilisations worshipped Mother Earth. The giant Easter Island totems. All are such places. Aires Rock too – revered by the Aboriginal people well before the arrival of westerners – is another. Even in the most arid of lands, earth energy is present.

'There are many more points where ley lines converge, where the Earth's resources are potent. Places which are undiscovered, are too remote, or perhaps have not yet been recognised. Except by those living close by, of course.

'That, in a nutshell, is what The Source here in Welham is. Damara was simply constructed for protection, and to house The Guardian near to The Well. You understand?' Slight nods confirmed comprehension. Jake's eyes were fixed on her, his concentration intense.

'The building here has simply absorbed the energies within and around it.' Maggie took a sip of her hot chocolate. 'These sacred places have appointed Guardians,' she continued. 'Protectors were designated long before time as we know it began, charged with safeguarding and managing the natural assets, the responsibility and privilege passed from generation to generation. We, the Peel women, have the honour to shield The Well from external wickedness – from contamination – because this power can also be used for ill.' She paused, gauging reactions, but they remained focused, offering no interruption.

'The Bruntons, for example. They wish to harness the force for personal, or destructive, reasons. It's always been thus, through the ages. Good versus evil. The battle for power. It happens all around the world, but thankfully the challenge is rarely successful, and usually squashed without others even knowing of it. Destruction and disaster averted once more. It's an ongoing war with those such as Luke Brunton.' She stopped, taking another sip from her mug, before speaking again. 'But gaining control of one source, having the power of The Well and The Chronicle, would give him a huge advantage should he decide to move on to another such place, or to target a different source.

'And now Alice is back. Which means that descendants of her murderer are once again pushing to attempt control of The Source here. Only that intention could have summoned her. She is here to prevent that happening. Her obligation is firstly, and always, to The Source. She will help those of us who follow in any way she can.' The very air crackled with anticipation. Still no interruptions, for none were needed. Both Jake and Lottie hung on her every word.

'George and Luke Brunton – ancestors of James, The Witch Finder – have long had aspirations to manipulate these energies, but they have wrongly assumed that finding The Chronicle is the way forward, an entry to The Source. The Chronicle is merely a tool, a place to begin. The only real power lies in connecting to the energy directly. As the raven did when he healed from wounds which should have proved fatal.

'Now, kids, hold on to your hats, because this is the bit I'm not so sure about. I think – following your experience tonight in The

Wishing Well, Jake – that the blunderbuss hanging on the wall – the one that George sets such store by – may have once belonged to James. That The Witch Finder's spirit is using it as a conduit to gain entry into our world. I have no proof, but the words spoken by George tonight make it a sensible assumption. If that is true, it can only strengthen the Bruntons' assault.

'You must take care, Jake. Protect yourself. Has Lottie shown you how?' At their nods, she continued. 'Does Anna know about shielding herself? Is she strong enough?'

'I'll show her tonight.' 'She's strong enough.' The couple spoke in unison.

'I know she is,' Jake continued more gently. 'Look how much she's come through already.'

She could tell he wanted to believe it, so much, but she shook her head.

'What she's already been through will have depleted her resilience, Jake, not strengthened it. The Source magnifies the uppermost emotion more acutely than any other. It will all depend on what reserves she has left; on how robust her personal resources are, and on whether her strengths can be boosted by the power of The Source. If grief, or anger or self-pity are uppermost, then they will be amplified, rather than her positive traits.'

'She's strong. I know it,' he reiterated, obviously trusting in her without doubt.

Maggie knew he had seen her push through the most dreadful of situations, with still enough left to carry him too.

'She just needs to be told how. She's stronger than any of us here,' he finished defiantly.

Lottie nodded. 'I agree, Mum. She's got a core of steel underneath the gentleness. Look at how she handled that day when Luke came to Damara. How calm she was with Albert afterwards.'

'Luke is targeting Anna for two reasons,' Maggie interrupted, remaining unconvinced, outwardly at least. The pregnancy, the fact that Anna was carrying the child of their enemy, must be taking its toll emotionally, but she couldn't speak of that in front of the youngsters, couldn't betray the confidence of a friend.

'The main one,' she went on, 'is that she's the owner of Damara. He thinks to worm his way into her affections and manipulate events that way. But the other is that he sees her as the weak link. The loss of her soulmate has left her vulnerable. Control of Anna would give him the upper hand. And he may be right.' She frowned again. 'Can you bring your mum here, Jake? Tonight. Both Lottie and I will work with her; teach her techniques to ground and centre herself, and also more help to protect herself from Luke's mind games. You stay too.' She smiled, finally allowing some softness into expression and tone. 'A little more practice won't do you any harm either.'

TO THE WILD WOOD

As days passed and his strength returned, Albert's wing gradually lifted, hugging more tightly to his body as healing continued. By the following weekend, he was attempting gentle half-extensions, hesitantly unfolding the glossy feathers, trying and testing his restoring potency.

Ten days after Luke Brunton's unwelcome visit to Damara, Albert was managing to fully spread the magnificent wings, causing Jake to pull the table aside so as not to hinder the raven's movement.

He'd behaved himself beautifully during his recuperation, the perfect houseguest. He ate everything put before him including, for the first few days, the droplets of green potion which Maggie continued to provide, and which Anna religiously added and mixed into his food. He sat quietly watching the comings and goings of Damara from his spot on the blankets beside the Aga, giving occasional low caw-caws to acknowledge any comments addressed to him directly.

Anna found herself chatting quite naturally to him as she washed the dishes or prepared a meal. Jake spent much of his free time sitting on the dark flagstones of the kitchen, back propped against the wall, hand resting on Albert's broad back, in the hope of gleaning more information about Doctor Grassington's death. It never happened though. It seemed that the connection between bird and boy, in that respect at least, had been severed. Either that or the message had been delivered in its entirety. There was nothing more to say.

Sometimes Lottie joined them, and the young couple would sit at the kitchen table, chatting through ideas and plans for the future as the bird relaxed contentedly on his bedding. For the small amount of time Albert was left alone during daylight hours, he slept, allowing his broken body to heal and his vigour to return.

A week to the day following the accident, Jake came downstairs to find Albert awake, alert and standing by the porch door. The raven's quizzical black eye met his friend's gaze, and Jake knew immediately.

'It's time then?'

The bird took two long strides towards him and Jake knelt, his fingers stroking softly the tufty halo of downy eyebrows.

He had been dreading this moment, had grown used to the quirky presence of the raven in Damara. He knew, though, that it could never have been forever; that Albert would have to return to the wild, to his rightful place in the grand scheme. It could have been such a different outcome for the injured bird without the power of The Source and the help of The Guardian, and he was delighted that the magnificent creature would have another chance at liberty, at life.

'You know where we are if you need us. We'll be here,' he said quietly, swallowing down a click of emotion. 'There's some strange stuff going on out there, and some even weirder people.' The raven bobbed his wise head as if in complete agreement. 'It's been an honour, Albert. A real honour. You take care.' Jake's voice caught, but with a wink of his knowing eye, and a jaunty hop towards freedom, the raven made clear his desire. He waited patiently for Jake to stand and open the door before step-hopping nonchalantly into the morning sunshine. The boy followed him to the threshold, watching spellbound as the raven stretched his great wings to full extent, beating the air as he tested their power one final time before flight.

With a last, and Jake thought, mischievous glance over his shoulder, Albert took one, two, three ungainly hop-flaps before suddenly, gracefully, rising upwards, climbing over the fence and gliding majestically away above the treetops.

He was gone.

Jake experienced a strange feeling. A hollow mixture of elation and desolation. How fantastic that this precious life had been saved, that he could now have freedom, the chance to find a mate, to be a regular bird again. How empty Damara would feel without the unique and charming presence of the raven.

Albert would be missed.

With a sigh, Jake turned back into the kitchen to find his mother watching from the window.

'It won't be the same without him,' she said simply 'but it's for the best.'

Jake merely nodded.

20

WITCH FINDER

She hadn't yet been brave enough to do a pregnancy test, and going to the doctor was, for obvious reasons, unavailable to her. But she knew. Without a doubt, she knew. All the signs were there. Still, she was unable to reach any decisions, make any plans, or to even think of speaking to Jake about it. It was enough – too much – that she had to deal with it herself, without burdening her son also. Although she knew she was being cowardly, his likely reaction had also played a part in keeping the news to herself.

She had talked to Maggie though. Maggie already knew, had guessed, the night of Albert's injuries and was as calm and unruffled as always when Anna arrived on her doorstep, tear-stained and frantic. She had spent an afternoon of weeping and self-recrimination at Welham Farm in which she bared her soul to the other woman. Maggie had listened, allowed her to vent, to release some of the tension, and then hugged her close, murmuring words of sympathy and understanding. What Maggie couldn't do, though, was make the final choice for her.

Do I keep this baby?

The day in the glade, what she had thought to be a dream, and since then her torrid illusory love-making with *him* each time she closed her eyes in slumber, had all been dragged into the light and dissected. Still, she had been unable to decide what to do. The baby was blameless. The sins of the father should never be reason to curse an unborn child. Yet to carry, to raise, a son or daughter of Luke Brunton? Unthinkable. Resolution seemed as distant as the moon.

Since that time, however, as though speaking of it had broken the connection with him, Anna's dreams had been blessedly ordinary and run-of-the-mill. Random, disjointed, and instantly forgettable, rarely staying with her beyond waking. For that, at least, she was grateful.

Now, though, she was back in that place. The amorphous place of knowing that she was sleeping, whilst experiencing all around her with acute clarity and awareness. She looked around her and smiled.

The noises roused him from sleep, but were sufficiently random and intermittent that he couldn't at first identify what had woken him. He lay in a comfortable half-doze for a few more minutes before another sly scraping from below snapped him to attention.

There was somebody in the cottage. Whoever it was seemed to be taking scant care to be silent.

There! Another soft thump. Jake guessed at the movement of a door, probably the cellar directly beneath him. Instantly alert and lithe as a cat, he was out of bed in one easy movement, hand closing around the shaft of a baseball bat – a gift from his father on his fourteenth birthday. He crept forward, his initial goal the head of the narrow staircase, and hopefully without alerting the intruder to his presence. What he would do if they met face to face he hadn't yet thought through, but the hefty weight of the bat in his hand gave him some comfort.

His mother's door, he noticed, was open – a throwback to his childhood – and the curtains too were drawn wide as usual, allowing the glow of an almost full moon to illuminate the room with a gentle light. He could see her still figure beneath the duvet, apparently undisturbed by the furtive movements from downstairs. He left her sleeping. To wake her would risk alerting whoever was below.

The upstairs hallway was a minefield of creaking boards and uneven flooring and he held his breath, heart hammering against his ribs. He had almost managed to negotiate a path without a whisper of sound signalling his approach to whoever was below. At the head of the stairs, however, a floorboard groaned beneath his weight and he froze, the sound seeming over-loud in the silence. He froze with weapon raised on the moon-slick landing, a caricature of a pantomime villain, and strained forwards, listening for any clue that the intruder may have been alerted to his presence.

Nothing. He crept on, the flooring not betraying him again. Halfway down the narrow staircase, he paused and listened again.

Silence.

The ancient oak door at the foot was closed, as he'd expected, but he could see a glow around its ill-fitting edges. Not bright enough to be from the kitchen spotlights – the trespasser hadn't pushed his luck that far – so presumably from the same natural moonlight which had assisted his own progress thus far.

Breath catching in his throat, fingers whitened in a vice-like grip around the raised bat, Jake moved again. Gently, slowly, taking care to test for creaking boards before placing his weight down fully, he edged downwards step by step.

Colours, sounds, smells, all appeared vivid and crisp. She could even taste a faint sweetness of blooming heather as she inhaled.

Around her, the moors stretched in seemingly endless purple beauty. Anna exalted in a feeling of completeness, of wellness and vitality, which flowed through her once more, filling and healing her. A midsummer sun shone from a sky of clearest blue – not a cloud marred the azure canvass – and the heat it shared was soft and warming against her skin. The drone of bees added to the whole as they busied themselves gathering heather pollen.

There was a path before her, leading gently downwards. She walked towards it now, the spring of the heather and moss giving way underfoot to a single, but well-worn, track which disappeared into trees further down the slope.

All was well.

Anna was only a little disappointed to find herself suddenly at the foot of the moors, and now approaching a cottage. Chocolate-box pretty, it was single-story with rough lime-washed walls and a thatched roof.

It was empty though, only recently vacated. She knew this without being told. It had an air of loneliness, of abandonment, for all its rustic charm. Sadness filled her momentarily although she could not say why.

The path now led her past the cottage – her desire to look inside strangely quelled before it ever had life – and onwards towards... what? Something was ahead, she was certain. She wanted, needed, to know.

A man walked before her now, his stride long and confident. He was tall of stature and well-muscled, a wide-brimmed black hat pulled low on his head. She was reminded of someone, but recognition escaped her. Although too far away for detail, she could see that his clothing was dark, the cloak long and heavy. Even if she quickened her pace, she would not be able to catch him but nevertheless she followed, towards the copse which lay before them.

Sounds came to her intermittently, drifting on the soft wind. Voices. A hum of people. More loudly now as she passed through the small wood which both muted sound and masked what lay beyond.

The darkly clad man had vanished as she stepped from the shade of the copse into a wide, grassy space, enclosed on three sides by a horseshoe of trees. A small brook burbled across one length before disappearing below ground once more. The place seemed familiar, although she was sure that she'd never seen it before.

In the distance to her right was a hamlet, the cluster of dwellings rippling in a heat haze. Before her, in the clearing, a crowd ebbed and flowed, their clothing simple, coloured in duns, creams and browns, a style known to her only from history books or films. They whispered behind hands, glancing and pointing. Anna followed their gaze.

A platform of rough planking squatted at the rear of the glade, wide, sturdy and built for purpose. Gallows and noose rose above it, appearing flimsy by contrast.

'Witch. Whore, witch, whore.' The chant started quietly at the front of the throng, gaining strength as more joined the chorus. She recoiled at the fanatical passion within the sound.

In a blink, she was above them now, looking down at the mob from her place on the scaffold. Twisted faces raised to her in religious bigotry and misplaced zeal.

She had been here previously, had lived through this memory before.

Her thoughts were crystalline in their clarity, every nuance remembered, each emotion recognised. Fear and anger.

She took a ragged step back in an effort to distance herself from the mob, her bound wrists making movement jerky, unbalanced. A painful catch on her heel caused a slight stumble, and she looked down at feet bruised and bloodied, testimony to the enforced barefoot journey from Damara. A raised knot of wood, unusually heart-shaped, had snagged her, adding yet another small injury to the many already inflicted. A wry smile twisted her lips. There was nothing of love in this gathering.

And as the voice, *his* voice, issued from the back of the multitude, she raised frightened eyes to the iron-grey of his gaze.

Recognition was instantaneous.

James.

The silent cry filled her soul. Intense love, fleeting memories of passion shared, of what could have been. A knowledge then, hurtful and wounding, of his intent.

Betrayal.

Loathing slid within her, replacing any gentler feelings. Fear again, too, enormous in its purity.

His lips were moving, but all was silence now. Colours faded to sepia and edges blurred. She saw, in slow motion and through the salt-sting of tears, the nod of his head, felt a harsh thump of fists at her shoulders before the ground disappeared and she was falling... falling...

Jake lifted the latch slowly, easing it from its housing with the dexterity of a surgeon. The door pushed outwards, allowing more of the ambient light to spill onto the narrow staircase. The sitting room was empty. He could see that straight away, but the hackles on his neck were telling a different story. Peeping through the crack, he checked, as best he could, that no one was hiding behind the door, but shadows were deep where moonlight couldn't penetrate. The cellar door, too, remained outside of his line of vision in the far corner of the kitchen.

He remained in the doorway, motionless, listening. The silence was complete. The intruder had either made their escape already – and Jake hoped fervently that this was the case – or they were taking great care to remain quiet.

The door to the kitchen stood half open, moonlight doing a much better job on this side of the cottage, furniture and cabinets etched in silver. Half of the room was clearly visible, but behind the door was still a mystery.

Reaching forward, he pushed gently, more of the dining area itself revealed as the door swung open to its full extent.

Nothing.

Relaxing slightly, he moved forward into the kitchen. A soft breeze touched his cheek and he turned towards its source.

Both front doors, inner and the sturdier outer, stood open.

Suspecting a trap, Jake approached hesitantly, fingers clasped tightly around the neck of the bat, nerves stretched taught.

Outside the throaty roar of an engine sounded, breaking the stillness. The driver accelerated hard, wheels spinning for a moment on the loose surface of the track before finally engaging. Jake broke into a run, reaching the doorway in time to see a gleam of moonlight on highly polished bodywork as the car disappeared into the shadow of the trees. A black sports car, he was certain. Although he hadn't managed sight of the driver, he was fairly sure to whom it belonged, and for what he was searching.

Feeling slightly sick now, the stress of past minutes suddenly catching up with him, Jake returned to the kitchen, taking care to lock and bolt both front doors firmly behind him. Sweat stood out on his upper lip and forehead, and his hands were only now starting to shake slightly.

Noting that the cellar door was also firmly closed, he filled a glass from the tap, sipping slowly, before dashing more cooling water over his face and neck. Gradually, the nausea passed.

Taking his courage and his trusty bat with him, he explored the cellar, thankfully without further incident. It was empty of all except storage boxes. After quickly checking around both the downstairs rooms for damage or theft, and finding none, Jake made his way back upstairs, the bat now hanging loosely in his hand.

He would speak to his mother tomorrow. Together they could investigate the break-in further and decide what to do next.

It was as he reached the top of the stairs that the hairs on his forearms and nape began to prickle once more. There was nothing physical to cause this reaction – no sound, nothing to see – and yet his internal warning system was alerting him.

Danger.

His fingers tightened once more around the shaft of the bat.

Anna slowly drifted up through clouds of sleep, the terror of those final moments of the dream staying with her as she surfaced into wakefulness. Shivering, she realised that her nightdress was soaked in sweat, and she could feel the same dampness in her hair, on her face. Eyes still closed, she raised herself to a sitting position, intent on nothing more than finding a clean nightie. She pushed lank hair from her forehead, and opened her eyes.

Her scream sliced the air. Jake started forwards along the landing at a run, fear for his mother overriding caution. At her door, he paused, shocked into immobility at the scene before him.

A dark figure, silhouetted against the window, loomed over the bed as she cowered, pressing back against the mattress in a desperate attempt to evade a shadowed hand which even now reached towards her.

Jake's roar was torn from him as he raced into the room, bat raised high, prepared to do battle to protect his mother.

But the figure was gone. There was nobody there. A stillness filled the room, as if time had suddenly paused. Jake stopped short, confused. He turned full circle, makeshift weapon still at the ready, but the threat had gone.

His mother's relieved sob drew his attention, and he crossed to her in an instant, wrapping his arms around her. They held on hard, drawing strength from each other. No words were spoken, for what could they say? Tomorrow was time enough to try to make sense of it. For now, it was enough that they were both safe.

The incursion into Damara Cottage, and into Anna's bedroom, had been doubled-edged this time. One, physical. Whether only to frighten, or with a greater purpose, they could not tell. The other, from a shadow realm. A hole punched between the worlds of reality and of dreams.

Had something slipped back with her when his mother had returned from her slumber?

THE BENCH

The bench had come with the cottage. Made of gnarled and weathered wood, sturdy and comfortable, its surface was unprotected and now grey with age. Since their arrival, it had quickly become a spot for contemplation and relaxation for both Anna and Jake, situated as it was at the end of the garden, hidden away to the rear of Damara Cottage. Albert, too, had used it as a perch in the early days of his visiting.

Now Jake sat in the late morning sunshine, seemingly relaxed, eyes closed, head bowed, arms resting loosely in his lap, as if in a daydream or perhaps a light doze. This was very far from the truth though. Jake's thoughts whirred and spun, concentration intense, as he tried to make sense of life post-Winchester.

At times now, he felt out of his depth, swimming in deep, dark water, with no sense of what lurked beneath and, more importantly, of his ability to face the dangers moving ever closer to the surface. At others, he was aware of himself expanding, growing to meet those challenges, his strength and power seemingly without boundaries. At those times, he felt like a super-hero. Always, though, the doubts would return.

That Lottie was a major part of this new-found confidence, he didn't doubt. It was she who picked him up whenever those perceived inadequacies threatened to sink his ship. But it wasn't only about her support, or the knowledge and encouragement she shared with regard to aspects of his life which previously he had taken great care to keep hidden.

The reality was that he had never before, in all his young life, felt so comfortable, so free to be himself, as he had since their meeting. It was a connection of minds and bodies, of course, but so much more. With a growing maturity, he acknowledged that he had met his soulmate. He wanted nothing more now than a future which allowed them to travel into the unknown together.

Of course, his parents had always been there for him. They had been proud and encouraging, allowing him opportunities to follow adolescent dreams. Firstly, the primary school football team, his height and dexterity making him a skilled little striker. Then followed photography and all that it entailed. Initially a hobby, but quickly becoming a passion.

Now there was just his mother, and he was the focus of her life. He accepted this, especially since it was only the two of them. Sometimes the pressure of her love seemed a little overwhelming. It was a lot to live up to, being the centre of another's universe. Meeting Lottie had relieved a little of that responsibility somehow, and he had begun to feel himself loosening, bit by bit, as their love blossomed.

Occupying most of his thoughts now though were The Brunton men, including that shadow-figure of his mother's bedroom last night. He could only assume it to be their forebear, James.

And The Chronicle, of course. Central to everything was The Chronicle, and Alice.

He had talked to Lottie, again and again, about options, scenarios, what had happened thus far, and what might lie ahead. Although always encouraging, and eager to help him hone his inherent abilities, she could only guess at what form any conflict may take. Even Maggie, on the few times he had spoken with her, had been somewhat vague.

'This is new territory for us too, Jake,' she had said, the last time they had discussed the Bruntons. 'We've been waiting for something to happen, for The Chronicle to reappear, but what comes next is still to be written.'

So no help there then, thought Jake, his fingers idling on a raised knot of wood on the bench seat. It was a case of wait and see. Having little or no input into what the future might hold, though, didn't sit easily on his young shoulders. He wanted to be able to plan, to prepare, to at least have some knowledge of what he might face when, as Maggie put it, 'the battle proper' began. Apparently everything until now had just been 'testing the water'. This worried Jake more than anything else that Maggie had said. He was playing catch up already, flying by the seat of his pants in every confrontation or new experience.

It was a fact. He was a novice at this magic stuff. Apparently Luke Brunton and his weird relations, past and present, had waited and prepared for many years – centuries in the case of James – to get to this point. They knew exactly what they were doing. Perhaps Jake's presence was merely an annoyance. He, the small fly, to be swatted aside whenever he became too irritating. At this point, not so much the super-hero as a worried, and pretty frightened, teenager.

He was distracted from his thoughts momentarily as a sharp edge on the knot snagged his finger. He looked down.

Strange shape, he thought vaguely. *Heart-shaped. Aren't they usually round?*

The builder of the bench had, by design or chance, placed the knot centrally within the seat, and he found himself strangely drawn to the texture and beauty of nature's artistry. Tracing the outline with a fingertip, he was caught unaware by an unexpected surge of emotion that washed over him, intense in its suddenness. Sadness, and fear, but to what it related he was unable to say.

Movement from the cottage caught his eye. Glad of the distraction, he suppressed the feelings and smiled a welcome. His mother was approaching from the far end of the garden carrying a tray laden with two glasses, a jug of orange squash, and a small plate of biscuits.

'I wondered whether you'd like some company...' she said,

sitting beside him and placing the tray on the grass at their feet, '…whether you'd like to talk? I might not be able to help much, but you know I'm a good listener if you want to offload.'

The offer was genuine, he knew, and he was grateful, but if he couldn't yet make sense of everything in his own head, how could he voice it logically to another? Even to his mum. Jake shook his head.

'I need to go and see Maggie again. I've so many questions bouncing around after last night. I might walk over this afternoon if you fancy it?'

'Actually, that's what I came out to tell you.' Anna smiled. 'She just phoned. Said she's read through The Chronicle, and has some stuff to talk to us about. She sounded quite upbeat.'

'Did she say what?' Jake asked, a nervous excitement beginning in the pit of his stomach.

This was it, he knew it. Now they'd find out what they were dealing with, what would happen next, and what part, exactly, he would have to play. His mother shook her head.

'No. I did ask, but she said it was complicated. She's expecting us after lunch to chat things through.'

'I wonder what she's found.' Jake's thoughts started circling again. He wanted to set off for Welham Farm straight away, but arrangements had already been made. Every delay was a frustration.

Anna leaned forwards, filling each glass with the cool juice before handing one to Jake and taking the other for herself. They sipped their drinks in companionable silence, each lost in their own thoughts, Jake's fingers still toying unconsciously with the knot of wood by his side.

Her cry came from nowhere. Nothing had changed. No one else had appeared. All was still and quiet, a perfect summer's day in the privacy of their own garden. Jake looked to her, startled. Something had shocked his mother sufficiently to make her face pale and her hands tremble. The glass tumbled from numbed fingers unnoticed, as if in slow motion, rolling unbroken on to the lawn before them, contents spilling and disappearing into the grass. Anna's hand went unconsciously to her mouth as her gaze remained frozen on his fingers. His eyes followed the path of hers. The knot in the bench.

'Mum? Tell me.' He was shocked to notice a sheen of tears starting, a solitary droplet spilling onto her cheek.

Shaking her head, she seemed unaware of his words, lost inside some other world where he could not reach her. Slowly, trance-like, she reached out and traced the edge of the heart-shaped knot with trembling fingers, her touch almost caressing.

'Mum!'

The sharpness of his tone dragged her back into the garden with him, and she raised eyes filled with questions to meet his own confused gaze.

'I've seen this before, Jake. Last night.' Fingers continuing the tender stroking, her voice was barely above a whisper. 'In the dream.'

ANCESTORS

Maggie had spent hours poring lovingly over and reading through The Chronicle at her own pace. The information contained within was valuable and complicated. It couldn't be rushed, and she needed time to assimilate all that had been kept secret within its pages for so many centuries.

The appearance of the name 'Brunton' in Edith's entry, and especially him being specifically named as murderer of Alice Peel, had been expected, for Maggie at least.

That George and Luke were descendants of this evil forebear was certain and that events were gaining speed, escalating towards some form of climax was now undoubted, especially in the light of Anna's condition, and the recent behaviour of both men.

The elder had become, quite suddenly, grumpily erratic, beginning with the unsettling incident in The Wishing Well with the blunderbuss from which he was, according to Linda Fowler, 'mending nicely'. Although apparently recovered, he had changed, and not for the better. Gone was any pretence at genial landlord. Instead he kept mainly to his rooms, barking orders when necessary, and allowing Lottie and Jake to run the pub – or not – as they saw fit.

Luke's actions, however, had been covertly unpleasant, swaying between an almost imperceptible insolence when witnessed by outsiders, to stingingly personal insults whenever chance engineered a meeting with either Coopers or Freers alone. The only exception was Steve. It seemed that Luke was not quite brave enough to confront the brawny farmer face to face.

Then there was Anna's frightening encounter to be considered. Although unproven, the intrusion into Damara yesterday night, which Maggie had just this morning been told of, was almost certainly to be laid at his door. Presumably he was still searching for The Chronicle, was not yet aware that it had left Damara and was now in her possession.

He must be getting desperate, to enter the cottage whilst the Freers were inside. There had been plenty of chances over the years – which Maggie knew that Luke had taken – when Damara lay empty, to search for his prize. He was unaware, though, of Hulinjalmur – The Helm of Darkness – which had made all of his seeking to no avail. The ancient magic had served them well. He could never have found either The Chronicle or The Source while they were thus protected. Her lips curved in a smile of satisfaction.

Now, here they were again, sitting around her table in their usual seats, discussing what could only be called Battle Plans.

Maggie took a sip of coffee. 'Shall I go first?' The Chronicle lay beside her, its closed cover guarding secrets within. Beneath lay an equally impressive tome, also seemingly of a great age, and of a similar size and appearance to the original. She lay a protective hand on the carved leather binding of the elder journal, drawing strength from its presence.

'We all read Edith's last entry. It was fairly self-explanatory. *This* Chronicle,' she indicated the lower book, 'was started by Margaret Peel. Alice's niece, Edith's daughter. She became Guardian on the death of her mother at the grand old age of 86. Margaret will have been in her mid-60s by then. Edith didn't keep accounts of her Guardianship. Or they may have been lost with the passage of years. Margaret, however, did.' Maggie paused, feeling her face flush with excitement.

'And it's all written here…' she indicated the later Chronicle. '…all documented from Margaret onwards, and finishing with me. I'll pass it forward to Lottie when the time comes. But this,

I've always known. It's been in the possession and control of the Guardian from Margaret's time forwards.' She took a steadying breath before continuing.

'The missing information, the parts that we need to know about, I found in the elder Chronicle. A sheaf of loose pages, hidden there somehow by Margaret, and dated fifteen years after Alice's death.

'How it was returned after The Chronicle was hidden, I can't even begin to guess at. Certainly, Margaret would have had great difficulty putting it there herself. The Guardians were banished from Damara on the death of Alice. Life would have been hard for them.' The statement was blunt.

'Edith was a widow with a young child to support. They had no menfolk to protect them, and they were also tarnished by the shadow of Alice's death. They were at the mercy of the kindness and charity of neighbours, and lived a nomadic-type of existence around Welham for some years, begging food and shelter where they could. It must have been a desperate time for them.' Lottie reached over to squeeze her mother's hand and Maggie smiled her thanks, eyes shining with love.

She continued. 'At the time of writing this account, though, Edith was still Guardian.' At the Freers' confusion, she explained. 'Margaret would not have been *compelled* to stay away from Damara. Only the true Guardian is constrained in this way. Maybe Margaret managed to slip down to The Well herself, or perhaps asked someone she trusted to deliver her words to their destination. My best guess would be Margaret, though, because someone with knowledge of the ancient craft placed the Helm of Disguise above The Source to protect it. It was strong magic. It's shielded both The Well and The Chronicle for centuries. What matters, though, is what she wrote.' Maggie paused but, far from feeling tired by her narrative, she positively thrummed with vitality and health.

'Basically, Margaret's account tells us what happened to Alice,' she said simply. 'What *really* happened. The awful truth. In much more detail than Edith's hastily-scribbled final entry.' She paused again. 'There's no pleasant way to say this. Alice was pregnant when she died.' Maggie worked hard to keep from glancing at Anna. Apart from a gasp from Lottie, those around the table remained silent, but the colour drained from Jake's cheeks. They waited, too shocked to comment.

'James Brunton was the father of Alice's unborn child, of course. He was her betrothed, as we know, had promised to marry her.' And now the tears sprang unbidden to Maggie's eyes, Alice's pain transferred through the words, and down the years.

'Who can say whether his intention was always, and only, to possess Damara. Or whether he was a weak soul who became corrupted over time by the power at his fingertips. Whatever the reason, Alice was betrayed. Betrayed and murdered, if not by his own hand, then by his design.'

Maggie glanced around the table. Anna, too, understandably had paled visibly. Anger was now apparent on Jake's face. Lottie leaned, elbows on the table, chin on hands and eyes closed in concentration or emotion, Maggie could not tell which. All waited quietly for her to continue.

'We knew already that he was a figure of some standing within the community. He was the local judge, which meant that his word carried weight. In those days too, every region had a Witch Finder – a man who was trusted by the Crown to discover and destroy anyone suspected of practising the Black Arts. James Brunton also carried this title.

'When the rumours of witchcraft started, Margaret wrote, no one was sure from where they originated, who had started them. But the lies took hold, fuelled, no doubt, by the Witch Finder quietly fanning the flames.' Her voice hardened as she recounted Alice's fate, even as tears flowed.

'His opinion would have mattered to the villagers. They would have believed him. They followed his orders, says Margaret, to take Alice from Damara by force. Her wrists were tied, and she was dragged into Welham to be tried as a witch. There was no trial, though.' Maggie dashed her wet cheeks with fingertips.

'At Brunton's word, she was hanged.' The words were brutal, and Lottie stifled a sob, but there was worse to come.

'He knew, too, about the baby.' Maggie's emotion threatened to overtake her, and she gulped down the constriction in her throat. 'Margaret speaks of scenes that she herself witnessed. Of her Aunt Alice and *him*, James Brunton. Of his apparent joy at the pregnancy, and of plans they were making to be wed. Quickly, of course. They were already betrothed, and it didn't do to have a child out of wedlock, so haste would have been essential. They were to live at Damara.

'He would have had all of that power within his grasp. It seems he didn't want to share it though.' She shook her head. 'Wanted it all for himself.

'After Alice's death, he took possession of Damara – as we knew already. It was his prize, as Witch Finder and judge, to claim the property of those he condemned.' Maggie stopped, reaching into her pocket for a tissue, and dabbing ineffectually at her streaming eyes and nose. A deep breath, and she continued. 'The Bruntons couldn't hold on to it for long though. It was gambled away, according to Margaret's later entries, and lost then to both the Guardians and the Bruntons.'

All three women were silently weeping now, Anna and Lottie moved beyond words at the Witch Finder's callous actions and the unspeakable outcome.

Jake, however, was furious. 'He got away with murder, though. Not only of Alice – of her unborn baby too. Doesn't it say,' he gestured to The Chronicle, 'what happened personally to James Brunton?' The name was spat with venom.

Maggie smiled then, but there was no warmth.

'There was the curse, Jake. Alice hexed him, you see, as she was about to die. Him, and all his family to follow. Oh, he had a few good years. Married, to a local girl of reputable station. He had a family, of course – otherwise we wouldn't have the problem of present-day Bruntons to deal with.' And now she did glance to Anna.

'And he managed, probably by virtue of his office, to sidestep any awkward questions about the paternity of Alice's pregnancy after she disclosed it on the day of her hanging. But his life was not long, according to Margaret, or happy. He died in poverty and sickness. A sickness of the mind, apparently. Damara sent him insane, I'd guess. Its energy will have been too much for a weak mind to cope with.'

Anna spoke then, her voice small with the effort of speaking through an emotion-choked throat. 'I dreamed. Last night. I dreamed of Alice's death. I followed *him*, the Witch Finder. Saw him give the order. She still loved him. I could feel it. Even then, she loved him.'

Maggie bowed her head. Poor, poor Alice. The effort of recounting the dreadful history, of learning of Alice's terrible end, was beginning to take its toll. At their encouragement, though, she told the final part of Margaret's account.

'James' son was the gambler, the one who lost control of Damara. By then, the dwelling was all but ruined through lack of care, and the family's good name destroyed. There was not much physical wealth left to lose – only Damara's essence, and all that lies within her.' She shrugged. 'I'm guessing that the Bruntons have been trying to regain that control ever since. The same as the Guardians, but for very different reasons.' Sitting back in the chair, her vitality was undiminished, but her energy had been much depleted by the emotional telling.

'Then it's the Bruntons. All along, it's been the Bruntons,' Jake stated.

'Instinct and intuition are weapons that will serve you well,' Maggie nodded. 'What form the battle will take, we have no clues, I'm afraid. But it *will* come… and soon. All the signs are there. Alice has appeared to you all now in her true form, allowing you to see her beauty of spirit. The Chronicle is returned to me, The Guardian, after all the years of being lost to us. Damara has strengthened us all in different ways for what is ahead.'

Again, Anna shook her head in bewilderment.

'To have you is to possess Damara Cottage,' Maggie explained again. 'What his family have been reaching towards for centuries.

Control of The Well. Luke Brunton is a master of his art. The power of The Source strengthens both good and evil with impartiality, making him a strong adversary, unfortunately. He knows his craft and uses it with impunity.'

A picture of the glade, fresh as if it had happened only yesterday came to Anna then. Now would be a good time to tell her secret to Jake. Something so very special should be shared, she knew. Soon. But not now. Courage failed her. The words stayed within, would not come forth.

'Alice was very clever,' Maggie went on. 'She knew the true power of Damara, and merely left the Brunton family's future to the mercy of The Source.' She reached for her cup again, but the coffee was now cold. She pushed it away in distaste. 'The Source enhances what is already there,' she explained, 'so James' nature, his evil deeds and intentions, came back to haunt him – and eventually broke his mind. Likewise, with his son, William, the gambler. His weaknesses, his need to barter with things precious to him, led to him losing it all. It works the other way, too, though.' She smiled. 'It enhances goodness and positivity. The work of The Guardians has always been about helping and healing. Using the power of The Source to assist others.'

'Did you always know that this would be about the Bruntons?' Jake asked.

Maggie nodded her head.

'Of course. There has always been conflict between our families. It's catalogued in here,' she gestured the later Chronicle, 'over many generations. And even as children, Luke and I couldn't get along. It has never been spoken of openly though. I've always been aware of, and immune to, his gifts. I've have watched him work his wiles many times for his own ends. Warlocks aren't created. It's a life choice. They channel earth magic, as I do. It's how they use the knowledge, and what natural gifts they are bestowed, that decrees whether they follow a path of good, or of evil.'

She paused, taking a deep breath. They needed to know, to be told, what was at stake. 'The great conflicts and natural disasters globally – think historically of events like Atlantis, Vesuvius, the greats wars of the last century – all, and more, have been as a result of evil gaining control of one of the natural sources of power. When that happens, the Guardians must stay close to their own Source. To prevent the falling of another has to be the priority. We can use earth magic and send positive energy, of course, to bolster the strength of the Guardian under attack. Can try to help from afar. I've already alerted those nearest and they will pass on our need.'

Maggie squared her shoulders, preparing to impart her final bombshell of the day.

'There's just one more thing that I must tell you, that you must be aware of…' She hesitated. '…and I don't know whether you'll already have worked this out for yourselves.' She glanced at Lottie, who nodded for her to continue. 'The battle for control will take place near to The Source. Because of this, because I'm forbidden entry to Damara, I can't physically be there to help with whatever lies ahead. My part in this must be as a bystander only.'

A brittle silence greeted her words, the implication crystal clear to Jake. She tried to soften the blow. 'I may be able to influence how events unfold with earth magic and The Chronicle, but that will be all. Only influence, and from a distance.'

Lottie gripped Jake's hand, understanding his shock completely. For Anna, though, it was a moment of intense clarity.

'So…' Anna asked quietly. 'So, are you and Lottie descended from Alice, and Margaret, then? Are all the Guardians of the same family?'

'My middle name is Peel,' shrugged Maggie, 'as is Lottie's. Yes, is the simple answer. All of the Guardians here in Welham have been Peel women.'

23

BUSY BODY

'Yoohoo. Anna!' The sound carried over the supermarket car park, but she couldn't at first place the voice. 'Anna. Over here.'

She turned, catching sight of a half-familiar face approaching. Heavily laden with shopping bags, Linda Fowler, neighbourhood busybody from Welham whom she'd met a couple of times in The Wishing Well, was bearing down like a galleon in full sail.

Anna sighed.

Her own provisions already stowed in the boot, she hurried to lend a hand. The older woman smiled her thanks and gestured with her head in the direction of her own vehicle, a 4x4 parked in the corner spot.

'One of the great joys in life, the food shop.' She sighed theatrically and rolled her eyes. 'I only went in for a loaf and a pint, and now look.' She hefted the bags to demonstrate. 'I'm so easily tempted by a two for the price of one bargain.'

After they had deposited the purchases, Linda suggested, 'Fancy a coffee? Have you time?'

Anna glanced at her watch. She'd been intending a visit to the library – she had an idea which, on speaking to Maggie, needed some research – but a chat and a sit down sounded pleasant. Perhaps Linda had some anecdotes about Welham to share, and it would sensible to get to know other folk in the village apart from the Coopers.

'I know a nice little café just around the corner,' she coaxed. 'Great cappuccinos. My treat.'

'Sounds lovely.' Anna smiled, and parked her misgivings for later inspection.

The Copper Kettle turned out to be a cosy tea-room a mere two-minute stroll away, just off the bustle of the High Street and hidden away down one of the town's many atmospheric little alleyways. They settled themselves comfortably at a corner table.

'They do fabulous scones here too. My guilty pleasure, but so delicious. I always have the cheese, but the cherry ones are lovely if you have a sweet tooth.'

With coffees and warm scones ordered, Linda got down to the serious business of gossiping. Anna had never been one for tittle-tattle, especially of the malicious type, but since the move from Winchester she had missed the company of friends. This could be a more productive way to discover more about Alice Peel, too, after many fruitless hours spent in the library thus far. Her personal research – a task she had willingly adopted at Maggie's suggestion – kept hitting brick walls. For such a well-known local legend, there seemed surprisingly little written about 'Mad Alice', despite George Brunton's earlier assurances.

Rightly suspecting that it was a ploy to avoid a recurrence of Luke Brunton finding her alone in Damara once more – that actually Maggie probably already knew more than any library book about Alice – Anna had nevertheless enjoyed keeping her mind busy and her thoughts away from the decision she had to make. Her predicament was never far from her thoughts, but the distraction was proving welcome.

As expected, it seemed that Linda delighted in sharing what she knew, whether or not it was appropriate or seemly to do so. No sooner had their drinks arrived than she started, in the obligatory hushed tones of an acknowledged know-it-all, to speak of the incident in The Wishing Well, when 'poor George had another of his funny turns'.

'Your boy – Jake, is it? – was a marvel. Calmed the whole thing down. For a youngster, he did really well.'

'Well, thanks,' replied Anna. 'I am proud of him, of course, but it was a bit of a shock, to be honest. He's only working in the pub to earn a bit of pocket money. Now, between him and Lottie Cooper, they're practically running the place. I wouldn't have expected him to have to deal with situations like this. Does it happen often? With Mr Brunton, I mean?'

'No. Not often. But he's never been quite right since he lost Helen.' She shook her head conspiratorially. At Anna's questioning look, Linda lowered her voice still further. 'My husband's elder sister, Helen, was George's wife. She died, oh, around twenty-five years ago now. Tragic, it was.'

'I'm so sorry. Helen was Luke's mother, then?' Anna kept her voice muted out of respect for the topic they discussed, but refused to adopt the dramatic cloak-and-dagger approach of her companion. Theatricals did not sit well with her, especially where real people were involved. 'He must've still been a boy. How awful – for all of you.'

'He was around ten, I think,' Linda's brow wrinkled in recollection, 'and it was Luke who found her. Must've been horrible, especially being so young, but he seemed to cope better with her death than poor George.'

'The resilience of youth, perhaps?' Anna suggested. 'Losing his wife must've been a terrible shock for Mr Brunton. Was it expected?'

An image of the evening of Peter's death, the knock on the door, the strange disjointed feeling which had hit almost as soon as the words left the policeman's mouth, flashed into her head. She knew only too well about dealing with sudden loss, and felt a reluctant pang of sympathy for the widower still struggling to come to terms after so many years. She hoped that, in time, she would find a way to move forward and cope with her own grief, and in a more productive way than the publican apparently had managed.

'Accident,' Linda replied, matter of factly, tugging Anna back to the conversation. 'At least, that's what the Coroner decided. Couldn't have been otherwise, although poor Helen. I wouldn't have wished that for her.' She was warming to her theme now, and Anna wondered about the type of woman who could speak so calmly about 'poor George' and 'poor Helen'. How she could take such enjoyment from relaying the tragedy of others, and to someone who was little more than a stranger. Her opinion of the woman, not terribly high to begin with, was falling rapidly.

'Truth be told, she was ten years older than Brian,' Linda went on, 'and I never really liked her that much. She was a bit, I don't know, cold? Not an easy woman to talk to. Still, she was Brian's sister, and dying like that was awful.'

Linda had Anna's attention now. Much as she hated to lower herself to the level of gossipmonger, she really did want to know more. Anything concerning Luke Brunton or his family were top of the agenda. But how to voice the question? Linda seemed keen to share every detail apart from the most important one. How did Helen die? She decided to grasp the bull by the horns.

'So…'

'You want to know how it happened, don't you?'

'I don't want to pry, if it's personal… or painful.' She struggled to find the best approach, still unsure of the other woman's reason for sharing such intimate family history, other than the obvious answer of being centre-stage.

'Oh, it's common knowledge around here. Caused quite a stir at the time.' Linda took a sip from her mug, and glanced up. 'There was a lot of talk. Questions asked. Speculation about the way she died. The same thing happened when Doc Grassington passed away. On the surface, a terrible accident. Nothing ever proven otherwise. But people talked behind closed doors, if you know what I mean?' She paused again, as if preparing for a big finish.

Anna raised her eyebrows.

'She drowned,' Linda said, bluntly. 'In the bath. Lost a lot of blood too, although that wasn't the cause of death.'

At Anna's shocked silence, she continued. 'The inquest found that she'd probably slipped getting in the bath, smacked her head on something – probably the taps, the Coroner said, because there was blood on the taps – and knocked herself out.'

'I'm so sorry, Linda. That's awful.' Anna tried for, and hopefully achieved, a note of sympathy, although it was difficult to know what to say to a woman who was so obviously relishing the wretched tale.

'The blood loss stopped her from fully regaining consciousness, the Coroner said, and she slipped under the water and...'

'Poor Helen,' Anna finished for her. 'Hopefully, she didn't know anything about it.'

'Well, that was the thing,' Linda continued leaning forwards, her voice dropping again to a whisper. 'The verdict reckoned that she'd been half-conscious, but too weak to pull herself up from losing all that blood. The bathwater was crimson, they said. She'd have known she was dying, alright, but was unable to save herself.' Linda heaved a sigh and shook her head in apparent distress, but Anna still caught the sly sideways glance to gauge the reaction of her captive audience.

Both women were silent for a moment, a picture forming in Anna's mind of a bath full of blood, and of Helen Brunton trying, and failing, to save herself.

'That was when young Luke found her.'

Anna's head snapped up. Linda had obviously not yet finished with her grisly story.

'She was still alive at that point, apparently, and he shouted and shouted, but no one heard him. He didn't have the strength, bless him, to pull her out alone. She was black and blue with his efforts. By the time George heard his cries, Helen was gone.' She sighed deeply. 'George found the boy with his arms still around his mother - trying to lift her up, obviously – but it was too late.'

Linda subsided in the afterglow of a tale well told, her expression virtuously smug, while Anna struggled to make sense of what she had just heard. Had this tragedy moulded Luke into the man he was today? Could finding his mother like that, being unable to save her, hardened and warped him? Or – and here she tried to stop, but was unable to prevent the thought – had Luke played a part in the death of his own mother?

The Fowler woman hadn't quite finished yet though. She

leaned uncomfortably close to Anna once more, the need for personal space and good manners obviously not registering on her internal radar, voice positioned in that place between stage whisper and overly-concerned relative.

'He's had such a hard time, poor lamb. First his mother, bless her heart, and then his wife. Not had much luck with his womenfolk, has our Luke.'

'His wife?' Anna could scarcely breathe. 'I didn't even know that he'd been married.'

'Oh, yes. Lovely woman. At least, that was the picture painted for the world to see.' Linda pouted, as if personally insulted by the perceived sins of the long-dead lady. 'Elaine, she was called. They met at university, both studying medicine, although she went into counselling in the end. All that studying, and then to end up working with those poor unfortunates in Saint Matthew's.' Linda shook her head. 'What a waste.'

Anna knew of Saint Matthew's. The largest psychiatric hospital in the area, it had a reputation for innovation and progressive research, pushing boundaries in mental health and welfare.

'Psychologist. That was it. She was a psychologist,' Linda went on. 'Anyway, they had what everyone called a 'whirlwind romance'. Were married within a year of meeting, and moved back up north, near to York. She went to work in St Matthew's, and him to that big hospital. The Minster Hospital, is it? I can't remember the name of it for certain, but you know the one I mean.' Anna nodded. 'Well, everything seemed fine for a couple of years, as I remember. The perfect professional couple. I can't quite pinpoint exactly when we started to hear that she wasn't too well. Somewhere around the Christmas of their second anniversary, I think.'

Remembering fairly specifically, Anna thought, for one who wasn't quite sure of timings.

Linda grasped Anna's forearm suddenly, ensuring her full attention, before miming the age-old, and horribly offensive, gesture of circling a finger around her temple.

'Not right in the head,' she hissed, as though no more

explanation were needed. 'Poor Luke. He did all he could, of course, but she was hell-bent. On a mission to self-destruct, I've heard it called, and by folk who know more than me about such things. We learned afterwards that Luke had found her several times, when she'd tried to... you know.' Linda nodded sagely.

'Tried to what?' asked Anna, a thirst for knowledge about Luke Brunton outweighing a hearty disgust at the woman before her.

'Top herself.' That sibilant hiss again. 'Do away with herself.' Every word was over-exaggerated, obviously to ensure that Anna was not in any doubt as to their meaning.

Even though she'd been expecting exactly this, the words were still a shock.

'She'd tried all sorts, according to Luke. Ever since they were first married, apparently.' Again, Linda was in full throttle, relishing disclosure of every sickening detail. 'It all came out afterwards. Pills, poison, alcohol. Or all three at once, I heard. Twice, he found her in the car, doors shut, engine running. He saved her each time, but the last was just one too many. Obviously, she simply didn't want to be saved.'

Anna didn't want to ask, to feed into Linda's evident delight of such disturbing gossip, but she had to know.

'So, what happened? How did she die?'

'Jumped.' A flat word, filled with gratified smugness. 'Off the cliffs at Saltburn. Luke was there, with her, but even he couldn't talk her out of it that last time. It fair near broke him too. Had to leave that smart position in York, and come home. The only luck he had, poor boy, was that Doc Grassington died soon after that. He died in your house. Did you know that? Anyway...' The woman was unstoppable, a tattling force of nature. '...the position of GP became vacant, and Luke slotted into it as though it were made for him.' She wasn't even pausing for breath now, the sorry details falling like snowflakes in a blizzard.

Anna listened on, aghast and horrified.

'Elaine died instantly, of course. Those rocks on the beach made sure of that. I can't help thinking that it was a blessed release for our Luke. All that time of doing his best, caring for her, poor deranged creature.'

She finally ran out of steam, sitting back and sipping her coffee as though they'd been discussing the weather. Anna had a question though.

'She must've had help though. Elaine? Apart from just Luke, I mean – what with working at the Psychiatric Hospital? Surely there were treatments, medications, that could've at least calmed her, helped to alleviate her symptoms when she felt that way?'

'Oh, no.' Linda was loyal in her own way. 'Luke – him being a doctor and everything – he looked after her himself.'

'Then there was no record. Nothing to show on her medical files that she'd been depressed or suicidal?'

'Well, there wouldn't be, would there?' Linda spoke slowly, as though explaining the glaringly obvious to a small child. 'Luke knew how to help her, knew what tablets and such like to give her. Why would he ask another doctor, when he knew it all himself?'

'Quite,' Anna replied drily. 'Why, indeed.'

With some relief, she left The Copper Kettle and the indiscretions of Mrs Fowler behind, and decided at once to stick with her original plan of visiting the library. She'd only lost an hour or so in the unpleasant company of Loose-Lipped-Linda, as she now thought of her. Tales of Brunton skeletons now provided an even greater reason for wanting to search and peruse past records.

She had already read what little information there was to be found about Mad Alice, Welham Village and Damara Cottage – the lack of it had been disappointing – and the Brunton family history, provided today from the flapping gums of Linda, had reset her compass to 'true north'.

After the day in the glade, that lost afternoon, memories of which she had so far failed to recapture in anything more than a dream-like haze – probably a self-defence mechanism, she told herself – Anna had promised herself that she would do this. That she would try to find out more about the enigmatic, charming, and undoubtedly wicked, Doctor Brunton. Anna could now add 'rapist' to that list of adjectives. And 'father of my child'. She shuddered.

The realisation of her pregnancy had made the task so very important to her now, but so much had happened since that day that she had been unable to do anything but maintain an even keel. She'd needed time to think, too. Time to allow the knowledge to settle.

For herself and her unborn child, she felt a renewed determination to learn more. She had a huge and life changing decision to make, time was of the essence, and she wanted to have all the facts at her fingertips before she shared her news with Jake.

A gentle hand went again to her still-flat tummy. The conversation was not one which she was looking forward to, whatever choice she eventually made.

With a fair amount of misgivings on what she may, or may not, uncover, Anna turned towards the far end of the High Street and headed for the library.

Late afternoon found her seated to the rear of the study area – the 'Reference Room' according to a small brass plaque above the door – with an array of pen, notebook and printed A4 sheets spread on the table before her.

The staff member she had approached had been most helpful in assisting with her queries, and it had not taken long to find the newspaper articles relating to the death of Elaine Brunton. Likewise, she also had recovered details of the Coroner's Report relating to Helen Brunton's unfortunate demise, although this had taken a while longer to access because of the passage of time.

Anna again perused the first sheet. It had obviously been a good story for the local paper at the time, appearing on the front page, and they had covered the doctor's death in detail.

"The body of a young woman was recovered by Coastguards yesterday from the rocks at Saltburn following a call to the emergency services. She was

named later as Dr Elaine Bell (27), a psychologist employed by St Matthew's Psychiatric Hospital near York.

An eye-witness statement provided by her husband, Dr Luke Brunton, confirmed that she took her own life. Dr Brunton was questioned by officers at the scene, and also afterwards at Middlesbrough Police Station, but was later released without charge.

An inquest into Dr Bell's death will be held, but at this time police have confirmed that they are satisfied that there was no foul play and that there will be no further investigation into this matter.

Dr Bell, who kept her maiden name for professional reasons, had apparently suffered recent mental health issues, although there appear to be no medical records to corroborate this claim made by close family.

Colleagues at St Matthew's described Dr Bell as a 'a talented doctor, and a lovely young woman' and added that 'her death and apparent suicide is a tragedy and a shock.'

Doctor Bell leaves behind a husband and extended family."

Anna also had before her a paragraph from the same newspaper revealing the verdict of the inquest. Page six. Short and to the point. Suicide.

She shook her head, unconvinced.

The piece on Helen was in much the same vein as that covering Elaine's passing, although the verdict in this case was, of course, accidental death due to drowning. Much was made of the efforts of *'son, Luke (10)'* to save his mother. Obviously an eager journalist using the tragedy to tweak at readers' heartstrings. Not much more information, actually, than Linda had provided earlier. Thought-provoking and unsettling, but proving nothing. Anna began to gather her things together just as a head popped around the door.

'I found something else, if you're interested?' The librarian, fresh faced and – in Anna's opinion – looking young enough to still be at school, fluttered another type-filled sheet. 'Identical name, and at about the same time. It must be the same person. I printed it off for you.'

Anna smiled her thanks as the young woman laid the paper on

the table. With a cheery, 'Let me know if there's anything else you need', she left Anna alone again.

There were two pieces, printed on each side of the sheet.

The first heading read: *"Local Medics Investigated."*

Two grainy photographs were inserted into the text. One, a woman, head down and mac billowing as she scurried along the pavement, obviously trying to avoid having her face captured for posterity.

The other, a youthful Luke Brunton. A head shot, looking for all the world as if he had posed for just such an occasion, eyes twinkling and perfect teeth gleaming through the black and white image.

She found herself staring at the likeness, that younger Luke. Those hypnotic eyes still projected a dilution of his charisma even through the distance of a camera lens. Tearing her gaze away with difficulty, she scanned the article through quickly, before re-reading slowly and thoroughly.

The unexplained deaths of several patients at The Minster Hospital in York had been investigated by an external panel following complaints by numerous relatives. All victims had had heart bypass operations, which had apparently gone well. Problems seemed to have occurred during the after-care stage, in the days following surgery. The junior doctor implicated was, of course, Luke Brunton. He was on duty at the time of each of the apparently-suspicious deaths.

The other photograph was of a staff nurse, named as Susan Rust. She had also been a common denominator, present at all the relevant times.

The article implied a relationship between the two staff members, although took care not to state this specifically.

The piece finished with names and ages of all patients involved, and a suggestion that the investigation was awaiting post mortem findings before proceeding further.

Anna reached out and flipped the A4 sheet over. The next article was a follow up, headed:

"Nurse of Death" and with a sub-title *"Murdered in Their Beds"*.

Again, she scanned through quickly, and then again carefully, taking in every word.

After a thorough investigation, Luke had, somehow, deflected all blame for the patient deaths away from himself, and on to Susan Rust. He had been completely exonerated of any wrong-doing (although the newspaper did suggest that he would be moving to a new position in the near future, to *'escape any stigma attached to his professional involvement with Staff Nurse Rust'*).

The post mortem findings verified that, in all cases, a saline solution had been substituted into the patients' drips. Records proved beyond doubt that Susan Rust was responsible. Her signature was found in the notes authorising treatment. Initials of consent also found on the document, and originally thought to be that of Dr Brunton, were demonstrated to have been forged. Her plea that she *'couldn't remember'* was considered an absurd ruse to escape justice, although it was noted grudgingly and in very few words that Ms Rust was presently undergoing psychiatric treatment following a complete mental breakdown.

Anna sat back in her chair, thoughts tumbling and twisting as she tried to assimilate all that she now had before her.

He got away with it.

And yet nothing was proven. The evidence told a different story, one of misfortune and innocence. Of being in the wrong place at the wrong time. Nothing more. Not a single death could definitively be laid at the door of Luke Brunton.

Feeling slightly nauseous, she gathered the detritus of the afternoon, folding the paperwork in half to slide it into her handbag, her head still swimming in waters of the past. Whatever the conclusions of yesterday's police, coroners and journalists, she herself was in absolutely no doubt.

First Helen.

Then the blameless heart patients in York.

Finally, shortly afterwards, Elaine.

Had the young wife suspected? Was that the reason that she had to die? Had she challenged him? Or had he merely grown tired of her, wanted to move on without the distraction of a moral and principled wife by his side? Many questions still remained. Of the one, though, she was certain.

Luke Brunton had murdered. Not once, but many times.

24

SHADOWS

The morning had started well. Clear and fresh. One of those bright summer gifts that promised of good things to come.

He had woken with a feeling of optimism and energy, deciding almost immediately that his proposed chore, that of hacking back the chest-high weeds at the far end of the garden, could wait, and that he was heading for the moors – hopefully with Lottie by his side. His camera, and the magnificent vistas of Welham Moor, were calling him. They deserved some downtime after all the stress of recent days. With more strife undoubtedly ahead, it would be sensible to spend time together, relaxing, gathering strength, and coming to terms with what was to come.

In that other life, the normal life, the home he'd left behind in Winchester, his father had converted one of the spare bedrooms into a makeshift dark room. A blackout blind at the window, infra-red lighting, and a seal around the door ensured there was no light leakage from the main house. Jake had learned his craft with enthusiasm, both in that small room and at the Camera Club after school. Many happy hours had been spent developing his own work. In those far off days, he had photographed almost anything, from old people chatting in the park to sunsets over the church tower. His passion, though, as talent emerged, lay in the grandeur and majesty of landscapes.

Today had not been a day for carrying the bulkier DSLR, however, or the tripod and lenses which accompanied it. Instead he'd opted for his tiny, but very high-spec, compact camera, a present from his parents last Christmas. Less than a month before that fateful evening when his father's life had ended, and his own had changed for ever.

For a moment then, grief had threatened to overwhelm him, and he had permitted himself the luxury of silent remembrance. A tear quietly slipped down his cheek – something he had never allowed the rest of the world to witness, not even his mother – and he'd wiped it away gently, aware always of the hole left in his life by the death of his father.

He had shaken away the memories though, with effort. It was too fine a day to dwell on sadness, and he needed to look to the future. Although still early, he had reached for his mobile phone. At the other end, it was picked up on the second ring.

'Lottie? Are you busy?'

Their previous day out on the moors had ended with a headlong, frantic dash back to Damara Cottage. He had been hoping, after all the strangeness since their arrival in Welham, for a quieter, less eventful period to spend with Lottie today. They needed some time to themselves, to think only of each other, without any outside interference. If he managed to catch some of the spectacular scenery on this beautifully clear day to add to his catalogue, then it would be an added bonus.

Where his future would take him was still unclear – events in Welham and with the Bruntons were seeing to that – but he knew with certainty that, if he were lucky enough to have any choices at all then he wanted Lottie by his side, and with photography as his occupation of choice. He needed to be ready if, and when, opportunities arose.

A spring in his step, he'd taken the tiny footpath which joined Damara Cottage to Welham Farm from the back of both properties, saving himself the short walk to the fork in the track. Already he was admiring the flora and fauna around him with the eye of a seasoned photographer.

Lottie had been ready, waiting for him with a packed lunch

stored in her rucksack. They'd set off from the rear of the farmyard towards the first inclines of the moors, happy and relaxed in each other's company, looking forward to a rare day spent together.

Their time had panned out as Jake had envisioned. In talk – of things deep and personal, of both The Chronicle, of what the future may hold, and of themselves. The connection each now felt to the other had clearly intensified, become stronger, even in the short time they had known one another.

They had made love twice, the soft heather and moss cushioning them – as comfortable as any feather bed – the overhanging grandeur of Welham Rocks and the undulating moorland shielding them from casual view. Initially, and almost as soon as they were out of sight of the farmhouse, it had been with a heat and urgency of their short separation. The next time, picnic lunch eaten, feeling replete and satisfied in the heat of the afternoon sun, was slower, and with a confidence and intimacy which their young years belied.

Thoughts of her – glossy auburn hair fanning out around her, face becomingly flushed, passion-darkened eyes locked with his own, and all framed by the heath beneath them – made him smile now.

What a picture that would make! But this vision was for him alone, captured forever in his memory.

He had also snapped, on his little compact, when the light was good and the view exceptional, what he hoped were some outstanding landscape shots. The Rocks, of course. The play of light upon the huge limestone boulders should make for some unique vistas, and the simple splendour of the moors stretching to the horizon were equally impressive. He'd been keen then to get back to his laptop to download them.

They had returned down the slopes as the late afternoon sun warmed their shoulders from the west, a pink glow of happiness touching their cheeks.

A whisper between lovers, a chaste peck on Lottie's cheek as they'd caught sight of Maggie smiling approval from the vegetable garden, and he was once more heading down the track towards Damara, excitement at seeing those magnificent views on the larger screen of his computer causing his pace to quicken.

Wolfing down the meal prepared by his mother, early evening now found Jake seated at the desk in the corner of his bedroom, laptop open and prepared, and camera attached and ready to download.

He had already created a file entitled 'Welham Moor', and he watched now as the photographs downloaded to their new home.

Deciding to open them in sequence, scroll through, and assess his efforts in total before working on each shot specifically, he opted for 'slideshow', elbows resting on desk, chin on hands, to appraise the day's work.

The first picture was a disappointment. A dark smudge to the top right-hand corner which he hadn't noticed at the time marred the image. Perhaps a stray cloud had picked the wrong moment to pass the sun.

The second, too – Welham Rocks this time, from below at ground level – showed an identical glitch. A dark mass atop the boulders. Jake groaned. His camera must have picked up a fault. Maybe a small crack on the lens.

Confusion and disappointment clouding his brow, Jake used the mouse to scroll forward manually, frown deepening as the weird shadow appeared in each sequential shot, resolution hardening with the progression. Not until the shape began to resemble that of a person did he realise that something unnatural was occurring. He no longer thought that his camera may have been compromised. This was far more sinister.

That it was, at a distance, the developing figure of a man could not be disputed. That he appeared to be watching them from afar could only be conjecture, but a prickle of unease crawled up Jake's spine as he continued the slideshow. With each subsequent landscape, the figure clarified, became more solid, the edges of the shape gaining definition.

As the day's filming progressed, so the watcher also moved

closer, little by little. The figure, deep black now, gave scant detail other than in silhouette. Jake guessed by the shape that he wore a cloak and hat, but could glean nothing further at this stage.

The last shots of the day showed the observer nearer still, the density of shadow intensifying even further at his approach, but giving no clue as to face or feature.

The final landscape appeared, at first glance, to be the only one unspoilt by the mysterious onlooker. But no. On closer inspection there was a small square of darkness on the right lower corner. Jake sat back in his seat. It looked like the flick of a hem. Of coat – or cloak, perhaps – captured for eternity as someone moved past the photographer and out of shot.

He worked all evening, shaken and unnerved at the thought of being spied upon throughout their time on the moors, trying to enlarge and enhance the mysterious figure. Mostly this was to no avail. The larger he made the shape, the darker it became, until all that filled the screen was a dense blackness, inky and unfathomable.

It was the first frame, his initial picture of the day, which finally gave up some small detail. Blurred, murky and indistinct, there was, within the misty outline, the suggestion of a visage. Jake tinkered and tweaked until, finally, there was nothing more he could do to improve the image further.

What he found provided cold comfort. He almost wished that he had left well alone. The expression revealed was one which would haunt Jake's dreams that night.

It was a face half-remembered from nightmares. An anguished and haunted expression. A wounded and tormented soul.

A FLIPPED SWITCH

The lowering clouds hung bruised and heavy, their swelling underbellies promising an imminent deluge. Silence had descended. Trees and foliage imitated art in their stillness. Birdsong had ceased with a suddenness borne of innate awareness. Sensing the closing storm, wild creatures, winged and earthbound, had sought shelter with time to spare. The air was now hushed and expectant.

Through this breathless landscape Jake pounded, the thud of his feet echoing loudly on the parched track as he hastened towards the village.

He had bridges to build – yet again – and the thought made him cringe inwardly as he recalled for the umpteenth time the angry words that had passed between him and Lottie earlier. He shook his head. *His* rage actually, he amended honestly, and his alone, for Lottie had contributed little. She'd struggled to make a dent in the tirade, once the floodgate of his temper had burst open.

It seemed to be a recurring theme recently, chasing after the women in his life to make amends. Yet before arriving in Welham, he had been the most placid, the calmest, of men. His father had often teased him as he grew. Even the early teenage years, hormones rising, couldn't puncture his reserves of tolerance, his patience.

'The longest fuse in the world' his dad would say, and his

parents had laughed. What would he think of the new Jake? This grumpy, edgy and – he had to face it – belligerent version of himself which seemed to have become the norm since moving into Damara Cottage.

He didn't feel angry now though. Or frightened. Far from it. Excitement churned in his belly, and he could hardly wait to share with Lottie that all their efforts had paid off. If she was still speaking to him, of course.

It had worked. Finally.

After poring over the laptop and those frighteningly vague images, they had spent the morning in the garden, a usual activity of late, seated on the bench in the sunshine as Jake tried to hone and expand the inherent ability which they all knew he possessed. That he was psychic was beyond doubt – past events and experiences had confirmed it – but, try as he would, he seemed incapable of pushing through to the next level of competence.

All of Lottie's encouragement, her helpful suggestions and ideas, had today served only to annoy him, probably due in part to the recent stress of the laptop and those pictures. That was no excuse, of course.

He had reached the end of his patience. End of story. He felt a failure. Everyone was counting on him to produce the goods. Each time that he crashed and burned was another step nearer to the day of reckoning, and he was frightened. Frightened that he wouldn't be ready. Wouldn't be able to even face their enemies, let alone confront and conquer them.

When Lottie said again, for probably the fifth time that day, 'Just relax your mind, Jake. Look inside yourself,' he had reached the limit of his tolerance. His now-very-short fuse had ignited, and he had vented considerable frustration on the person he loved most in the world.

Lottie.

His parting shot, after many other stinging epithets, yelled straight into her face as he towered over her, 'Do you think I'm not trying? How can you be so dense?' had seen her quietly collect her cardigan and turn away, a dignified silence failing to disguise the sheen of unshed tears as she left him alone.

Her departure had shocked him. He'd had many lesser meltdowns during their short time together, and always she'd waited for the storm to pass, for him to calm down again. For 'Nice Jake' to win the battle over 'Nasty Jake'.

He'd half-expected for her to return to him in the garden, but as the minutes passed and he remained alone on the bench, he recognised that perhaps this time he'd gone too far. Lottie should never have to put up with, or be subjected to, such behaviour.

The realisation came as a surprise. It was a moment of complete personal honesty. He sat for quite some time, lost in thoughts of her, and of the awfulness of his conduct, aware that something had to change. The 'something' was himself, and specifically, his temper.

Within the self-awareness, something else rose to the surface. Something positive. He recognised it immediately, although how this was so he could not have explained.

It was an emerging, an expanding, within him. As if a switch had been flipped into the 'on' position allowing passages to open and channels to flow.

With renewed enthusiasm and a fresh confidence, he had turned once more to the items lined up on the grass in front of him. Random objects designed to test his skills, to hopefully assist his progress. A knife, an encyclopaedia, a broom handle, and a small coffee table, ranging from small to large, left to right, before him.

He'd tried again.

A glance at the heavens predicted that this would be a monster of a downpour, and he quickened his pace both to avoid a soaking and to speed towards Lottie. She would, he knew, be working the teatime shift in The Wishing Well, and he couldn't wait to share with her his news. To explain that the outbursts, his sharpness, and the many self-centred sulks, were a thing of the past. That before her stood the new-and-improved Jake. Or rather, the previously calmer version of Jake – the pre-Welham Jake – but with certain significant adaptations and upgrades.

A smile curved his lips as he turned on to the High Street, his attention focused solely on his thoughts and on getting to the pub to see Lottie.

The car came out of nowhere. One moment silence, the next a throaty roar of engine as the accelerator was depressed violently. The burnished black of the Audi hurtled towards him, wheels screeching and smoking in protest.

There was no time for thought. He merely reacted. Throwing himself sideways, he landed painfully on a garden wall, ribs bearing the brunt of his weight, before momentum tipped his feet and flipped him awkwardly into shrubbery on the other side.

He heard a ragged scraping as the front wing of the TT grazed brickwork exactly where he had just been standing. From his prone position in the foliage, he saw sparks fly above the wall, the impact of metal on stone sending dozens of tiny infernos soaring, before the car ricocheted back into the roadway to continue on its journey.

Jake quickly pulled himself to his feet, using the wall as a prop, in time to see the rear of the vehicle drawing away from him. The black Audi.

A further squeal of tyres as the sharp right turn into Mad Alice Lane was executed with the confidence of a stunt car driver, confirming the unthinkable. That Luke Brunton was on his way to Damara Cottage.

It did not occur to Jake immediately that he'd been the victim of attempted murder. His thoughts were with his mother. At home, alone, and completely unaware of the threat racing towards her.

He vaulted back over the wall, a fresh and acute pain in his side causing him to suck in his breath but not slowing him at all. His immediate reaction was pursuit of the Audi, and he ran a few steps towards the lane before stopping short in indecision. He needed help. Physically he was no match for Luke Brunton. Although tall and fit, Jake had yet to fill out and acquire the strength of muscle that came with manhood. It would be like a match between a greyhound and a Rottweiler. Much as he pictured himself, and quite regularly of late, smashing that arrogant face into a bloody, pulpy mess, the reality would most likely be a reversal of this vision, with himself taking the role of punch bag.

He reached into his jeans for his phone. He had to warn his mother that Luke was on the way. Tell her to get out, to hide. Then Maggie. She should know that events were moving more quickly than they had ever expected.

Not there! His phone was gone. Confused, he patted every pocket jerkily. Nothing. Think, Jake, think! Hope rose, and he looked back over the wall. There it lay, in the shrubbery. He lunged for it urgently, ignoring the pain in his ribs as he again connected with the brickwork. Without conscious thought, he hit the memory button for Anna's mobile and waited for it to ring. Silence. Confused, he looked properly at the screen. It was smashed, a crazy-paving pattern zigzagging outwards from the central impact point. It, too, had suffered as a result of contact with the wall. He swore quietly under his breath.

'Shit.'

He turned towards The Wishing Well. He had to get to Lottie. Had to let her know what was happening. She would have her phone, and could warn his mother, could rally the troops.

Then he had to get home. To Damara.

THE WARLOCK COMETH

The TT crunched to a stop on the gravelled driveway of Damara Cottage. Heavy clouds made twilight of the afternoon, and way off on the horizon lightning forked across the heavens. All was preternaturally still around him, but a storm of some magnitude was almost certainly on its way.

The calm before the storm.

His lips twisted in a sardonic grin.

Most fitting for what lies ahead.

Making no effort to disguise his arrival, he wasted no time knocking, nor waiting to be invited inside. He merely pushed open the front door and entered.

Anna was not there, and this slowed him momentarily. He had not accounted for her absence. Her co-operation, her assistance, was needed to complete the next step of his plan.

A noise upstairs drew his attention. Raising vulpine head, sensing the vibrational energy swirling about him, he took a seat casually in the rocking chair to await her appearance, his manner utterly relaxed.

He was content to pause in his quest, confident that ultimately the prize would be his. Sounds of muted movement above him continued, until a step on the wooden staircase promised her return.

Anna entered the kitchen humming softly to herself, the shadows of lowering skies concealing his presence from casual scrutiny. In one effortless movement, he rose. Her cry of alarm broke the silence of the pre-storm lull, and the harsh sound bounced off the thick stone walls before dying abruptly.

'Luke! You shocked me. I didn't hear you knock.' Anna worked hard to keep the tremor from echoing in her words.

'That may be because I didn't. Knock, that is. Should I apologise for frightening you? I hope I'm always welcome here, Anna. You are pleased to see me, are you not?'

His voice, that deep and melodic resonance, was as hypnotic as ever. Even having knowledge of his intention, his reason for being here, she still found herself struggling to resist the pull of his magnetism. Yet beneath the physical beauty, that intense charm, there lurked a hint of his true character. She focused her mind on noticing the small, tell-tale signs of a bestial nature. The curl of his lip, a flare of nostrils, and those hands. Large and strangely tapered, the nails were polished and unusually long for a man. More than that, more than the physical, though, was an underlying aura of danger and... she searched for the adjective... malevolence.

She was more frightened than she dared to admit, even to herself, for she knew that the time that they had spoken of, in the safety of the Welham Farm kitchen, had now come. She prayed that she would be able to hold him at bay until help came. She knew beyond doubt that assistance would come. Whether it arrived in time, however, was not at all certain.

She countered his question with attack, feeling a need to appear strong, if only outwardly.

'Our last meeting didn't end well, Luke. I thought you'd got the message that I'm not interested in a relationship with you... of any kind. I'm more than a little annoyed that you feel you can just walk into my house without invitation.' Her tone strove to be indignant, and just about achieved it.

'Ah, but Anna, surely you know that our friendship is special...

has the potential to be very special. To me at least. I had hoped that you felt the same?'

Those words, his voice, almost pulled her in. Almost, but not quite. A picture of Jake, of Maggie and Lottie, and of herself, speaking in low tones of this exact situation, rose before her. Their support, their strength, focused her mind, helping her to erect the barriers needed to repel this assault on her emotions. She played for time.

'Perhaps. At some point. But you're moving much too fast for me.'

Maggie had informed them all that Luke's weakness would always be his arrogance, his inability to see past his own prowess. She could use the knowledge to her advantage if she was clever.

'You are a lovely man, and I am *so* flattered by your attention, but walking into my home like you live here is not the way to win me over.' Her voice hardened. 'It's not what I'm used to, and it's not what I want. You'd better leave now, and we'll pretend this never happened.' She strove to maintain an irritated tone.

'Ah, sweet Anna, if only you sounded sincere I might actually believe the words you're forcing yourself to say.' He took a step or two towards her, confidence in his own ability to seduce apparent in every gesture. 'I know you want this as much as I. Why not just let it happen? Stop fighting me. Let me love you.' His hand, those long, long fingers, cupped her chin, his thumb brushing her lower lip gently.

Her resistance was weakening. She could feel it draining from her as she looked into the azure-blue of those magnificent eyes, and was unable to help herself.

A movement from behind him drew her gaze. Alice, hand upon the cellar door, stood as if just entering the room. When she spoke, it was for Anna's ears alone.

'Stay strong. Your son is but minutes away. The warlock thrives on your weakness.'

Anna blinked and she was gone, as if never there, but her words had been enough.

Anna placed her hands gently upon his chest, mirroring that other time when she had pushed him away in fear and anger. This time, however, she merely turned her head from the sensual pressure on her lips, patting his lapels in a familiar, almost affectionate, gesture.

'Luke, no. Please. You must give me time. I value your friendship, but I just can't give you more at the moment.' She moved away from him, putting a small and vital distance between them but, more importantly, breaking the hold of his eyes. That hypnotic gaze could, would, have been her undoing if not for the timely intervention of Alice. If she could just keep him at arms' length for a short while longer, she knew now that Jake was on his way.

Luke was not to be so easily dissuaded from his mission though. Once more, he approached, from behind her this time, laying hands upon her shoulders and leaning in to nuzzle her nape.

'You feel it too,' he murmured into her hair, 'this connection we share. We were meant to be together, you and I.'

Away from the power of his gaze though, the contact of his mouth on her neck made her flesh crawl. The hot touch of his tongue against her skin, such an intimate and seemingly loving gesture, caused an involuntary shudder, a mixture of fear and repugnance.

Luke, misreading the signs, tried again. 'I feel it. You're longing for it too. Our union is meant to be. Let me love you, Anna.'

She stepped away from him with purpose and more than a little relief, leaving him frozen in time, hands still resting on her now-removed shoulders, head bent to continue the serious business of seduction. She turned to face him, resolve now strong, as he straightened.

'You must hear me, Dr Brunton.' She emphasised the formal term of address. 'This is not something that I want, or can even contemplate. You've misunderstood. If I've been giving out the wrong signals, then I apologise, but it's really best if you leave right now.'

He changed in a split second, the speed of transformation alarming. She knew that she had overplayed her hand. The suave shell fell away to reveal the beast beneath. The distance between them was crossed in an instant – she was barely aware of him moving – and one massive hand closed, claw-like, around her neck. With the other, he pulled her to him, bending her backwards until her spine felt it might snap.

'Do *not* play with me, woman. No more games. I shall have The Chronicle, and you will take me to it.'

Anna's breath came in red-hot gasps as his fingers tightened on her throat. The room began to spin around her. Just as blackness crept around the edge of her vision, he loosened his grip, allowing barely enough air into her lungs to keep her from unconsciousness.

'You know where it is hidden, do you not?' The voice, no longer smooth or caressing, growled from his snarl of a mouth. 'You will take me to it now.'

'I … don't know… what you mean. Luke… please…' The room was fading in and out of a red-black haze, her grasp on reality slipping away, as he toyed with her neck. A cat playing with its helpless prey.

'Take me to it, woman, or your usefulness ceases – and with it, your life.' He spat the words with contempt, dropping her to the floor to lie in a crumpled heap of agony.

She sucked in blessed air through a bruised and swollen windpipe.

'Those who think to best me have learned the hard way.'

He looked at her then, eyes like bottomless pools of corruption. His grin was beyond despicable, and Anna shrank beneath the evil before her.

'Enough! It is time, woman. Show me. You know for what I search.' He reached down and, grabbing her by the upper arm, dragged her to her feet.

She felt her shoulder wrenching as it took her full weight, her whimper of pain drowned beneath the moan of the rising storm outside.

She stood before him, head bowed, injured shoulder hanging at an odd angle.

'It's not here. Not anymore.' Her voice was defeated, barely more than a whisper, and he had to lean close to hear.

'Liar.' His anger, ice-cold, frightening in its quietness, brooked no disobedience. 'You will tell me now where it is.'

'I will not.' Her words were a surprise, even to herself. The warlock had not expected to be denied, and especially by such a pitiful adversary. His bellow of rage briefly drowned the song of the storm before the back of his hand slammed into Anna's cheek and she sank into merciful oblivion.

The stab of her injured shoulder dragged her, time and again, from welcome darkness as she was carried, as if without effort, down the familiar stone steps to Damara's cellar. A soft groan was dragged from her as pain speared once more and she heard a guttural chuckle from the one who bore her downwards.

Low ceiling, feeble light from the low-watt bulb, came and went above her as she struggled to maintain a grip on consciousness, but as he dropped her roughly in the shadows at the dank, darkest end of the room, her head connected hard against something cruelly solid. She again embraced freedom from pain and travelled into a void of nothingness.

MEMORIES

Jake ran hard. He had outpaced Lottie, last seen on the High Street with her mobile glued to her ear. She was somewhere behind him and heading for Welham Farm, but he couldn't spare more than a fleeting thought for her safety at the moment. There were bigger fish to fry.

His arms were raised to protect exposed skin from the worst of the wind's games, which picked up and flung small debris with seemingly vicious intent. Moving forwards was becoming instinctual, eyes covered by his forearm.

Twice, lightning struck uncomfortably close. He'd smelled charred vegetation, heard the sizzle and pop of tiny explosions, which had carried even above the howl of the gale. The rain had still to arrive, but all indications promised it joining the party before too long.

He noted as he passed, and without too much surprise, the pool of Mr Brunton's blood. It wasn't real, he knew that. At least not yet. This confrontation had still to happen. There was no awareness within him of the reason for the blood, but he recognised to whom the injury belonged, and the understanding pleased him. It confirmed his progress of the morning and gave him confidence. There was an acceptance of this fresh knowledge, this power that was his, without question. Barely pausing, he pressed onwards towards Damara. His ultimate goal, he knew, would be the cellar.

Jake finally caught sight of the pale outline of the cottage with relief, standing solid and robust, through the dust-filled, shrieking air ahead. His lowered head and raised arms giving him many blind spots, he almost collided with a large, dark shape before him. The Audi. He skirted around the car, abandoned rather than parked diagonally across the track. As he passed, he noted an ugly graze marring the once-glossy bumper, the sight causing a twinge of recognition in his ribs as his body remembered its recent tangle with a stone wall.

He surprised himself then by veering around the side of the building towards the back garden, guided by intuition and a wisdom greater than his own.

The fury of the dry-storm abated abruptly as he rounded onto the rear lawn, the space protected by the barrier of structure, hedge and trees. Although the gale continued relentlessly all around, within the cocoon of the garden there was an unexpected respite from the continual buffeting of his journey. Jogging the last few yards, he sank gratefully onto the bench, wiping grit from his eyes with his sleeve as he did so. The wind seemed softer, less cruel, on the lea-side of Damara.

He had no idea why he should be so, sitting here in the garden when his mother was under the control of a monstrous fiend and undoubtedly in peril. Yet he knew what he had to do now, what must happen next. He needed more weapons in his arsenal, otherwise facing the warlock would be nothing more than a gesture, and all would be lost.

Thinking of earlier, that morning, in the aftermath of Lottie's departure when all had returned to serenity and quiet, he again calmed his mind by sheer effort of will. Placing hands on the bench to either side of his thighs, palms down for optimum contact, he closed his eyes and focused his thoughts. Towards Luke Brunton.

He felt the click within him, the precise moment when he connected to a higher realm, and he released his conscious mind with ease.

Images came to him immediately, the sensation that of

viewing a cinema screen on the inside of his own skull. He, the spectator looking in on another time and place, unperceived by the star of the show who went about his grisly business with concentration etched on an angelic young face. The resemblance was unmistakable. The distance of thirty-something years could not disguise the blond beauty of a nine-year-old Luke.

The scene – inside a garden shed, probably. Door closed. Slatted walls. Hooks and shelves displaying garden tools and cobwebby plant-pots. There were no windows, and a single weak bulb threw a sulphurous and sickly light on to the seated boy beneath it. A single mewling whimper came from a source hidden by the slight frame of the child. The Luke-boy shifted his weight then to reveal a penknife clutched in his right hand, and the body of a huge grey-brown rat on a low table before him. The creature was still alive, but barely, and not for much longer as a flash of steel confirmed the blade's purpose. Blood gushed darkly and covered Luke's fingers as he sliced expertly into the creature's abdomen, his expression of clinical attention seeming out of place on the face of one so young. Without pausing, the boy lifted bloody fingers to his lips and licked, his pupils darkening in delight at the taste of…

The vision was gone. Jake now watched from the corner of a large bathroom, the black and white-tiled walls dripping with condensation as steam rose from a claw-footed tub. The woman, fair-haired and delicately pretty, dropped a towel to the floor and stepped elegantly into the hot water.

A man entered. A younger, slimmer version of Mr Brunton, dark auburn waves covering what would later become a balding pate, stepped quietly from beyond the open doorway, his manner relaxed. As he approached the woman, she turned a head over her shoulder, confusion briefly clouding her brow before, with the agility of a predator, he stepped briskly forwards, hands rising to connect in a forceful shove against her upper back. Jake flinched, but there was no time to react even if he'd been able. His was the part of witness only.

The pale lady crashed forwards, feet finding no purchase

below her. Her head connected with a sickening crunch against the Victorian-esque taps, body folding limply down, perfumed water immediately beginning to stain red from an unseen injury. She was still now, crumpled and face-down. Mr Brunton turned without another glance and left the room.

Helpless, Jake could only watch, an appalled onlooker to the horror. Then the woman moved, rolled over. The wound on her forehead was ghastly, edges resembling lips opened wide in song, revealing the sickening gleam of bone beneath. It spewed a steady, pumping waterfall, covering her face and exposed breasts in a grotesque mask of scarlet. Only half-conscious, she reached with one hand to the bath edge, began to pull herself up and into a sitting position.

The same beautiful boy – Luke – possibly just a little older now, entered and she made a soft moan, perhaps thinking him her salvation. He dropped to his knees at her side, a picture of tender concern, hands moving apparently to help her. To save her. Strength was ebbing from her limbs, though, as her life force spilled from the wound. When he locked his small fingers around her throat and pushed downwards, there was only token resistance from the semi-conscious woman. Her tenuous grip on the bath rim was broken easily, and she slipped for a second time below the water. She could summon only enough fight to surface once more, before again succumbing to the pressure from above. He held her down, slight arms quivering, as the small movements beneath the bloody water slowed and finally ceased.

He hadn't yet finished though. Fledgling muscles straining to complete the task, he raised her again, propping the inert form against the back of the bath, her sagging mouth just clear of the gory liquid. Thick blood still seeping from the wound signified proof of life, however tenuous, and Luke reached out a hand, stroking his mother's cheek gently in a parody of tenderness, before pressing fingers deep into the lesion…

The fluorescents overhead flickered into darkness as the woman clicked the switch to OFF. The only light now was from various monitors, and a subtle leeching through viewing windows from the corridor outside.

The nightshift.

This ward had six beds, four with occupants, all men. The patients were sleeping, connected to various apparatus, and all had drips inserted into the backs of hands.

The nurse, a tight curly perm framing an unremarkable and vacant face, moved from bay to bay, her movements stilted, robotic, eyes blank and impassive. She was obviously performing the evening observations, and at each bedside, she executed a similar ritual. Straightening sheets, taking a pulse, checking readings.

At the final booth, however, she also removed and replaced the suspended bag of fluid connected to the patient before her. She completed this final task and, as if on cue, the door swung inwards.

Startlingly handsome in white coat, obligatory stethoscope hanging stylishly around his neck, a twenty-something Dr Brunton entered. He spoke softly to the nurse. Without further response, she collected the discarded fluid bag and left by the same door, her face devoid of expression.

Luke approached the last patient and studied the monitor above him. A red warning light had started to flash already. In one lithe movement, he reached behind the bed and flicked a switch. The machine subsided into blackness. He stood then, quietly, seemingly lost in thought as he observed his ailing patient.

Hearing his voice was a shock.

'I can feel you, whelp.' The words hissed towards Jake, although Luke's lips had not moved and he remained facing towards the helpless man in the bed.

'You watch me, thinking yourself invisible. You hide in shadows, but I know you're there. I've always known.'

Nonchalantly he sat then, perching on the edge of the hospital cot. Using his thumbs, he gently raised the man's lids and leaned in close to look directly into the dying eyes.

'Come. Face me now, brat. I am so very much stronger than you', he challenged. 'Do you dare?'

The scene changed again.

Late dusk. An almost full moon hanging low in the sky. A wind was blowing now, pushing lonely clouds across an otherwise clear sky, stirring the coastal grasses around him. It flowed straight through Jake yet chilled him to the bone. He knew what was to come next.

The cliff top was deserted save for the couple standing a few yards from him. The man was facing away, towards the horizon where sky merged to sea. Still, the blond head and set of shoulders confirmed his identity.

She was frightened, her face contorted with emotion, and was backing dangerously close to the crumbling edge in an effort to put distance between the two of them. Luke stepped forwards, and she countered again with another ragged pace back.

He turned then, his face a cold mask, features set and hardened, looking directly at Jake, acknowledging his presence, truly *seeing* him this time.

The voice had substance too, came from lips now tightened in icy fury.

'Well, well. The brat gatecrashes once more. This is becoming a habit.' The lightness of tone belied a rage not quite hidden beneath the supposedly calm exterior.

'Elaine? Meet the whelp.' He didn't turn his head from Jake. 'He has come to witness your demise, my dear.'

The woman, clearly able to hear her husband, yet understanding only the final intent, made a last bid for liberty. She darted to Luke's left, the surprise of her attempt almost gaining her freedom, but with the speed of a cobra, his arm snapped out and captured her wrist, immediately twisting in a hurting grip designed to subjugate and damage. They all heard the crunch as tiny bones shattered, and Elaine slumped to her knees, head bowed, seemingly beaten.

She was hauled roughly to her feet again without pause. Luke walked purposefully towards the cliff edge, dragging his injured wife behind him. Elaine was not defeated yet though. With the last of her reserves, she fought him all the way, twisting and pulling. Her strength was no match for his. They reached the cliff edge as she continued to squirm and struggle, the pain in her crippled wrist deterring her efforts not at all.

Luke stopped and turned, holding his writhing, kicking wife with ease, and spoke again, softly.

'This will be worth a front row seat. You watch now, Jake.'

The use of his given name from those malign lips shafted a freezing spear through Jake's soul.

With free hand, Luke lifted Elaine's chin, leaving cruel red welts on the delicate skin, forcing her to face him. Their eyes locked. She quieted instantly, her struggles ceasing, uninjured arm dropping limply to her side.

'There, there, darling. You see how easy this all could've been if only you hadn't challenged me?' He caressed her cheek with his fingers before, with a gentle tug on the ruined wrist, she toppled, ragdoll-like, over the edge and into blackness.

At that moment, Luke turned, gaze locking with intent with Jake. A gleeful malevolence shone at the hideous wet-thud of his wife's body hitting the rocks below. Those eyes, that evil, followed Jake as he spun away from the scene, forwards through the years, back to Damara's garden.

He opened his eyes. The storm still raged above and around.

'No time's passed. Nothing's changed,' he whispered.

Except me, Jake thought. *I've changed.*

How long had his journey into Luke's memories taken? Probably no more than minutes, perhaps even seconds judging by the still-ferocious weather.

He knew that he should feel fear now. Should be horrified at what he had seen, been forced to witness. Certainly he didn't underestimate his adversary, this man-monster who, at this very moment, was holding his mother captive somewhere within Damara.

But the fact was that Luke had betrayed himself during his final performance. For performance it had been. He had played to his audience. Had adored having his masterpiece seen by another, his genius observed.

The last scene – Elaine's murder – had given Jake an idea – a much needed edge – and a possible means to defeat his nemesis. For he had found the enemy's Achilles' Heel, had seen it exposed before him.

Luke was strong, but no one was invincible.

Jake stood and walked towards the cottage as the first fat drops of rain fell.

GEORGE AND THE DRAGON

George Brunton lifted the blunderbuss carefully from its brackets on the wall. The time had come. He had already collected the lead shot, acquired long ago and safely hidden away in his bedroom until just a few minutes ago. Now he loaded the dragon with a precision borne of much practice and an obsessional adoration. He stroked the glossy stock with reverence.

The coming hours had been long awaited, and anticipation of actually firing the weapon in conflict excited him in a way that sleeping with that silly wife of his never had. The loaded blunderbuss aroused in him a carnality which could never be echoed with any woman. His cheek rubbed against the flared barrel in an erotic caress, eyes half-closed in pleasure.

Already intending to follow Luke to Damara Cottage, he had then fortuitously overheard the young couple's conversation, had hidden himself behind the door when they thought themselves alone; but Old George had got the better of them this time. He sniggered quietly at his own cleverness. For once, his eavesdropping had paid off. Luke would be well pleased on learning every detail of their pathetic plan. He'd be able to use the information to combat their pitiful hopes. Every word had been registered and noted. His burly chest swelled at the thought of the certain praise coming his way later.

He'd then seen Jake tear away towards Mad Alice Lane, Lottie in hot pursuit, before locking the front door of The Wishing Well behind them immediately.

He had ignored several attempts to gain admittance by regulars arriving for their daily drinking session, cunningly remaining out of sight, crouching behind the bar. The customers finally left, puzzled and irritated at the pub's unexpected closure. He tittered again, the thought of his own guile, and of their bewildered faces pressed to the windows, hands cupped around eyes in an effort to pierce the interior gloom, tickling his funny bone.

Scooping up the blunderbuss, George left the pub via the back door so as to remain unseen, and also made his way towards Mad Alice Lane, although he travelled across a mixed terrain of planted and fallow fields that ran between the rear of the High Street properties, and the outer rim of Welham Wood.

Scurrying in and out of the shadows at the periphery of the copse, his bulk making movements clumsy and ungainly, he was enjoying himself hugely. Imagining himself a soldier scouting ahead of his section, his mission high risk and perilous, he stopped every few yards to ensure that he remained unobserved.

There had been very little rain over recent weeks, an odd torrential downpour the only relief to the long hot summer, and the ground was firm and easily covered. Storm clouds had gathered above though and the wind had picked up. It would be a much wetter walk home, he thought to himself, unless he could persuade Luke to give him a ride back to the pub in that snazzy little sports car.

Luke had been a most unusual child from the first. Always headstrong, his gift of manipulation and mind control was apparent from a very early age. George had been smitten from the first, proud beyond reason of his beautiful and intelligent boy. Helen, though, was less easily swayed, and this had always puzzled George. That she couldn't see their boy in the same way that he did was a mystery to him.

Perhaps the birth had tarnished her view. It had been a particularly difficult time, even George would acknowledge that.

But weren't women supposed to be able to cope with these things? Shouldn't a mother's love overcome even the worst of pain?

Luke's birth had damaged her irreparably. Helen's insides had been torn and lacerated beyond the consultant's ability to mend, a partial hysterectomy – the removal of her womb – the only option.

He could still remember the baffled expression on the midwife's face too. She'd never seen anything like it, she'd said. How could a new-born gash and split his mother's soft tissue, and to such a degree, on his way into the world? Yes, his toe and fingernails were unnaturally long, and yes, he did have a full set of tiny, pearly teeth, but surely this could not have played a part in his mother's condition?

Whatever the truth of the matter though, the injuries had ensured no more siblings could follow. This had been a disappointment – for George, too – but there was nothing to be done about it. From that moment onwards, his perfect, bright and beautiful boy had been his whole world.

The couple had argued long and hard about their gifted son from the first, their approach to rearing him differing by a distance too great for compromise.

Endlessly thwarted by his mother – her tough-love method of parenting sitting badly with the lad – over-indulged and spoilt by his father, it was little wonder that relationships within the Brunton household suffered. Luke learned early how to play off his parents against each other.

A twig whipped past his head, carried on the rising wind, and George's messy brain easily shifted to a memory of *that* day. He tittered once more. The very special day when Helen had 'slipped' in the bath and ended their putrid excuse for a marriage. It was still fresh in his mind. A hefty shove had gone a long way – he snorted again – her feet slipping on the slick surface helping her along nicely. She fell hard, and with the added, and unforeseen, bonus of her head connecting with a satisfying crack against the taps. There had been an extraordinary amount of blood. George licked his already wet lips, eyes glazing at the recollection.

What he hadn't expected though was the part his son had played in the drama. A proud moment, and no mistake. His face now split into an unpleasant grin as a picture of the ten-year-old Luke, heaving his half-conscious mother back into the water, came to mind. She'd almost made it out of the bath too.

Shame, that.

He chortled again.

Another loud crack of thunder echoed through the trees. He ducked his head instinctively, and then laughed aloud at the reflex. It'd take more than a clap of thunder to scare him. He pounded forward, feet planting firmly, the dragon cradled lovingly before him.

The shortcut from the rear of the pub to the lane would gain him some time, a diagonal and more direct approach, rather than the dog-leg of the youngsters' journey. He reasoned that he shouldn't arrive too far behind Jake and Lottie. He'd wanted to give them a small head start though, principally so that he could make a grand entrance at an appropriate moment. Wielding the dragon at this point was vital. Their terrified expressions at sight of his pride and joy, a loaded and potentially lethal weapon, was something he was itching to witness.

Passing to the rear of the cemetery, the woodland encroaching much nearer to the village here, George began to have an uneasy feeling that he was not alone. Worse, that someone was watching him from beneath the trees. Someone with a knowledge of his destination and his intentions. Someone who may be able to slow his progress, if not completely foil his artful plans.

He paused, fevered eyes darting erratically in an effort to penetrate the shadows around him, the dragon clutched before him, aiming randomly into the gloom. A fork of lightning flared above, momentarily throwing the scene into brilliance.

The Peel witches' plot was illuminated only a few yards from where he stood. The hag was there, behind the gravestones, as he had always known she would be. He recoiled in fear. She observed him, motionless, her hideous visage partially concealed by the hood of a voluminous cloak. He could see her eyes though, glowing red from within, and he shrieked as the skies darkened once more, the spectre vanishing into enveloping blackness.

He backed away, weapon waving haphazardly towards the spot where the Witch had apparently been standing, but she was gone. Thunder crashed again on the back of lightning. The storm was much closer now, the bursting of clouds imminent, and George cowered, his recent bullish bravado waning, and a childish whimper escaping as fear mounted.

Gone now was the brash exuberance, his excitement at confronting the whippersnapper and his slut of a mother fading more than a little. The appearance of Mad Alice confirmed that the interlopers would not be fighting this battle alone. Were it not for the fact that Luke had commanded, he would, at that moment, have turned tail and run. Fear of his son, though, made this an impossible choice. He would rather face a hundred hags than the rage of his only offspring.

A fresh lightning-strike, and somewhere very close, followed instantly by booming thunder, made him recoil once more.

With a last anxious squint into the shadows – mercifully, no sign of the Witch – he turned on his heel and stumbled on, picking up the pace as best he could. Precious time had been lost by the unwelcome distraction of Alice glaring at him by the graves.

Gait uneven and lumpy, an unwelcome tightening starting in his chest, his accelerated strides were beginning to make breathing difficult. He had a dull pain down his left arm too – where he'd cradled the dragon too tightly and for too long, he reasoned. He couldn't linger in that spot though. Not with the Witch standing sentinel. Luke was expecting support at Damara too. George pressed onwards, the weapon clutched before him.

At last, spotting the gap in the hedge that opened on to the lane, he lurched on to the track on the last approach to the farm and the cottage.

That he was observed from above he had no inkling. For in the uppermost branches of the tallest tree in the copse, the raven stretched his newly-healed and strengthened wings. He made ready for flight just as the first fat drops of rain began to patter on leaves and dapple the dry earth beneath him.

A couple of minutes behind Jake, Lottie had wasted precious time standing on Welham High Street trying to make contact with Anna. Or with either of her parents. Even knowing that her father would be no help at all, fifteen miles away and helping out a fellow farmer with the harvest, hadn't prevented her from trying. Had he answered, he wouldn't be able to make it home in time to be of any help, especially with the skies darkening by the second. She would have worried him for nothing, but still, just hearing his voice, knowing that he was on his way, would have been some comfort. She sighed.

All three mobiles were going straight to voicemail, probably due to the magnetic disturbances caused by the storm, she reasoned. The landline at Damara was ringing out, this causing a small frisson of fear to stab deep in her stomach – Anna should be there – and answering. Why wasn't she? What was stopping her? The answer was all too obvious. Luke Brunton was stopping her. Welham Farm was constantly engaged, causing her normally serene temper to spike.

'Just put the damn phone down, Mum. *Please,*' she whispered as she pressed the screen again, the familiar number glowing mockingly, the strident 'busy' tone scorning her efforts once more.

The absolute waste of time, when time was of the essence, was agonising. Finally admitting defeat, she turned with a groan of despair towards home.

Both mechanically and physically, it seemed, the heavens were working against her. The ferocity of the weather, as she left the High Street and veered into a wind howling straight down Mad Alice Lane, slowed her progress to a snail's pace in an instant. She was, for the first time in her young life, genuinely afraid for her own safety as dust was sucked from the ground, and small articles of flying debris filled the air, picked up with ease by the updraughts of the gale.

Lightning now forked with ridiculous regularity, followed always and immediately by an ear-splitting crash of thunder. Terror forced her into an ungainly crouching gait, an impossible and futile effort to make herself smaller, less of a target.

Breath dragged from her by the force of the gusts, head dipped to protect her eyes from the sandstorm-like conditions, she had no warning of the falling bough, didn't hear the crack as it separated from the trunk and tumbled earthwards. The tree was, thankfully, just a sapling, and it was only a tiny branch, but solid enough to cause damage. It caught her with precision, and a loud crack, across the temple.

She dropped like a stone.

ONE MORE STEP

The roiling darkness of the storm overhead prevented any glimpse, any warning, George should have had as the great bird took flight. The landlord quickened his pace still further, the gentle hiss of first rain belying the deluge to come. Thoughts of completing the Brunton men's eternal quest, of Luke's approval – and of avoiding a good soaking – spurred him on.

The pain in his chest had worsened though, and his breath was now coming in short jagged gasps due, he rationalised, to his efforts thus far to ensure speedy progress. He wasn't as young as he used to be. Still, not far now, and then he could sit back and watch Luke, his pride and joy, take centre stage once more. His own role in the forthcoming performance was likely to be one of back-up only, as was usually the case. He was the understudy, Luke, the star of the show.

There had been several occasions over the course of many years when he had been the gratified observer of his son's artifice and originality. The number of Welham pets and spring lambs that had mysteriously gone missing during those early years to satisfy Luke's endless-questioning and insatiable appetite for knowledge; and his other, more base, cravings too, of course. He chuckled, rubbing his aching arm once more, the memories distracting him slightly from an increasing discomfort.

Then the day in the bathroom, with Helen. Luke had only been a child, barely turned ten, and his ingenuity and composure had been wondrous to behold. George had been a proud father that day.

There had been another memorable evening too. Here, at Damara. They'd worked as a team that night, his own promotion to supporting artiste welcomed and, he felt, earned. Poor old Doc Grassington. A snort of mirth escaped as he recalled the look of surprised terror, viewed from his location in the depths of the cellar, as the elderly GP tumbled gracelessly down the stairs. Not a pretty sight. That remaining eye staring accusingly in death, strangely glowing in the half-light, would have sent lesser men skedaddling.

He shuddered. Not the Brunton men though. They stood firm against all adversaries. He unconsciously squared his shoulders. It'd take more than a spot of rain and a long-dead hag to slow Old George down. Lowering his head against rain that had quickly become a deluge, he pressed forwards.

The screech took him by surprise, and he thought fleetingly that Mad Alice was again before him, her flapping cloak blocking what little failing light remained as the storm gained strength. Powerfully clawed feet locking around his arms quickly gave lie to the witch notion, and a blade-sharp beak stabbing at his exposed pate made him wish that his attacker *was* of the spirit world. This assailant was all too real, the sting of claws piercing through cloth and into skin, beak slicing easily his balding scalp, causing him to wave his arms frantically in an effort to shake off this foe. Its grasp seemed unbreakable, and he shrieked his pain to the lowering skies.

Lifting his head was a mistake though. The raven struck immediately at his exposed throat, tearing and gouging with its razor of a beak. George felt a trickling of hot blood mingling with the cool of rain, and he roared his fury aloud. How dared this creature attack, injure, a Brunton man? And to draw blood? Unthinkable.

He dipped his head once more in an effort to protect his face, whilst grappling ineffectually with the creature connected, limpet-like, to him. His struggles did little to free him of the tenacious grip. Rather the bird took full advantage whenever exertions left skin exposed, and the dagger-like bill slashed again and again.

A soft pop. Excruciating pain skewered through his brain, and then the warmth of something viscous sliding down his cheek.

With renewed strength borne of rage, he flung his arms wide, the speed of movement surprising and dislodging his adversary. The bird flapped away, arcing gracefully above the trees before circling for a second assault.

George raised his darling, his dragon, and cocked the weapon. Unaware of the injury, his right eye watering with a stinging mixture of rain, sweat and blood, he swiped in vexation with the back of his hand. The sudden intense pain to the left side was a surprise, as was the slimy fluid which he smeared inadvertently across his temple. Puzzled but not distracted, he squinted to take aim.

The raven came on, great wings beating only occasionally as it glided effortlessly downwards, its span filling the sky before him.

As lightning forked the clouds once more, throwing the scene into harsh brilliance, thunder rolled in quick succession. In that same instant, the trigger was pulled, the resultant report crashing and merging with the roar of the heavens as the dragon discharged its deadly load.

The bird was stopped dead by the impact, as if colliding with an invisible barrier stretching from earth to sky. It cartwheeled, wings wide and messy, to land behind the hedge, an untidy heap of black feathers.

'Ha!' George nodded in satisfaction. To his wounds he paid no attention at all, blood running freely down his face far more quickly than the rain could wash it away. His white shirt was now a becoming shade of pink. His left eyeball, attached to the socket only by a thread of glistening white sinew, dangled jauntily.

He reached into his pocket for the emergency packet of lead shot.

No point in arriving for his grand entrance unprepared.

How much time had passed since the branch felled her, she had no way of knowing. She thought – hoped – that it had not been too long. The heavens still raged above, but rain now drummed on and around her with a violence to match that of the wind.

Reaching soaked and shaking fingers to probe the point where the branch had struck, she was relieved to find no blood. Only an impressively-sized lump which, although tender to the touch, did not seem to be affecting her at all now. Not even a headache. Her thoughts, surprisingly, were clear and concise. She knew what had happened and, more importantly, where she needed to be. As soon as humanly possible.

Bracing herself against the still-howling wind, she rolled first on to her knees. Taking care to compensate for the rigour of the elements, she stood then, knees bent, one arm outstretched for balance, the other shielding her face.

One step at a time, one foot in front of the other, she pressed again for home.

A feeling of having been on this journey forever began to seep into her consciousness, sapping her resilience, weighing her feet with lead. Nothing seemed more appealing than to curl up in the relative shelter of the hedge and wait out the storm. She recognised, however, that keeping her away, slowing her down, would be exactly what the warlocks wanted and needed. She knew that her physical strength was ebbing though, every pace a challenge. The fork in the path was not far now. The initial goal? Her mother, home and shelter. One last effort.

There was something on the track ahead, blocking her way. She paused, squinting through the slanting silver curtain of rain, before her breath released in relief.

Albert!

He squatted – that was the only word that came to mind – in the middle of the track, drenched, bedraggled and sorry-looking. Like a huge black toad. Water streamed from his plumage, forming into muddy rivulets beneath and around him. The bird was injured, that much was obvious by his stance, but he was alive and alert. Lottie pushed forwards and stooped. Knees bent, feet planted wide, braced against the relentless pressure of the wind, she wrapped soaking arms around him, hoisting him clumsily to her chest. He made no protest, merely tucking his head trustingly against her neck in an effort to protect himself from the sting of rain.

Soon be there, not far to go. Soon be there, not far to go. The mantra was a constant tempo inside her head. She forced her footsteps to the rhythm as the ceaseless pounding of the gale sought to slow, perhaps even stop, their progress.

Carrying Albert was harder than she had expected. His size, his sodden weight, and the loss of her arms for balance on the mud-slick track, made any movement hazardous. And now she was half-blinded by the slicing rain, making each pebble, every rut, an obstacle. Vicious Medusa-like lengths of her own hair whipped around her head, targeting eyes with malicious intent and finding their way into her open mouth with unpleasant regularity.

Twice they almost went down, saved from falling only by lush foliage of the hedgerow by the side of the path. Welts on Lottie's exposed skin bore witness to the contact, but remaining upright was a greater priority. There was no time, and she had no energy, to tend scratches.

Feeling much like a pinball, lurching from one obstacle to the next, Lottie finally attained the relative shelter of the copse. The dense canopy afforded some small protection from the violence without for what seemed like an all too brief interlude.

A short way further, though, and they would be safe. The sturdy walls of Welham Farm beckoned her on. So close now, and yet the final stretch seemed a Herculean task.

Pausing a moment more to gather her strength beneath the cover of the trees, Lottie sucked in her breath and, head down, arms wrapped tightly around Albert, made a final push for home.

The crash of the outside door spun Maggie, bending over the telephone, towards the sound, her face a pale mask of concern.

'Oh, thank goodness.' She almost threw the receiver into its cradle. 'I've been trying to call ever since the storm broke. Are you okay?' Maggie had never been quite so thankful to see her daughter, quite so grateful to have her home. Lottie nodded, dislodging a spray of droplets which speckled the flagged floor and ran down her face to drip on the soggy mess of black feathers still clutched tightly in her arms. Maggie saw tears of relief glazing her daughter's eyes, and a noise which was half-hysterical-laugh, half-sob escaped her lips.

Albert lifted his head slowly from beneath Lottie's chin and gave a low croak of greeting as he was dumped, rather unceremoniously, on the kitchen table.

'Your head. Love, what happened?' Maggie grabbed a thick towel and wrapped it around her daughter's shoulders before gently pushing the thick mass of wet hair back to inspect the injury.

'I'm okay, Mum. Honestly. I know it probably looks bad, but it doesn't hurt at all now. We can worry about it later.'

Maggie nodded, trusting Lottie's judgement, and turned her attention to the raven. He allowed the quick ministrations without objection. The only obvious damage was to his flight feathers, broken on the tip of the left wing. They had been snapped about halfway down, and now dangled uselessly, attached to the whole only by threads.

'But the blood?' Lottie looked down at the gore and clots on her reddened hands, the same still drenching the raven's undercarriage even after his soaking. The injury, at first glance, appeared to be Albert's, but this was obviously not the case.

Maggie shook her head. 'I don't know, love. Not the bird's, for certain. But time's short.' She was all brisk efficiency once more. 'Is Jake there already?'

Lottie nodded, her face ashen, and her mother understood. The girl was so afraid for him. Yet she also knew what she must do now, and that knowledge frightened her even more. Maggie hoped that Lottie's courage was sufficient. She had been through so much already.

'You know that I would go if I could,' said Maggie, emotion catching her voice and making it ragged, 'but it has to be you.' She reached to cup her daughter's chin, fingers stroking and caressing, needing this final physical contact. This was the hardest thing she had ever had to do. To send her beautiful girl back out into the storm, injured, weakened, and exposed to dangers such as neither of them had ever faced before. Lottie returned the gesture, a small smile saying more than any words, before turning away.

'I'll get The Chronicle,' she said.

Maggie closed the well-worn pantry door behind her, allowing the raven to hop from her arms to the table. He was beginning to dry in the warmth of the farmhouse, and downy feathers fluffed around his forehead like a dark halo. The sound of the storm, muffled by the thick stone walls, raged on outside.

Prepared days earlier there lay, placed neatly on the surface before them, an array of objects and implements, the most notable of which were four small, wax dolls, laid side by side. They bore more than a passing resemblance to the members of the Freer and Brunton families.

Lottie had left a few minutes before, The Chronicle wrapped neatly within three tough plastic bags before being placed in her backpack. Their best hope of protecting it from the elements.

Only through shear effort of will could Maggie focus on her own tasks. Her thoughts kept straying outside, into the storm, to her daughter striving towards to Damara and The Source. Lottie's mission was now out of her hands, though. She had to trust that years of preparation, that the fortitude and resilience, which she had always known her daughter quietly possessed, would be enough for the trial ahead.

Maggie, however, had her own part to play. She may be excluded from Damara, but there was still work to be done here. Her influence on events today may be enough to edge the conflict in their favour. Perhaps. If Fate smiled on them. Pushing unwelcome images of a storm-thrashed Lottie away, she bent to her task.

Albert, though, had other ideas. Hopping directly before her, head almost on a level with her own, he met her gaze with one beady dark eye. Twice she tried to push him gently aside. Twice he paced back.

'What, Bird. What is it that you want?' Maggie's tone was clipped, edged with her anxiety. Worry for her daughter, and for the Freers, clouded her usually sharp perception, and she was in no mood for games. The raven, though, would not be diverted. He pushed a rain-fluffed head beneath her palm, guiding her hand to slip to his shoulder. At once she felt the vibration.

'Okay. You have my attention.' Her voice quieted. 'Show me, Bird. What do you see?'

And as Albert's other, milky, orb began to glow lilac, Maggie closed her eyes.

In the cellar of Damara Cottage, one more book in the infinite library of Jake's mind opened its cover for the first time.

TERMINUS

Rather than a traveller through dreams, this time he played host. Albert – and Maggie by proxy – were timely visitors.

The situation was grim, and Jake scanned the room slowly for them, the whole desperate scene laid bare before him. It was comparatively easy, he found, allowing the bird to see through his eyes. More a decision than a feeling that, once made, required no further thought or energy.

Things were not going well here. Perhaps this well-timed development, the raven's eavesdropping, may go some small way towards tipping the scales of Fate back in their favour. Perhaps Maggie may glean some clues to help them. They needed all the help they could get.

He was kneeling on the damp earth at the furthest point from the cellar stairs, where shadows were long. At his side lay his mother, who was only now beginning to revive. Ugly bruises on her cheek and around her throat had already started to colour. Her arm, even to his unpractised eye, hung too low against her body. He guessed that her journey down, into the bowels of the cottage, had not been easy. His jaw clenched in anger as she groaned again and tried to sit up.

'Don't, Mum,' Jake whispered, pressing a hand to her healthy shoulder. 'Stay down.' He tried to keep his voice low, but at the far end of the cellar, strategically placed beside the steps and blocking any hope of escape, the Brunton men turned their heads to the sound.

Not that leaving was top of Jake's 'to do' list at this moment, but he would sooner have had the option of a swift exit should the need arise. Attracting their attention was something he would have rather postponed for as long as possible. He needed time to formulate an alternative strategy. Plan B was something that hadn't ever been discussed during their long meetings around the table. Time had escaped them. Plan A, he acknowledged, was a bit random at best, and already things were not going quite as hoped.

He had known exactly what he was doing when he made the decision to descend, without preamble or precaution, into the basement. He'd known also that the warlock was expecting his entrance. There simply wasn't another option that he could see. The dice were cast. Until that point it was as they had discussed… kind of.

Luke, waiting at the foot of the steps, had simply waved him past theatrically, with a jolly 'how very kind of you to join us.' Had even pointed out where his mother lay, in the shadows at the far end of the cellar. 'She's there, whelp. Waiting for you,' he'd sniggered nastily.

What Jake hadn't anticipated was the severity of his mother's injuries. Or the fact that she was, at the time of his arrival, deeply unconscious.

Nor had he expected the elder Brunton, complete with blunderbuss, to join the party mere minutes after his own arrival. George had half-stumbled, half-slid clumsily down the moss-covered steps, reaching the cellar floor more with the help of gravity than his own propulsion. And although his appearance wanted for much, there was still the weapon to consider. Jake did not underestimate the old man's eagerness to use it.

The Brunton men then stood together, whispering, for some minutes, George swaying like a reed in a breeze, before Luke moved forwards to inspect his captives.

As soon as he was no longer the object of Luke's attention,

George immediately took the opportunity to sit on the mossy stairs, shoulders and head slumped as he continued to massage his left arm. His obvious, and sickening, injury was clearly taking a toll. He must have lost a lot of blood already judging by the oozing socket and his unpleasantly stained clothing.

Apart from the gruesomely dangling eyeball though, he seemed also to be struggling for breath. Sweat-slick skin had taken on a waxy greyish pallor, emphasised unattractively by the sulphurous lighting. The constant rubbing of his upper arm had not gone unnoticed by Jake. Luke, however, appeared unaware of his father's evident distress. Nor, bizarrely, had he even mentioned the glistening globe still adorning the pallid cheek.

Although clearly weakened, George was alert enough to cradle his beloved dragon though, and twice already had aimed the weapon in Jake's direction in a menacing, if slightly arbitrary, way.

Luke's velvet-smooth voice now echoed hollowly around the enclosed space. 'Ah, the whore awakes,' and he approached still closer, arrogantly unafraid of any perceived attack by Jake, to the darker end of the cellar where the weak bulb failed to penetrate fully. This was where Anna had been lying, apparently lifeless, when Jake had arrived, and in horror he had rushed to her side, ignoring the warlock's mock welcome and giving up, in that moment, any hope of gaining the advantage with position or surprise.

The battle lines had been drawn. Luke was, for the time being, in the ascendancy and Jake would have to trust that his own newly awakened gifts would be sufficient to turn the tables. To hope that the warlock was unaware of the huge step forward he had taken this very morning

Was it just this morning?

If they were very lucky – and only *if,* Jake conceded – the thought of an easy victory, and his own overbearing arrogance, might sway Luke to underestimate the challenge.

Anna was lying directly over The Well. Had she been placed there deliberately, or was it just divine chance? The Hulinjalmur had been lifted by Alice, so Luke was presumably now able to see where The Source had been hidden? Whatever the case, deep shadows, and his mother's inert form, successfully concealed the edges of the cover, disguising its exact position from casual glance.

Luke sauntered still closer to the Freers now, tauntingly so, confidence writ large in his swagger and the haughty tilt of his brow.

'Anna.' His voice caressed the name. 'I've missed your sparkling company since that unfortunate bump to the head.' He sniggered again. 'I do hope you're feeling a little improved?'

She hauled herself into a sitting position, cradling her elbow to support the injured shoulder, but kept her head bowed and eyes downcast. Sweat-limp hair curtained her face.

He snorted his distain. 'I've seen you look better, my dear. But...' and he paused for dramatic effect, '...I'm just a tad surprised. No challenge? I had thought it would take more to break you.' Then dismissively, 'Apparently not.'

He turned his attention to Jake and his tone changed in a heartbeat.

'The Chronicle, whelp. Let me have the book, and I may yet let you live.' Jake grunted his scepticism. 'What? You doubt me?' Feigned and extravagant disbelief. 'You think I may kill you just for the pleasure of it? For the sheer delight of watching you suffer?' He received no reply, but a derisive sniff from Jake spoke more than words. 'You may be right,' he conceded, grudgingly. 'You've already witnessed where my inclinations lead, after all? Did you enjoy the floor show? Did it excite you, make your juices flow?'

Jake refused to be drawn, to respond or encourage the monster in his posturing, but Luke continued nonetheless.

'Yes, I'm sure it did, young Jake. To watch a master craftsman at work? What honour, what privilege.'

Luke was enjoying himself now, his power over them apparently complete. He strutted and gestured as though performing to a theatre audience, the dirt-floor his stage.

'It serves me not at all to have you survive,' he continued, 'a constant thorn in my side. Yet the joy of seeing you begging for mercy, where no mercy will ever be given?' He turned and looked straight into Anna's eyes. 'Well, it gives me a hard-on just thinking of it.' One long-fingered, claw-nailed hand went to his crotch where a growing bulge was now horribly apparent. He rubbed suggestively, his eyes never leaving Anna. She flinched at the vulgarity and he sneered at her distress. 'Oh, so prim and proper now, whore, in front of your runt of a son. You weren't so prudish that night in The Wishing Well, as I recall.' She gasped and glanced at Jake. He could feel his mother's shame. 'Or in the glade. Couldn't wait to open your legs for me then.' He licked his lips provocatively as her eyes returned to his once more.

'An opportunity missed, Anna...' He leaned in to her, '...for both of us, I think,' Luke finished in a stage-whisper and, before Anna could reply, his hand whipped forward and grasped a breast hard, twisting viciously.

She cried out, and Jake reacted immediately, lurching forward. Seeing his mother humbled and hurting, his own inability to protect her, tested his endurance to the limit. He moved without conscious thought, and his striking hand connected fruitlessly with air. Emptiness now, where Luke had so recently been. Nimble as a cat, the warlock was astute enough to recognise when swift withdrawal was required.

'Too slow, whelp. You'll have to do better than that,' and he turned his back on them with disdain, faith in his own power, in their weakness, supreme.

Jake subsided reluctantly, helping his mother to a more comfortable position. At his questioning look, she nodded and mouthed 'I'm fine'. Clearly she was far from 'fine', but was fast recovering her wits.

A noise from the kitchen caused all to look upwards, and a suddenly distracted Luke rushed the length of the cellar to the steps.

'Come out, come out, wherever you are,' he taunted, his voice sing-song and child-like.

'I feel your presence, Charlotte Peel. I've been expecting you.'

More unhurried sounds from above, before Lottie's mud-caked sandals and soaked jeans appeared, slowly descending the mossy steps. Jake gasped as her hands came into view.

She bore The Chronicle before her.

George rose unsteadily from his perch, backing up to allow her to pass. His remaining eye, marble-like, was glued to the prize so suddenly and unexpectedly before him.

Reaching the bottom, she stepped into the cellar and quickly found Jake's gaze. He read in her eyes a message meant only for him, and understood instantly what must now happen.

'Lottie, NO! You can't let him have it.' He leapt to his feet, hoping his voice sounded convincingly panicked. 'We have to try. Please. Don't do it.'

She answered quietly, the tremor in her words hinting of anguish, of misery. 'This is the only way. I'm so sorry.' Her amber eyes filled with unshed tears. 'We don't have strength to defeat him. The victory must be his.' She turned, a single salty drop tracing down her cheek, and held out The Chronicle in both hands.

Offering it to Luke.

The warlock fairly crowed in his glee. Snatching the book roughly from her fingers, he stroked its ancient binding reverently. His face contorted in excitement, lips pulling back in a hideous grin and exposing unfeasibly long, sharp canines.

'So long,' he murmured, as if unaware now of those watching. 'I've waited for so long.' Raising The Chronicle before him, a long and oily tongue slipped from his mouth. He slowly licked the leather, tasting. Marking it as his own.

With a gasp, Maggie snatched her hands from Albert's back, his glowing eye quickly returning to its normal milky opaqueness, the link between them broken. This last vision had physically sickened her, to see The Chronicle in the grip of darkness and so abused. She couldn't allow personal feelings to compromise their plans though.

'I really hope that's not the end of the connection, Bird,' she said, pretending a brightness she did not feel, 'because we'll need to do that again very soon. I take it George Brunton's attractive eye condition was your doing?' He blinked as if in answer. She reached out and gave his dark halo a complimentary pat. 'Well done!' And she meant it.

'We need to get Anna protected now, though, and quickly. And there's the binding to be done.' Words trailed off as concentration took her, and she busied herself with the primary task. As she picked up the first of the poppets, Albert hopped to the side of the table to watch.

This was the Anna-doll. Cuttings of her fingernails and hair from the brush on her dressing table, helpfully provided by Jake at Lottie's request, had personalised it. A prettily embroidered handkerchief from beneath her pillow – again, Jake had come up trumps – provided a shift dress for the tiny figure. Maggie's dexterity had made the facial likeness unmistakable.

The figure, worryingly, already displayed various dents and dimples, its previous smoothness marred by existent injuries of the real Anna. The shoulder was lopsided too, as though the image had been made in a hurry, and without thought for precision or form.

Maggie reached behind her for a Kilner jar and gently placed the poppet within, along with a sprig of sage and a black tourmaline crystal. These same protections – sage and a tiny tourmaline – had also been hung in a small leather pouch around her daughter's neck as she battled her way, bearing The Chronicle, through the elements towards a foe far more dangerous than any storm, waiting for her at Damara. Maggie pushed the thought aside. She had to remain focused, or Lottie's supreme effort may be squandered. She could only hope that Jake was astute enough to understand their hastily scratched together plan – and that his abilities were sufficient to make it work in their favour.

Stretching to a high shelf, she retrieved two candles. The white one she lit, and placed beside the jar. Its soft illumination licked the clear surface of the container, and caressed the tiny figure within. She placed her hand atop the lid and, quietly but clearly, spoke the words:

> *'Jar of glass and herb of sage,*
> *deflect evil and keep safe.'*

The lid of the jar clicked shut with a satisfying *snap*. The Anna-doll looked out from within her glass shelter.

'This should shield her – at least for a while,' she murmured.

The Jake-doll she left alone, for to tamper in any way could impair the strength of his newly acquired gifts. This was an unknown quantity, and she had to trust that he would have the resilience both to implement, and to then control, his fledgling powers. That he protected against himself against external evils, that he achieved this without conscious thought, was a blessing. One which she had never before encountered. Another sign that he was The Chosen? She hoped so.

The George poppet was disintegrating almost before her eyes, seeming to lose substance from the inside. Its waxy sides were pocked and flaccid, and an ugly stain marred the face. She pushed it to one side. No magic would be needed here. Nature was taking its own course. A thought occurred though and, reaching to Albert, she pressed her palm to his under-carriage. He cocked his head in an effort to see her purpose. Her hand came away red, a glob of congealed blood adhering to the index finger, and she carefully detached the clot on to the George poppet's chest. No harm in helping nature along a little. A distracted smile curved her lips as she wiped the residual blood from her hands.

The last doll was clearly Luke Brunton. A blond hair, discreetly lifted by Lottie from the bar in The Wishing Well, had customised it. A natty waistcoat-and-trouser ensemble, fashioned from a green paisley scarf 'lost' weeks since, provided his outfit. She lit the black candle and lifted the Luke-doll.

The Guardian wound a thin black ribbon around the effigy's mouth, securing it in a tiny knot to the front. Pressing her index finger to the nub she had created above the poppet's lips, she chanted softly.

'*Sostantivo, silenzio, maschile. Sostantivo, silenzio, maschile.*' The intention was to prevent speech, at least of words gleaned from The Chronicle, and of a dark nature. She laid the doll beside the black candle, the light from its flame casting flickering shadows over the bound form.

'Enough for now,' she whispered, sitting back. She turned to the raven. 'Again, Bird. We have to try again.'

Albert's clouded eye was already beginning to glow as Maggie rested her hand on his shoulder once more.

MAGIC AND MAYHEM

An up-ended packing crate provided a makeshift lectern for The Chronicle. Luke's whole attention was on the tome, leaving his father to keep an eye, literally, on the three who crouched in the shadows.

George was not looking good. Slumped on the cellar steps, the dragon cradled in limp fingers, his head nodded to his chest with regularity, only for him to pull back to consciousness time and again. Were it not for the fact that Luke stood between them and the landlord, Jake might have attempted to remove the weapon from his failing grasp. Distance, and leaving the women to the mercy of the younger Brunton, made any current attempt a fool's errand.

At Luke's distracted instruction, Lottie had joined the Freers by The Well, and her hand, small, cold and very damp, now crept into Jake's and squeezed. He squeezed back, glad of her presence, but still unsure how surrendering The Chronicle to the enemy could be a sensible plan. He could only trust that she knew what she was doing and that there was sound reasoning behind the seemingly disastrous submission.

He was relieved to note, though, that his mother was improving by the minute, recovering more quickly than they could have hoped or expected. Clearly, as with Albert, proximity to The Source was supporting a speedy revival. Even the dislocated shoulder seemed to hang at a less dreadful angle, at least to his optimistic eye.

Being unable to communicate aloud was a disadvantage. Any suggestions, plans to outwit Luke, or to take him by surprise or force, would be immediately overheard and used against them. Jake knew that he would have to make some hard decisions, and soon. At this very moment, the warlock was stroking a long index finger down The Chronicle's binding, his lips moving in a silent chant, in preparation for opening the cover.

The squeeze on Jake's hand came again, but harder, with purpose, and he turned to Lottie, eyebrows raised in question. She met his gaze quietly, directly – and with eyes of deepest lilac. She carried a message, and he knew what to do immediately. Jake opened his mind to Alice.

She spoke within him, her voice a beacon of hope amid the raging sea of doubt. He felt her strength and goodness wash over and through him, calming and focusing him to the task at hand.

'George Brunton's time is almost past,' she said.

Jake looked to the far end of the cellar. The publican's breathing had worsened significantly and he plucked ineffectually at his shirt front. His single healthy eye bulged from its socket in terror, knowledge of his own mortality causing a stain of shame to appear around his groin as his bladder released.

As if propelled by an external master, one over which he had no control, he jerked awkwardly to his feet, the dragon still clasped tightly to his chest. They watched in horror as the weapon was clumsily raised and aimed in their direction.

But George's failing body could cope no more. His remaining eye tipped backwards, the iris disappearing, as his head slumped one final time to his chest. With a grace rarely captured in life, he sank elegantly to his knees before toppling gently sideways to rest on the damp cellar floor. He would never see the outcome of a lifetime's work, had fallen at the final hurdle, his misused heart too weak for the strain of battle. His dead hand still maintained a tight grip on his love, his dragon.

There remained though, in his place, a dark shape. As though

George had left behind a blurred and unnatural shadow. It heaved and rippled as it began to take form.

'There is another here.' Alice spoke again, her voice soft, yet urgent, in his mind. 'He was concealed, was out of bodily sight. His cover is now broken.'

Even as Jake acknowledged the words, a sound began around them. Softly at first, like the hiss of a fractured pipe, but growing rapidly to a roar. A wind to rival the storm outside rushed the confined space, bouncing from surfaces and pounding them into a protective knot, arms wrapped firmly around each other, muscles clenched against the force. Only Luke Brunton seemed unaffected. He loomed over The Chronicle still, hair lifting only gently as if on a summer breeze, his attention on the book complete, the death of his father passing without notice.

Lottie turned to Jake within the confines of their cluster, her eyes glowing deeply purple. Alice spoke again. A name.

'James.'

The wind ceased abruptly, a supernatural hush blanketing the cellar as completely as falling snow. As the three captives slowly unwound from their defensive ball the dark mass gained substance, became solid, and raised its head.

The Witch Finder, James Brunton, stood beside the cellar steps, eyes black and dead.

As her erstwhile lover forced his way into Damara's cellar, taking George Brunton's life as forfeit, Alice Peel left her own refuge and rose to meet him. Lottie slumped against Jake, her energy depleted by the separation.

A lilac sphere now glowed in tandem to the dark figure, appearing close to where the Witch Finder stood. Through the eddying mists within, Alice took shape and materialised, her beauty undiminished and ethereal. From beneath the well-cover, a glow of the same unsullied hue began to seep slowly into the cellar.

Their eyes met over centuries, and held. A union of love abused, of faith betrayed, and of lives ruined in hatred and greed.

Apart from the eerie sound of Luke crooning feverishly over

The Chronicle, silence reigned as Alice and James faced one another across the space of the cellar. Anna and Lottie clung together as they watched the emotive scene play out before them.

Jake, however, still maintained the link to Alice, and the dialogue between wraiths was as clear to him as if they were talking in the physical world.

James Brunton spoke first. Her name only, a caress of recognition, a whisper of anguish. She responded by moving closer, her progress smooth as silk, more floating than walking. The lilac halo remained with her, enveloping her within its protective glow.

Now within arms' length of each other, separated in time by death – his betrayal, her murder, hanging between them – the emotion of the moment was not lost on Jake.

'James,' she responded softly. A sigh, carried on a breath of sadness long held. 'Atonement is required for your actions.'

He dropped his head, could not hold her direct gaze. 'I meant it to be otherwise. I could halt not the beast of avarice once released. The fault was ever mine. I humbly beg your pardon, Alice.'

'The time for absolution is past. A reckoning is nigh.' Her voice hardened.

'Please,' he ground the word out. 'I am in torment. If payment were needed, surely the ages of guilt, of anguish, go some way toward penance?'

'Our child, James. She died with me. This deed is surely beyond forgiveness. Yours was the sin, yours the penalty.'

The dialogue seemed to be costing James Brunton much in the way of energy, and his form rippled constantly, losing cohesion with each response. Alice's lilac light, however, glowed more strongly, brighter and clearer, as she finally faced, and challenged, the spirit of her betrayer, her murderer. Her love.

'There is much I would change, Alice, were I able. My greed, my arrogance in life, ruled all. In truth, I know now that heaven was within my grasp. I bartered all for want of an illusion.' His distress was palpable, but she appeared unmoved by his suffering.

'My love for you was enough to sustain us,' she said. 'It was always enough. Should have been sufficient to bind us for eternity. Your betrayal saw an end to all that was meant to be. Now the harm must be made good.'

'Tell me, Alice, my love. How can I atone?'

'The punishment is mine to bestow. I cannot forgive the death of our child. For this, you must pay.' It was too gruelling, though, this anger, this bitterness, which she had nurtured through generations. She visibly softened then, the surrounding aura reflecting her changed emotion. 'Yet the love we once shared, it still holds sway.'

She lifted her hand towards him and he reached out, their palms touching, fingers entwining and clasping.

'I did love you, Alice. Truly. I have searched through the ages to find you once more. To make peace between us. My weakness, the corrupt nature that was mine, was to blame. I accept your price, whatever it may be. Forgive me, my love, for the ills I caused. Against the tenderness we once shared.'

There was but a slight nod in response before the light intensified, its pale hue darkening to a violet flame. Still, the couple's hands remained locked, but the figure of James Brunton grew hazy, began to lose substance. Their gaze locked once more, the demonic darkness falling away from his eyes to reveal the steel grey of physical life.

The man he had once been, before evil took him, emerged. The violet flame extended and enveloped him, and his form grew dim.

As if knowing that time was short, he stepped forward to her. Cradling Alice's face with his free hand, he kissed her gently on the lips before a dazzling while light engulfed what little substance was left of him, and he was gone.

Alice bowed her head for a moment before turning to Jake.

'My part is done,' she said. 'The next is for you.'

The halo began to fade, the figure of Alice within growing misty and transparent.

'Please, no. Don't go,' Jake shouted aloud, his voice echoing around the chamber, their spiritual connection forgotten in his disbelief at what was surely about to happen. How could she leave them now, at the crucial moment, when they needed her most?

'Come back, Alice. Please,' he yelled again. 'We need you.'

'Trust in your loved ones. Trust in yourself.' Even her voice was weakening, coming to him now as if from far away. 'You are stronger than you know. You can defeat him.' This final message, and Alice was gone. He knew that they would not see her again. She had made peace with James, had released him from the purgatory of guilt, and had forgiven his crimes against her. She was now free to move on.

Jake knew he should feel happy for her – and he did – but couldn't help but question her timing.

As Luke raised his head and turned towards them, his attention dragged from The Chronicle by Jake's ill-advised cry, he acknowledged that, for now, all of his focus must be on the task at hand. There would, hopefully, be time enough to lament the passing of Alice to another realm later.

Their own personal demon, Luke Brunton, was still very much at large. It would take more than a handshake and a healthy dose of forgiveness to vanquish this adversary.

As Jake watched, the warlock lifted The Chronicle's outer binding, and howled his possession to the heavens.

Instantly the pages began move, his long-fingered hand now redundant as the leaves fluttered and turned of their own accord, coming to rest eventually at a pre-destined position.

Anna leaned in and whispered, 'It knows. Which spell to use. For each person… it knows what to do. Maggie showed me.'

Jake nodded his understanding, eyes never leaving the scene before him.

Luke's elation was apparent. This seemed far too easy. He had expected to have to fight the whelp, fight the witches, even fight the book itself. Everything was falling into place with an ease borne of a belief in his obvious right to harness this power. He stroked the ancient parchment, a clawed nail gently tracing the intricate and archaic script. The spell chosen by The Chronicle itself. It knew what he wanted.

He chortled in glee, and readied himself.

There was a stillness, a nothingness, as if time itself were suspended. The three by The Well remained quiet. Very soon it would be apparent whether Maggie's interventions were robust enough to help them.

Luke opened his mouth to speak. His brow furrowed. The first sign of uncertainty he had yet displayed. He tried again to speak The Chronicle's words, but could produce no sound from a straining throat.

With a shriek of rage, he turned from The Chronicle and bayed to the heavens. 'You think to stop my connection to The Book, to stop me voicing the ancient words? Try harder, Guardian.' He raised an outstretched hand to Anna. 'Come to me. Anna, come.'

Keeping lids lowered, she turned her head from him. Jake could only watch. He had to trust that she could resist without his help as he gathered himself for the confrontation ahead.

Luke tried again, this time with more force. 'Woman, you will come to me,' his voice rising in anger.

When she did not, he again howled his vexation. 'You will not thwart me, Witch.' Raising vulpine head, he hissed the words upwards, the message meant for Maggie again. 'Watch now, vixen, how I brush aside your feeble powers,' and, seemingly without effort, fingers clawed to his lips, he pulled away the invisible cord which bound him.

He turned again to Anna, yet still his anger seemed aimed towards The Guardian.

'You think to shield her from me with your pitiful attempts at magic. She is mine. *This* is magic, Witch,' and he thrust his hand, fingers splayed, towards Anna. She was thrown backwards, landing hard on her back.

Luke walked slowly forward to claim his prize.

FINALE

Maggie, eyes tightly closed and hands still on Albert's shoulders, watched in horror as the conflict in the cellar spiralled out of control.

She was aware when the ribbon around the Luke-doll's head split and released, heard the sigh as it unravelled, and knew that time was short. They were in grave danger.

Keeping her grip on the raven – for to release the connection would render them blind to events at Damara – she trusted her intuition and dropped to the floor, pulling him down roughly with her beneath the protective lip of the table.

The Kilner jar exploded. Slivers of lethal glass sliced the air, several glittering shards embedding into exposed surfaces around the room. Splinters sparkled down like fairy snow around them, tinkling on to the wooden boards. Both candles, black and white, were snuffed out simultaneously by an invisible breath.

Silence.

Retaining the link with Albert, his eye still glowing, she edged from beneath the counter, taking care to avoid the glistening glass carpet. There remained only one more spell to try. A last effort to influence events in the cellar and help her loved ones. One of strength, of resilience amid adversity. It was so little, yet it was all that was left to her.

Her lips began to move, and she hugged Albert more tightly against her chest.

In the bowels of Damara, Lottie ran to the stricken Anna, who was again cradling her injured shoulder. Jake sensed his mother's pain. It sliced white-hot down her arm. He could feel her resolution too. She had steeled herself to remain strong, to show no weakness. Lottie's thoughts were also clear to him, and her spirit, her resilience, were beyond doubt. The connection between them, the knowledge that was now his, was power. He felt a growth and expansion within himself once more.

He rose, placing himself between his prone mother and the warlock.

As Jake turned to face his nemesis, Luke's lips peeled back in a grin of anticipation.

'At last, runt. You've finally discovered that your balls have dropped. I was beginning to think you'd been castrated at birth. Come… join the fun.'

Without another word, he spun on his heels, flamboyantly caricaturing stage magicians of ages past, and returned to the makeshift lectern. He began to chant immediately, words read from The Chronicle falling with ease now that Maggie's binding had been swept away, his voice resonant, silky, and with an undertone of poison.

Harken ye spirits to
gather here,
by ether, air, fire and earth

Jake felt only a fleeting uncertainty – what now? what should I do? – before the switch in his head clicked again. Instant clarity. He calmed, concentrating on Luke's voice, embracing the sound.

Imbue these waters
of the source
I bid thee now to do my worth

The warlock's arm shot towards his mother, fingers splayed once more, but this time the objective was The Well behind her. Violet-hued water began to spill silently and steadily from beneath the ancient cover. Jake saw Lottie help his mother to her feet and they moved quietly nearer to him while Luke's voice gained strength as the incantation progressed.

Send out ye servants
elements of yore
mine enemies be thine enemies true

Jake felt the words connecting, becoming a part of his essence. At once he recognised their power, acknowledging the portent concealed within. He understood what must now happen, what he must do. Luke continued, his voice rising with the waters.

Retribution I call thee
elemental waters
claim those who bring harm to you

Jake reached behind him, feeling for Lottie and Anna, needing their closeness, feeding on their strength. Their love for him, and for each other, would be the tipping point, he knew. The difference between defeat or victory, death or survival. Their resilience would bolster his own resources.

The women, huddled behind him, seemed to recognise his silent plea. The circle of three, Jake to the fore, clasped hands and stood united, facing their foe. Luke's voice rose once more, melodic yet dreadful.

Spirits of ether,
rise forth I bid thee,
Join the elements and have your way

The ghost-wind came again, softly at first, and hissed through the cellar kissing all it touched. Jake refocused his mind to The Chronicle. Loving energy from Anna and Lottie pulsed into him like a physical force through their grasped hands. He lost himself in the words, became a part of them, uniting with the elements, with pure spirit. All of the power, all of the magic being conjured before him, entered and suffused him. Diverse energies rose within him. His physical body shuddered in effort before deflecting them – mirroring them back towards their origin.

Luke's voice climbed still further, unaware or uncaring of his rival's endeavours, hideously screeching his elation as the incantation climaxed.

RETRIBUTION, I call thee
imbued waters and ether before me
Justice be served this day.

Abrupt stillness.

Lilac-tinged water from the source lapped gently around their feet, progress halted but not reversed. The wind ceased its movement, idle for now.

Yet within the calm, something throbbed, vibrating beneath the skin. Unheard at first but growing and pulsing as it gained strength. The warlock looked around him, his brow furrowing as if in puzzlement – clearly he had not expected this – and then to Jake, as a malevolent and triumphal smile spread across his features.

'The elements await my command, whelp. The deed is done. It would seem that your challenge fell short even of the feeble effort that I anticipated. And now, it is too late. The power is mine.'

He chuckled manically, stroking The Chronicle with clawed fingers.

'I am the victor,' he crooned. 'My first task as Lord of the Source will be to end the pitiful lives of you, whelp, and that of The Guardian's slut of a daughter. Quickly and mercifully? Or slowly and painfully?' He made a play of weighing the options in outstretched hands, snorting, Jake supposed, at his own dark humour. 'Slowly, I think, and without mercy; and with as much pain as I can conjure. As for you, my pretty Anna…'

He didn't finish. The throbbing intensified, swiftly building and hardening into an intolerable din as the waters moved once more. The wind howled from out of nowhere, and Luke stopped abruptly, face a mask of surprise, hands clapped to his ears.

'I did not order this. My control is absolute,' he howled, raising both hands above his head.

'Cease your movement. My dominion is recognised and unopposed. I bid you cease,' he bellowed. Still the waters rose, now knee-deep, as the wind moaned around the walls.

Jake half-turned to the women, eyes never leaving the warlock.

'Run. Now. Get out of here.' His voice could barely be heard above the clamour of the elements, but Lottie and Anna obeyed immediately, releasing his hands and wading awkwardly towards the cellar steps, their progress unmarked by Luke. He now searched urgently through The Chronicle, flipping pages back and forth in an obvious effort to locate an antidote to the chaos around him.

The women reached the stairs and began to ascend, his mother almost turning back into the waters. Jake understood, could feel her anguish. The need to stay with her son was overwhelming, Lottie urged her upwards though, an arm around her waist, and they disappeared from sight.

Jake turned to The Chronicle. His lips began to move in words as old as time. Wading slowly forwards through the lilac waters, he held hands wide, palms upwards.

'What do you think to do here?' screeched Luke. 'I have possession of The Book. I alone control The Source. Do not dare challenge me again,' but there appeared doubt in the bravado, an undercurrent of uncertainty in his defiance.

Jake ignored the warlock's threats and did not falter. He came onwards, concentration intense and, as he approached the packing crate on which The Chronicle lay, he raised his hands higher.

The wind-rippled waters rose at his command.

The warlock screamed his rage.

'You cannot. I have The Book,' and he snatched it from its perch, turning towards the steps. Escape from the cellar, from this flood which seemed bent on his destruction, was now the priority.

The boy raised his hands once more, the elements obeying his command, lilac waters rising still and the wind howling in union.

Luke lifted The Chronicle above his head and pressed forwards towards the stairs, the fierce currents beneath the surface dragging, pulling like the hands of monstrous mermaids, at his legs and hips.

The body of his father floated face-down before him, annoyingly blocking his way. In death as in life, it seemed. His lip curled in disgust. Dead arms moved gracefully in the eddies, patting and stroking at Luke's chest, fingers curling in mock caress at each contact. A parody of the fawning touch which had so irritated him in childhood.

Frustrated, he barged the limp figure of his dead father aside and it drifted away obligingly into the gloom, the purplish radiance and fluid undulations of the cadaver giving the scene a surreal and other-worldly appearance. Sparing the body a single, scornful glance, the warlock pressed again for the steps.

'STOP!'

Jake's voice was commanding yet calm and Luke turned, feeling a bizarre fusion of anger and shock. The sight which greeted him was, in all of his abuse of magic and witchcraft, beyond anything he could have predicted.

His nemesis must surely be standing atop the packing crate, for he rose above the waters and stood unaffected by the winds, his head almost grazing the dank ceiling above them.

Jake's eyes were wide now and shone with flawless luminance. A vibrant halo around him glowed a rich indigo. Luke saw with disbelief that, although the waters lapped around the boy's feet, he was unsupported from beneath.

As if to prove the point, the packing crate, moving at speed within powerful undercurrents beneath the surface, smacked with force into Luke's back, knocking him off his feet and plunging him into the cold and impenetrable depths.

The Chronicle slipped from his grasp.

Jake watched from above, removed yet connected. He could sense the movement of water, of wind. He controlled their flow without conscious thought or effort.

As Luke, and with him, The Chronicle, disappeared beneath the swirling maelstrom below, the gale instantly ceased its relentless moaning as if on cue. The waters though continued to swirl, small whirlpools forming and disappearing with regularity.

Jake's focus changed then, centred on the ancient book and its path through the purple depths. The Chronicle floated gracefully downwards, absorbing water and gaining weight. It settled, finally, on the earthen floor, saturated leather bindings wide, pages drifting and dancing in the ebb and flow.

A figure then. Blond hair shaded to brown by water and shadows. Pale eyes open, glazed and staring. The hand, long-fingered and claw-nailed reaching, stretching, almost touching the prize…

…and then it was gone. The connection severed, the link broken.

The waters receded with unnatural speed, returning from whence they came to the darkness of the earth. Smaller whirlpools melded into one enormous vortex, its centre churning and bubbling above The Well.

Jake saw the publican's body, spinning with abandon, the packing crate and several of its brothers bumping and colliding with each other, all gathered in the powerful flow, whirling in a dance of madness on their journey downwards.

His feet touched the floor, and he looked down in surprise. All waters now gone here, yet at the far end of the cellar chaos still reigned, as if gravity and the laws of nature had no influence in this place of energy and magic. The noise, the crunching and grinding as all was compressed into The Well and beyond, made Jake shudder, and he closed his mind to the turmoil before him.

Of Luke, there was no sign. Certainly he had not gained the stairs, and freedom. Jake could only assume that the warlock had paid the ultimate price for his avarice, his need to control and possess The Chronicle, and had joined his father in a shared descent to hell.

And yet... Jake still felt his enemy, could sense a faint glimmer of... something? He shook his head. It was gone.

The last of the water sucked away, taking with it the eerie violet light, and he was left alone in the feeble glow of a single bulb. All that had been in the cellar was gone, swept down The Well as The Source returned to Mother Earth.

Except for The Chronicle.

It lay in the centre of the room, on the earth, and Jake rushed to lift it from the dampness, fearing that all within be ruined by immersion in the magical waters.

He caught his breath in wonder. The leather bindings were dry, unspoilt by the ordeal. As he opened the cover carefully, ancient parchment crackled to his touch with the fragility of age. He closed it again, gently, but firmly.

One day maybe, with Lottie by his side, he would be ready to make this journey, to discover its secrets, and perhaps harness the power.

For now, though, The Chronicle must be returned to its rightful place. To The Guardian.

Hugging both arms around the great book, he moved towards the stairs, and took the first step up towards daylight.

EPILOGUE

DAMARA COTTAGE: 2023

The party, Ethan knew, was almost over. It had been the best day of his life.

Everyone had paid him lots of attention. His presents had been all that he'd hoped for, and they'd played lots of games which he'd been allowed to choose.

His cake was amazing. It was shaped like a green dragon with seven candles on its nose so that they looked like it was breathing fire. The red sponge inside looked like real blood. He was feeling just a little bit sick now, and knew that the last slice he'd eaten had probably been one too many.

That was why he was in the bathroom at Damara Cottage. Well, two reasons really. The first one was that he really did feel a bit queasy and was being sensible just in case the worst happened. Big Boys didn't throw up their birthday tea in front of everyone. The second was that he was trying to make his day last a little longer.

He knew that his special time was coming to an end. That when he went back downstairs, he would have to put on his coat. He would say thank you to his big brother, Jake, and Aunty Lottie for letting him have his party at Damara Cottage, hug his grandparents from Welham Farm, and then head home to The Wishing Well with Mummy.

It would all be over. He sighed. The best day of his life would be finished.

It was a nice surprise, then, to see the man in the mirror here, in Damara's bathroom. Ethan had always thought that Mirror Man lived in his bedroom's reflection at the pub. That there was only one magic mirror in the world.

Yet here he was. The familiar smile, the crinkling eyes. On his birthday too. Ethan grinned into the glass.

Mirror Man called him 'My Little Prodigy' then, which made him feel very grown up. He didn't know what a prodigy was, but was sure it was something very special. Maybe being seven now meant that he was old enough to be a prodigy?

He smiled back into the reflection and their eyes met and held. Mirror Man had some very special instructions today, he said, because now Ethan was old enough to be trusted.

The boy's narrow chest swelled with pride.

Things that couldn't wait any longer, Mirror Man said. Things that must be done today – now – or the chance would be lost.

Ethan nodded, understanding the instructions, but his usually unlined young brow furrowed in confusion.

'But I don't understand why you want me to do it?' he spoke softly to the glass. Tears were starting behind his eyes and he fought them down with effort. Big Boys shouldn't cry in front of other people, and especially when their best friend is asking them – *no, he's telling me* – to do something.

Mirror Man spoke again.

'I don't want to.' The last word caught on a sob, and a solitary tear spilled down his cheek. He could see that Mirror Man wasn't happy any more. His eyes looked hard and cold, and Ethan was afraid. The demand was repeated, and the boy nodded, his face ashen.

His voice was little more than a whisper.

'If I do this one thing, can we be friends again?'

In a pretty, lace-fringed Moses basket in her parents' bedroom, Alicia slept. Ethan knew that she would be here. He'd been disappointed earlier when Aunty Lottie had taken the baby away from his party for a nap.

Now he looked down on her tiny form, dark lashes fanning rose-pink cheeks, dainty hands thrown high above her head in the abandonment of slumber. He could hear each light breath whisper between her lips, could see her lids move as she dreamed. She was like a little doll. So perfect, so sweet.

He should be protecting her, taking care of her. He knew that. He'd been utterly smitten by his tiny niece ever since her birth only two months earlier. They were family, and they loved each other. But Mirror Man would be so cross if he didn't do it. Ethan was frightened of facing those icy eyes again if he failed.

Alicia looked so delicate, so fragile. She was sleeping so soundly. Perhaps she wouldn't know anything about it if he did it quickly. If he followed Mirror Man's orders properly, he was almost sure that he could be brave enough.

As tears fell in earnest now, he picked up an embroidered cushion from the foot of the crib.

Holding it tightly, Ethan stretched towards the sleeping baby.